Another Ch

By

Hazel Goss

Copyright © Hazel Goss
2024

All rights reserved. No part of this book may be reproduced, adapted, stored in a retrieval system or transmitted by any means, electronic, mechanical, photocopying, or otherwise without the prior written permission of the author.

The rights of Hazel E. Goss to be identified as the author of this work have been asserted in accordance with the Copyright Designs and Patents Act 1988.

All characters in this book are fictitious, and any resemblance to actual persons, living or dead, is purely coincidental.

A CIP catalogue record for this book is available from the British Library.

ISBN: 9798324344931

Utopia

Utopia is nowhere,
It cannot ever be.
A non-existent dream
humans will never see.

Writers can create one,
Where people are content.
But then there is no drama,
No disastrous event.

God created all the world,
Its beauty unsurpassed.
A perfect ecosystem
For ever it should last.

God then fashioned Adam,
And Eve to be his mate.
She ate forbidden fruit,
thus sealing Earth's fate.

Mankind developed, invented,
Until industrialisation.
Powered by burning coal,
Brought poisonous pollution.

As we destroy our world,
It's clear for all to see,
During man's existence,
Utopia can never be.

Hazel Goss
May 2022

Chapter 1

August 2022

The fissure looked deep, about two metres wide. If you peered into its depth, there was just a thin ribbon of blue, a river. The cleft in the rock was striated with different shades of grey, and green ferns grew in tiny crevices.

It looked as if someone had attempted to cross it on a plank that had given way, leaving jagged splintery edges. The plank was mahogany brown, but the splinters were bright shades of creamy white and pale orange, as if the break had been recent. People strolled past, looked at it and smiled. Some even dropped a pound coin into the artist's cap, upturned on a rug.

The artist had permission from the council to create the picture in the summer to amuse visitors. The riverside walk in Newcastle was wide, and a popular place to stroll at all times of day.

It was midnight as we walked towards the picture. The area was almost deserted. There was just one man, leaning against a lamp post, his hat pulled low, the brim hiding his face. We'd had a lad's night out and were tipsy. Rich and Mike were worse than me, I think. Anyway, as we got right up to it, Rich said, 'What the fuck's that? It looks real.' I noticed his ginger hair and beard shining in the streetlight as he giggled and said, 'Who's for walking the plank then?'

I laughed, 'I'm too drunk. I'd fall in. But don't let me stop you.'

Rich stepped onto the plank, hesitated, then jumped the gap. He wobbled on landing, steadied, and then raised both fists in the air, 'Yeah! Beat that, Mike.'

Mike grinned and braced himself to start. He ran, jumped the gap, and landed with one foot half on the plank and half on the pavement. 'Piss easy. C'mon, Phil. We've shown you how to do it.'

'Just because the two of you want to prance about on a picture doesn't mean I have to,' I said. 'Let's go.'

'No, don't be chicken. Do it, then we'll go back to the hotel,' said Rich.

I sighed and walked up to the chasm's edge and placed a foot on the plank. There was an ominous creak.

'That was realistic who made that noise?' I grinned, convinced my friends were making sound effects. I made to jump the gap, but the plank gave way and I fell, not onto the picture but into it.

The fall seemed endless. I hit the water, scarcely having time to breathe. before I plummeted right to the bottom. My lungs were bursting. I panicked, kicked out and swam up and up, until I broke the surface, sucking in as much air as I could, gasping. I was alive and feeling euphoric. I trod water, turning to look about. The grey cliffs towered vertically, and the sky was so far above, I could only see it if I floated on my back. There were twinkling stars and a clear, crescent moon, but I hardly noticed, shivering with cold. I was a confident swimmer, so now I put my head down and swam towards the cliffs. My arms were beginning to ache with the effort, so I stopped for a rest to check my direction. As my feet went down to tread water, they touched a rock. I waded awkwardly, sometimes sinking below the water where there were gaps between the rocks. Then there was sand. I stumbled out onto a narrow stretch of dry beach.

I was shivering and shaking with shock and sat, trying to think. There was no obvious path or steps up the cliff. No way out. Hypothermia was a real danger. Would it be better if I took off my sodden clothes? I decided to do that, ringing out each item before spreading it on the rocks. It wouldn't be long before the sun came up and they would dry. Feeling vulnerable in my nakedness and exhausted, I lay, curled on my side, my arms hugging me trying to find warmth. I thought I'd never sleep, but I did.

The dawn brought the sun. I woke hearing an engine above the steady flow and ripples of the river. As I moved, every part of me seemed to ache. I managed to stand and went to feel my pants and trousers. They were almost dry. I put them on. My shirt was not only dry but warm.

The engine was getting closer and coming from downstream. The craft was old, chugging along, with steam, coming from a tall, brass chimney, escaping into the air. It had a faded canopy like something used in the tropics. I waved both hands to attract attention. The boat turned towards me, then crunched onto the beach.

A man in a cap, wearing a raincoat, climbed over the rail, and jumped down.

'Hi, Phil. You made it. Any injuries?'

'No. I'm fine. How do you know my name? I've seen you before. Yes, you were watching us fooling about on the picture. How did I fall into it?'

The man ignored all the questions and held out his hand. 'I'm Adam. Welcome to the other dimension.' I shook his hand, his grip firm and reassuring.

'Put your socks and shoes on, Phil, then climb aboard. I expect you're hungry and thirsty and if you're feeling cold, there's a jacket you can put on.'

I clambered aboard, found the jacket, and put it on as Adam put the engine into reverse and the boat scraped off the beach. He turned it to go back the way he had come. I sat on the bench seat under the canopy and studied the interior. It had a large brass boiler in the centre, reminding me of an old film set in the war. It came to me then, 'The African Queen'. My mum had it on a DVD.

Adam left the tiller and went into the cabin. Was this dangerous? Should I take the tiller? I decided to do it if the boat veered towards the cliff. The course seemed steady and Adam soon reappeared with two mugs of tea, almost crushing a box of doughnuts under his arm.

'Tea and doughnuts. Just the ticket when you've had a shock. Eat as many as you like. I've more where they came from.' I ate two, gulped down the hot tea and felt more human after it. Adam sat opposite me, sipping his tea and nibbling a doughnut.

'Adam, is this a complete replica? Does it really run by steam?'

He smiled and shook his head. 'It's faithful in all aspects except the propulsion. She's battery driven. The chugging is a simple sound effect. If I want to run stealthily, I can turn it off and then it glides almost silently. I love this boat. We're nearly there, so prepare yourself for an ecstatic welcome.'

'What? Why?' Adam ignored my questions, concentrating on guiding the boat. The cliffs dwindled and around the next bend, there were trees, some buildings just visible through them, and a landing stage. Two fishing boats were moored further up but then I heard and saw a crowd of people smiling and cheering as we approached. Adam threw a rope that was quickly gathered, and we were safely tied, fore and aft.

'Why are they cheering?'

'They're pleased to see you. Wave and smile.' I frowned at him before I mustered a smile and waved. The cheering increased.

'Now let's introduce you to some of our leaders.' We walked along the jetty and for a moment, I almost lost sight of Adam with so many people surrounding me, shaking my hand and patting me on the back.

'Welcome, so pleased to see you.'

'We've been looking forward to you coming.'

'Everything's ready for you.'

'We want you to be happy here.'

I emerged from the crowd feeling bewildered, my head buzzing with questions, and I was then introduced to a burly man wearing a chain of office. The mayor, I assumed, introduced himself.

'Good morning, Phil, my name's Arthur, and I'm the mayor, as you can see.' He tweaked the chain that decorated his bulging waistcoat. 'Come and see our village, then we'll show you our new hospital. I think you'll be impressed.'

'Thank you,' was the best I could muster. I was being manipulated, in a kindly way, by everyone.

The crowd drifted away as Adam, Arthur, and a couple of councillors led me uphill from the river. Where the ground levelled, there were buildings, houses, a shop, a cafe, a school, a green space with playground equipment, and at the furthest end of the road was the hospital.

All the buildings were made of logs. It reminded me of the American outback, but there were no pickup trucks. In fact, there were no cars at all. I wondered how a hospital built like that could be hygienic. Once inside, I was pleased to see the walls were plastered, smooth and painted. The lighting was bright and there were few shadows. I began to feel excited.

'I can see you're smiling,' Arthur said. 'As they said in some film or other, you ain't seen nothing yet.' He flung open a door and said, 'Waiting room and reception.'

The space was generous with at least twenty chairs and a door with WC on it.

Arthur moved across to another door labelled: Consulting Room 1. He opened it and said, 'Have a look and tell me if anything's missing.'

There was a couch, that could be raised up and down and a curtain that could be drawn around it. There was a solid desk with drawers, paper and pens on its top and a large cupboard that contained stethoscopes, thermometers, a blood pressure machine, syringes and dressings. There was also a filing cabinet, labelled, 'Patient Records', its drawers labelled with sections of the alphabet

'As far as I can see the only thing missing is a computer,' I said.

'Ah, yes. In this dimension, there are no computers, electronic tablets, televisions or mobile phones. Ours is a simple way of life.'

'What about a defibrillator, heart monitor or electrocardiogram?'

'Don't worry, we are up to date with medical equipment. Now, let's move on to consulting room two.' We walked a few paces then I went in, glanced around it, nodded and said, 'Similar to the first, but no filing cabinet.'

We paused at an X-ray department, a pharmacy and then walked down a long corridor to an operating theatre.

'We can't all troop in there. It's an ultra-clean area. You can go in alone, Phil, once you've donned your scrubs.' He held his hand out towards a changing room. 'There's a connecting door from there. We'll wait here. Take your time.'

I went in and could hear the muffled voices of them chatting.

'What do you think, Adam? He seems perfect.'

'He's certainly gained top marks from me with the way he handled his difficult arrival. I'd say he'll make an ideal doctor for us. After this, we'll take him into Diane's Diner and introduce him to his staff. I've asked them all to be there at eleven o'clock.'

Chapter 2

2022

Phil's scream faded into the depths and both men heard the faint sound of a splash. They looked at each other in disbelief.

Phil, Phil, shouted Mike. There was no reply. 'Fuck! What do we do Rich? Should we call the police or an ambulance?'

'How can we call anyone? What can we say? Our mate, Phil, fell into the canyon in the picture?'

Perhaps there's a real hole, like a manhole without its cover, or something.'

They both peered closely, using the torches on their phones but there was no manhole.

'Where's that bloke? He must've seen it happen. He was watching us,' said Rich.

The man had gone.

Rich and Mike walked back to the hotel, arguing.

'We'll have to report Phil missing,' Rich said, 'He's got a family: mum, dad, and a sister. If he doesn't ring or text, they're going to ask why.'

'I still don't see how we can explain what we saw. Is anyone going to listen if we say he fell into a picture?'

'Perhaps we don't have to say that. We can say we had a night out, got drunk and he never joined us at the hotel. He still wasn't there this morning when we were due to leave, so we were worried.'

'Okay, let's do that in the morning.'

Sergeant Broadbent was at the front desk when the two large men entered.

'Good morning, gentlemen. How can I help?'

'Good morning, officer,' said Rich, 'We, erm, our friend, Phil's missing.'

Sergeant Broadbent pulled a pad towards him, filled in the date and then asked, 'What's your friend's full name?'

'Philip Clarkson.' This was recorded and then more details were added. 'When did you last see him?'

'Last night. We were on a lad's night out, been to several pubs and were well wasted. Mike and I said we were going back to the hotel. Phil was chatting up a girl and said he'd be along soon. Only he never came. We thought he'd got lucky, but we had to check out this morning and there was still no sign of him.'

'Where were you staying?'

'The Premier Inn.'

'The name of the last pub you were in?'

They hesitated and then Mike said, 'Sorry, I don't remember.'

'Me neither,' added Rich.

Sergeant Broadbent looked over his glasses at them, as if he didn't believe this last statement, but said, 'Have you got a photograph on either of your phones?'

Rich searched and came up with one of the three of them. He handed the phone to the sergeant.

'You're all rugby players, I see. Philip Clarkson's in the middle then?'

When Rich nodded the phone was whisked away for a few minutes.

'Our tech guys will just make a copy and you can have your phone back. Right, I've got your details so that's as far as we can go, for now. I'll post him as a missing person but if he should appear, please tell us so we can take him off the list.'

They nodded.

A young man, not in uniform, gave the phone back and they were free to go home. As they left the police station, Mike said, 'We have to tell his family. If we don't, they'll go to the police and find out we've already reported him missing. You've met Phil's parents, haven't you? I think you should do it.'

'Shit! I don't want to,' said Rich. Mike said nothing, waiting for Rich to realise it was necessary and he would have to do it.

'Okay, but I'll go home first and take some paracetamol. Then I'll be able to face them.'

The two men parted company at the Metro Station; Rich went to North Shields and Mike went to South Shields.

The three friends had grown up together and gone to the same primary and secondary schools. When they left school, they went different ways but continued to meet at the rugby club on weekends.

Mike was a lawyer, living at home with his parents and studying to become a barrister. Rich had become a civil engineer and was working on strengthening a bridge in Tynemouth. He was going home to an empty flat.

Phil also lived in a flat on his own in Tynemouth. He, like Mike and Rich, was not in a steady relationship. Phil, a junior surgeon, with his height, fair hair and dancing blue eyes, was considered to be a catch by all the nurses. But, at the time of his fall, there was no-one special.

When Rich got home, he made some coffee and took two painkillers. He cradled the cup and thought about last night.

Did it really happen? We heard him scream and then a splash as he hit the water. We didn't imagine it. What am I going to tell his parents and his sister, Olivia? I hate lying.

He drank the last of his coffee and stood up wavering slightly with the headache. He hoped the fresh air would help clear it.

Phil's parents lived in Tynemouth, so Rich walked along the quayside, past fishing boats and the Low Light, an early lighthouse, and then along the bank of the river Tyne. When the path turned inland, he had to climb the steep hill with the Sailing Club on his right, nestled below the cliff, topped with the Priory ruins. Tynemouth's main street was quiet, although some of the cafes had a few people sitting outside enjoying coffee or an early lunch.

The walk took him twenty minutes and all the way he rehearsed what he was going to say. When he arrived, he hesitated at the garden gate then opened it and walked along the short path not seeing the flower beds or smelling the lavender. When he rang the bell, it was Phil's dad who answered the door. 'Hello Rich.' He peered past him. 'Phil not with you? Come on in, Sheila 'll put the kettle on. Where's Phil then?'

He didn't wait for an answer, just led the way, shouting for Sheila.

Sheila, a short, plump woman, came downstairs, greeted Rich, and then went into the kitchen to make tea. While the kettle was singing, she came and sat down with them.

'Why are you here, Rich? Has something happened to Phil? Has he had an accident?'

Rich took a deep breath. 'We all got very drunk last night. When Mike and I said we were going back to the hotel, Phil said he'd come when he'd finished his pint. We went to bed assuming Phil would come in, but this morning, there was no sign of him. His bed hadn't been slept in and all his stuff was still there. I've got it here.' He indicated a small holdall he'd brought with him. 'We had to check out by eleven. We were worried so we went to the police station and reported him missing.'

Sheila's normally rosy cheeks were white. Her bottom lip trembled as tears fell.

Phil's dad said, 'You've rung him? Stupid question, of course you have. He's always got his phone on him.'

Rich nodded. 'When I phoned, the voice said the number was unobtainable. Our texts were not even received. Wherever he is, there's no signal.'

Sheila stood up and went into the kitchen. They could hear the kettle coming up to boil again and the clink of cups. Above that, they could hear her sobbing. Both men looked at each other.

'Should I go?' asked Rich. 'I've brought bad news. I feel I'm intruding.'

'I don't know what's for the best. Perhaps you should.'

Rich nodded and stood but then Sheila, her face red and blotchy, opened the door with an elbow and came in with a tray. 'I couldn't remember how you like your tea, Rich, so I've brought the pot in to pour it in here.'

Rich took the tray from her and before he sat down again, he poured tea for everyone and handed out the biscuits. Neither of them took one but Sheila said, 'Please have a biscuit, Rich. I made them and their Phil's favourite.'

She put down her cup and blew her nose loudly. He dutifully took a biscuit. There was a long silence punctuated with a slurp of tea and a crunch as Rich bit into the ginger biscuit.

Eventually, Phil's dad put his cup down and said, 'I think we should go to the police. You reported it in Newcastle, but we can do it here. If you've all finished your tea, we can go now. Better than just sitting here moping.'

Sheila nodded and Rich stood, saying, 'Thank you for the tea, Sheila. I'm sure the police will find him. Let me know if you get any news.'

Then he walked quickly to the door and let himself out. The air outside was sultry. Too warm. He wanted cold air so he could walk briskly to calm the tension and misery of the last half an hour. He set off towards home and his heart sank as he saw Phil's sister, Olivia, approaching.

Her smile was dazzling as she said, 'Hi Rich, are you hung over? Have you walked with Phil to our house?'

'Yes. No, I'm sorry, Olivia, I've just had to tell your mum and dad that Phil's missing.'

'What?'

'Yes, he didn't come back to the hotel with us last night and he didn't appear at breakfast, not answering his phone or anything.'

As he said that, Rich saw Olivia's incredulous expression, eyebrows raised, turn to a frown. Suddenly, he wanted to tell her the truth.

'Are you in a hurry? I'd really like it if you'd walk with me for a while.'

'Perhaps I ought to go home. Mum and Dad will be upset.'

'They're not there, they've gone to the police station.'

'In that case, we can go for a walk.'

They set off towards Northumberland Park and as they walked Rich's mind was frantically thinking how to tell her what really happened. He stopped, just inside the gates, and told her everything. When he finished with, 'I know it sounds impossible, but we were not so drunk that we were hallucinating. We both saw the same thing.'

'So, you haven't told Mum and Dad this, or the police?'

'No, it's such an unlikely story. We said Phil lingered in the pub and said he'd catch us up when he'd finished his pint.'

'I can see why you lied.' Olivia smiled, sadly. 'Thank you for telling me. I'd better go home now and be there when they come back.'

Chapter 3

2022

My head was reeling when I went to bed in my log cabin, just behind the hospital.

I'd met so many people. Jane, a nurse with long, tied-back, brown hair, Madeline, a middle-aged midwife, her black hair going grey, and Caitlin, a chiropodist with piercings everywhere. Then there was Gary, the radiographer, tall, dark and handsome, who doubled as an anaesthetist. Helen, blonde and petite, was the receptionist. There were several others, but although I tried, I couldn't recall their names.

I was exhausted, desperate to sleep but tossed and turned, trying to make sense of everything. Finally, I got up, went into the bathroom, and examined the contents of the cabinet. Sleeping tablets were on the shelf with painkillers. How irritatingly thoughtful. I took a sleeping tablet, wandered around the cabin, yawned and went back to bed.

I slept for ten hours. In the morning, I showered and discovered a wardrobe full of clothes in my size. I selected the casual type of clothes I'd normally wear to work and then noticed there were three suits and wondered if dressing smart might be expected. I was apparently the only doctor and doubled as a surgeon. I put on a shirt under a grey suit and was glad to see there were no ties.

In the kitchen, I opened the fridge and found milk, butter and eggs. The cupboards revealed some basic food, tea, jam and a small loaf of bread. I fried two eggs and ate them as a sandwich. They tasted delicious. I always thought eggs were eggs but had to concede I'd been wrong. As I ate, I thought about this new life and worried about my old one. *What did Rich and Mike do when I fell through the picture? Did they know I'd survived the* fall? How could they tell Mum and Dad I wasn't dead? Was anyone going to try and rescue me? Did I need rescuing? Yesterday I'd been a junior surgeon in the Royal Victoria Infirmary. Now, I was the head doctor and surgeon in a small but new facility.

I felt energised at that thought and walked the few steps to the hospital to begin my first surgery. The front door was unlocked so I went in, paused and surveyed my domain. It was very quiet, with no sound of anyone else there, so I moved across to the first consulting room and went in. I sat at the desk and then stood and opened the patient record filing cabinet. I pulled a record out at random and began to read it.

Eleanor, aged seven, had broken her arm six weeks ago by falling off a swing. Her X-ray showed a neat fracture. She had been treated with some painkillers and had a pot put on. So, which doctor did she see? Who had been my predecessor? I was trying to decipher a signature when I was interrupted.

'Hello, Doctor Phil. We have two patients waiting to see you, so I thought I'd check you were ready.'

'Yes, thank you, Helen. Send the first one in.'

Helen left without closing the door. I stood up ready to be pleasant and to find or create a record of the visit. An overweight woman with obvious breathing difficulties came in. After examining her, I prescribed an asthma inhaler and suggested, as gently as I could, that she should try to eat moderately. When she'd gone, clutching a diet sheet and a handwritten prescription, I added to her record, then put it to one side as the next patient arrived.

By lunchtime, my pile of records had grown considerably. Helen had brought me a cup of tea in the middle of the morning, but now I wondered what happened at lunchtime.

Helen was ready with the information. They closed the surgery for an hour, beginning again at 2 pm so I was free to go back to my cabin or go to Diane's Diner.

'I haven't much food in my cabin, and I have no money so I don't see how I can go to the diner. Come to that, I don't know who paid for yesterday's evening meal.'

Helen smiled, sympathetically, 'You had a lot to cope with yesterday, so you were not told how this dimension works. It's best described as a large commune. Everyone works so everyone eats. We don't use money. If you need milk or anything, just go to the shop and collect what you need.'

I was incredulous, unable to form a suitable comment, so just said, 'Oh' and then added, 'Thank you for telling me.'

I walked over to the diner. It was a much larger cabin with a counter and cakes under glass cloches. There was a noticeboard that I promised myself I would read when I heard a voice.

'Phil, come and join us when you've ordered,' said Adam. I did and when I'd sat down, he said, 'Did you have a good morning?'

'Yes, I was kept busy right up to one o'clock.' I turned to look at Arthur. 'What do you do, Arthur, when you're not being mayor?'

'I'm the minister at the church. I also help at any farm that needs me. We're just coming up to harvest time, so you won't see me in here then. It's an exceptionally busy couple of weeks.'

'What's grown here?'

'Wheat, obviously for our bread, soya beans for protein, oats, potatoes, carrots and other seasonal veg. Then we have huge poly tunnels for soft fruit, tomatoes, lettuces, cucumbers etcetera.'

'Cows, sheep, chickens?'

Arthur looked down, and wriggled, seeming uncomfortable with the question. Adam answered.

'We're trying very hard to keep a good carbon footprint here, so we do keep chickens but not sheep or goats. Everyone here is a vegetarian.'

'But I'm drinking tea with milk. You haven't mentioned cows.'

'It's oat milk. I should also tell you there are no alcoholic drinks and no smoking.'

'Oh. Thank you for explaining all that. Adam, Arthur I have a lot more questions but,' I glanced at my watch and stood up. 'It's 1:50. I'd better go back to work.'

Arthur and Adam agreed that Phil was settling down remarkably well.

'I don't think I've had any recruit accepting their situation as well as he has,' said Adam.

'Don't get complacent. Phil's a highly intelligent man. I think he's biding his time, finding out as much as he can, intending to escape back to his own dimension.'

'You could be right. I've got Helen keeping an eye on him at work.'

Just before six, when my surgery closed, Adam arrived. I was filing patient records and tidying the room.

'Have you got a medical problem, Adam? If you have, I'll pull your record out.'

'No, I'm fine but I wondered if you were.'

I looked at him and noticed how small and wiry he was, ferret looking. This was a man not to be trusted. I was tired and angry.

'That's a stupid question. No, I'm not fine. You kidnapped me. I could have died from the fall alone. I nearly drowned. You seem to think I will happily join your cosy set-up here if you make it comfortable enough. You pander to my ego showing me a beautifully equipped hospital that's all mine. I was just a junior surgeon, and now, suddenly I'm Chief Medical Officer, GP and Head of Surgery, because I'm the only one. You've managed to avoid answering all my questions, so I don't know what happened to the doctor you had here before. Another thing, did everyone fall through a picture to get here?'

My tirade was halted by Helen.

'I'm sorry to interrupt but there's been an accident. You're needed at Thistledown Farm. Jason B.'s been run over by a tractor.'

I grabbed my doctor's bag shouting, 'Adam, I need you to show me the way.'

'What about the stretcher?' asked Helen and ran to fetch it. Adam took it from her, and we ran out of the hospital. Adam turned right, past my cabin and up the hill.

My breath was coming in gasps as I said, 'So, no cars, means no ambulances. A huge flaw in your Shangri-La. Jason B. could bleed out and die while we're walking to his farm.' I sped up and overtook Adam. 'Come on, hurry.'

It took twenty minutes to reach the casualty. The tractor was on its side, half in a ditch. I wanted to ask how the accident happened, but my first concern was treating my patient. It was evident, after a quick examination, that he needed to go to the hospital. His wife, Mary, had covered him with a blanket and pressed on the worst wound. I applied a tourniquet, used some field dressings and steadied Jason's head when, on my instruction, he was lifted onto the stretcher. Four strong farm workers carried it as I sent Adam ahead to ask Jane, the nurse and Gary, the anaesthetist to meet us at the hospital. I then ran down the hill, reaching the hospital in time to change into scrubs and begin preparing the theatre for a probable operation.

After an hour and a half, Jason B. was recovering in a hospital bed. It had been a difficult operation, but he had not lost his leg which I had thought was a possibility.

'Thank you, Gary, and you Jane, for coming so quickly and doing a good job. I felt we were a team, even though we hadn't worked together before.'

'No problem,' said Jane.

'It was a pleasure to watch you work, Phil,' said Gary.

I thought, ruefully, that in my previous life, I'd have invited them to have a drink on me. That was something I couldn't do in a dry dimension that didn't use money. At that moment, I would have been grateful for a pint of beer with some cheerful company to help me relax.

I went back to my cabin and, as there was no television to watch, I went to bed. My last thought was, I'll go mad if I have to stay here. I haven't even got a book to read. I wonder if they have a library.

Chapter 4

Ten years earlier, 2012

Adam found the other dimension by accident. At least, he thought it was an accident but sometimes he wondered if the other dimension had found him – chosen him.

He had just taken ownership of a large warehouse and was wandering amongst the shelving, looking for a suitable space to create an office. There was one corner that must have had vehicles parked in it because there were oily marks on the floor. He paced a square roughly four metres in each direction and decided that would still give him space to park one or two forklift trucks. As he looked carefully at the floor, he thought one area was slightly raised. He crouched down and, in the grime, there was the outline of a trap door. There was no handle, so he used a key to scrape around it, but it was not possible to lever it with a key. He would come back tomorrow with a couple of flathead screwdrivers.

When he levered the trap door the next day, Adam saw a flight of steps disappearing into the gloom. He used his phone torch, shining it around, and saw the cave was huge. It also showed there was no handrail. He climbed through the hatch, steadying himself against the wall, and descended, shuddering as spiderwebs brushed his hands and face. *This had better be worth it,* he thought, as the flight of steps seemed unending, knowing he would have to walk back up. He counted 365 steps and wondered if it was significant.

At the bottom, the floor was packed earth, and the corridor smelled damp and musty. He walked on, his footsteps echoing in the vast cavern until he reached a wooden door reinforced with metal strips shaped like an X. The sliding bolts were stiff but eventually yielded. The shaft of sunshine, even filtered through the undergrowth, was dazzling as he tugged the protesting door open.

Adam stood for a moment, breathing in the fresh air, trying to see what lay beyond the thick branches of shrubs and trees. He tried to push his way through but the branches were stiff, unyielding so he sidled, his back against the rock, sustaining cuts and scratches but making some headway. *I'll have to come back with loppers or an axe,* he thought. He imagined himself an intrepid explorer, using a machete in the jungle and smiled.

After five minutes, Adam stopped and listened. He could hear seagulls and breaking waves. This garden, or whatever it was, was near the sea. Suddenly, he felt worried he was trespassing and hoped no guard dogs were employed. He moved again, still with his back to the rock and the land began to go downhill. As the incline increased, the undergrowth thinned, and he could see the waves glinting in the sunlight.

The going was easier now and Adam walked faster until he was at the seashore. Then he stood and looked about him. It was an estuary. He could see black rocks just poking out of the sea. *They're just like the Black Midden rocks at Tynemouth,* he thought. *But there are no lighthouses. From here, I should be able to see Lord Collingwood's statue and the priory up on that jutting headland but they're not there. Strange, it should all look so familiar but different.*

Adam sat down on a flat stone, facing the sea, just breathing, totally relaxed and calm. Perhaps it didn't matter where he was, geographically, because it was lovely. Eventually, he noticed there were no large ships or smaller craft and no dog walkers. It was strange to be so alone, but he knew he wanted to come back and experience this place again.

It was three weeks later before Adam could explore his secret place. He had been working hard, building his office within the warehouse, ordering goods to store and then distributing to factories, shops and homes. The number of people buying online meant he was kept very busy, but he was also getting very tired. He was in his office by 7.30am and rarely left before 7pm. This Sunday, he was going to give himself the day off and go down the steps.

Adam woke early as he usually did to go to work. He got up, had a quick breakfast, and then packed a large rucksack. He put a tarpaulin in the bottom, some rope, a small axe and tied a large felling axe onto the outside. In the extra pockets, he put small items like matches, a metal mug, a sharp knife, some packets of dried food, a large bottle of water, instant coffee and a set of camping pans.

He let himself into the warehouse and locked the door behind him. In the office, he moved his desk to reveal the trap door, pulled it up, and began a careful descent. At the bottom, he opened the door and left the rucksack half inside to stop it from closing. He hoped the fresh air might waft through the cave and clear the air of its mustiness.

Adam took his felling axe and was about to use it on the nearest hefty branch, then stopped. He wasn't sure why, but he felt this door needed to remain difficult to access, hidden from sight.

He squeezed along as he had done before for about ten metres, then chose branches to lop so he could forge a path. It was slow work and he looked at his phone to see the time, but his phone was dead.

After much hacking the narrow path was finished, and he was close to the sea. A strong, chill wind was blowing, and he shivered despite sweating with the exercise of chopping branches. Adam planned to build a shelter, so he explored the area. Moving uphill, he eventually found a flat place with two sturdy trees about three metres apart and soft grass beneath them. This was going to be his camp.

He tied the rope between the trees, threw his tarpaulin over it and guyed it down to the floor. He could just stand up inside and felt warmer, protected from the wind. Now he searched for stones to make a fire surround, recalling the delights of camping as a boy scout. He foraged for dry twigs and some larger branches and made a mound of kindling inside the stone circle. When the fire was crackling, some larger branches glowing red,

Adam filled his pan with water and then sat on his rucksack and waited for it to boil. He began to think about improvements. He needed a ground sheet, a plate and some cutlery.

Once the water had boiled, Adam poured himself a black coffee and then tipped the contents of a dried meal with rice into the remaining hot water. He had no spoon to stir it, so he used his knife but then realised it was going to be difficult to eat. He could use his fingers, but it was going to be too hot. The meal was bubbling so he took it off the heat and went out of his camp to look for a suitable branch. When he found one, he cut it off with his axe and shaped it with the sharp knife into a crude spoon shape. By the time he had finished it to his satisfaction, his rice meal had become cold and glutinous. It didn't matter. It was food and he was having fun.

Adam washed his pan and mug in the stream nearby and looked at his watch. It irritated him that he had no idea of the time. He looked up and saw the orange glow of the setting sun, so he ought to go back. *What should he do with his axes and other equipment?*

He was not generally a trusting person but decided to leave everything, except his rucksack, under the shelter. There had been no sign of other people and he now believed there was no possibility of anyone finding his things. This peaceful place appeared to be uninhabited except for red squirrels, rabbits and a shy deer he had seen.

Adam reached the door in the fading light. He paused, looked back through the trees at the last vestiges of the orange-pink sunset, and sighed with pleasure. This was a precious haven from the manic pace of life above.

Chapter 5

2012

Adam had improved his shelter and spent several nights camping in it. Whenever he arrived, he felt the pressure of work lift and a calm he'd rarely felt, settle on him. For just a few hours he forgot the busy warehouse with forklift trucks whining around it, delivery deadlines, goods in, goods out, and customers ordering or complaining.

One Saturday evening in September, Adam locked the warehouse, picked up his rucksack and went to his portal. He was whistling, looking forward to two nights under canvas. When he emerged from the door, he turned towards the river heading for the small area he had cleared in the woods. He found himself smiling with pleasure as if all the nature around him had healing properties.

At the shelter, he lifted the flap, went in, lit his woodburning stove and then picked up a pan to fill with water. It would take a while for the stove to get hot enough, but he had plenty of time. He didn't have to return to work until Monday morning.

As he walked uphill to the stream, he was pleased he had bought a cheap, clockwork watch. He had no need of time for two days but wanted to get back to work on Monday. Although, being the boss, no-one was going to ask him why he was late.

He filled the pan with fresh clear water and then stood, holding it, looking out towards the estuary and the river. Seagulls wheeled and screeched in the warm, still air and he breathed deeply and shut his eyes. *This place is some kind of Eden.* He became aware of the pan of water becoming heavier in his hand and opened his eyes. He set off towards his camp and saw something half-beached, a dolphin perhaps, too big for a seal. He put the pan on the ground and went down the hill to look. It was not a dolphin. It was a beautiful young woman with short black hair. Her face was white, eyes closed. Was she dead? Whether she was dead or alive, the river would take her out to sea as the tide was coming in. He put his arms under hers and hauled her further up the beach. Her dead weight and sodden clothes made it hard work and he was breathing heavily when she was well clear of the water. Adam knelt beside her and felt for a pulse. She was alive. He rolled her into the recovery position and then wondered what to do. A blanket. That was what she needed. He stood up to fetch one when she coughed, retched and was sick, bringing up a lot of water.

'Oh God, that's yuk.' She spat making a grimace and wiping her mouth on her sleeve.

'I'll get you some water.' Adam paused, took off his jumper and put it over her shoulders, then ran to the stream. When he got back, she was sitting up, hunched, her arms hugging her drawn knees. He knelt beside her.

'Here, drink this. It'll take that nasty taste out of your mouth.'

She took the pan and drank deeply. 'Thank you. I'm sorry...' She put the pan on the ground and began to cry, rocking from side to side.

'No need to say you're sorry. Don't cry, you're safe now. I know you're cold. If you can stand, I'll help you up the hill to my shelter. It's warmer in there.'

Adam's speech had no effect. If anything, she cried louder. He didn't know what to do so he sat down beside her, close but not touching, and waited. Her sobbing abated into shuddering gasps. She leant towards him, and he put an arm around her, pulling her cold, thin, wet body to him.

'It's my own fault. I wanted to die. I jumped into the river, in the dark and sank down and down, and then I panicked and began to swim. I was so relieved when I broke the surface, but it was dark. I couldn't see the shore. After what seemed like hours the sky brightened just enough for me to see the land. When I crawled over the stones I was exhausted and must've fallen asleep.' As she spoke, the girl had leant away from him, and he had dropped his arm.

'If you feel strong enough to get up, my shelter's just a short walk from here. You can get warm, and I can make us something to eat. Come on.' He stood and held out his hand. She took it and he helped her up.

At the shelter, he held open the flap to let her in.

'This is homely. You've even got a carpet on the floor.'

He nodded and busied himself stoking the stove. 'There's a blanket on the bed. If you take off your wet things, you can wrap yourself in it. Then your clothes can dry in front of the stove. I'll go outside while you do it. You're quite safe with me.'

'Thank you. Sorry, what's your name?'

'Adam.'

'Thank you for looking after me, Adam. My name's Evelyn but it's such an old-fashioned name I prefer to shorten it to Eve. Oh my God, I hope that's not some kind of omen.'

She smiled, fleetingly, then turned her back and began to remove her top. Adam left her and went back to the beach to collect the pan of water.

He thought about Eve, imagined her taking her clothes off and felt aroused, then ashamed. She was beautiful but she was also vulnerable. He couldn't understand why she would want to kill herself. She'd probably tell him, eventually.

He picked up the pan, went back to the stream and filled it almost to the brim. As he did so he examined his own feelings. Did he want anyone sharing his haven, especially a depressed woman? Eve was very attractive. She would be company and he was lonely. But she would ask questions. He'd have to show her the portal door and the way back to normal life. It was too complicated. He sighed, walked back to the shelter and shouted, 'Are you decent? Can I come in?'

'Yes, come in Adam.'

He entered and saw her sitting on the carpet, swathed in a blanket. Her clothes were draped on a camping chair, steaming in front of the stove. Adam put the pan of water on the top, trying not to look at her underwear or imagine her naked under the blanket.

'Do you like scrambled eggs?'

'I do and I'm starving.'

He fetched everything he needed from a cool box and busied himself making the meal. Then Eve asked the question he'd been dreading.

'Adam, I don't really understand where I am. I jumped into the Tyne at North Shields, but I've ended up in the countryside.'

Chapter 6

2022

I was feeling calmer. Jason B. was recovering well and would be able to go home by the end of the week. The poor man had been desperate to go back to work. He had barely regained consciousness from his operation when he was fretting about the harvest.

'There are only so many dry days in late September, and I had this window of perfect weather. By the time I'm fit, it'll all be ruined.'

'I'll speak to Arthur. He said he helps at harvest time.'

Jason nodded and closed his eyes. I stood for a moment beside his bed wondering what would happen to someone like him and his wife if he was too disabled to work. *Would the commune feed them? Would they be banished back to the normal dimension?*

At lunchtime, I set off to Thistledown Farm. When I got there, I found a gang of men, including Arthur, sitting down to a sandwich lunch. They were red and sweating from working very hard.

'Hi Phil,' said Arthur, 'Have you come to lend us a hand?' He was grinning but became serious and said, 'Only kidding, how's Jason B.? Hope you've come with good news.'

I smiled and encompassed everyone as I said, 'He's out of danger, no sign of infection and he might come home in a few days.' This provoked a murmur and a lot of smiles and nods. 'He's been worrying about this good weather and his crops not being harvested. Can I go back now and tell him you've got it in hand?'

'We have that,' said Arthur, 'I've never worked so hard in my life. It was kind of you to come and see the situation so you could put his mind at rest. Sit down, Doc and have a sandwich, cheese and pickle.' His eyes twinkled. 'Vegan cheese but it's okay.' He held up a box and I took a sandwich, then joined them, sitting on a bale.

'Thanks.' One of the men held out a bottle, after wiping the top on his sleeve. I took it and drank deeply. 'That's good stuff, very nearly beer.'

Everyone laughed. I felt accepted and enjoyed the camaraderie and banter. I couldn't stay long because I had afternoon surgery. As I walked my heart was lighter, almost happy.

My mood changed when I reached the hospital just a few minutes later. Helen was trying to pacify an irate young woman holding a crying child in her arms.

'Please, Helen, let me jump the queue. I've been up all night with her constant coughing. I'm frantic with worry.'

'I'll see you first,' I said, 'I'm sure the other patients will be happier to have you in with me than sit there listening to you and your little girl's distress.' I saw the relief in her eyes and felt a wave of sympathy and tenderness. I closed the door of the consulting room and took the baby from her. She was red and sweating but became calmer in my arms.

'Hello,' I said, smiling down at her, 'What's your name?'

'Her name's Sandy. You seem to have the magic touch. She's been coughing all night.'

I nodded, still looking and smiling at the baby. 'And what's your mum's name?'

'Alice.'

'Right, Alice. I'm sure Sandy has croup and there's a really simple way to relieve her symptoms. When she coughs, she needs moist air. Boil the kettle in her room and keep filling the air with steam. This will make her feel better and she won't cry so much. She'll recover in a day or so. If she doesn't, bring her to me at any time or fetch me and I'll come to your house. Have you, or rather Sandy, been here before? I need to update her records.'

'Yes, I had Sandy here in the hospital so we both have a file.' She stood up and took Sandy carefully from me. 'She's sound asleep. When I get home, I'll try to do the same. Thank you, Doctor.'

Helen brought me a cup of tea when there was a lull and said, 'Did you know that Alice's husband died just a few months before Sandy was born?'
'No! How did he die?'
'He was asthmatic and got a chest infection. He kept using his inhaler but didn't want to bother the doctor so when he collapsed and was brought here it had developed into pneumonia. Doctor Greg gave him intravenous antibiotics, but he had a heart attack and died. He was only thirty-two. Totally tragic.'
'So, what happened to Greg, my predecessor?' I saw Helen's face redden and her hands twist together.
'I'm not supposed to discuss this with you. But I'm going to tell you anyway. He hated it here. He was a GP, not a surgeon like you. When surgery was required, he felt inadequate. He did his best but sometimes that was not enough. In the end, Adam let him go back to the 'real' world.' She used her hands to indicate parenthesis around the word 'real'.
'It is possible to go back then. I've been wondering about that and was going to talk to Adam.'
'Please don't tell Adam I told you about Doctor Greg. He'll be livid. He told me there would be dire consequences if I breathed a word and ... and now I have.'
'I won't say anything, but I'm pleased you told me. Thank you.'

When the day's surgery was over, I checked on Jason B. and was pleased with his progress.
'You can go home tomorrow if you promise to take it easy. No physical work for a week but you can walk about. I mean a gentle stroll, not pushing hard up hills.'
Jason smiled and then said, 'I'll behave myself, Doc. There's not so much to do now the harvest's in.'

I went home and made a drink but was restless. The events of the day kept playing through my head. Alice kept coming to the forefront. She was attractive and needed help. Sandy had felt so warm and vulnerable in my arms. That was what being a dad must feel like.

Mum had often asked me when I was going to find a wife, settle down and give her grandchildren. I wished I could tell her I'd met someone I'd like to see again.

Mooning about the cabin was not productive. I needed food and decided to go to the diner.

The harvesting crowd were all there and as soon as they saw me, Arthur called, 'Come and join us, Doc. We'll make a space.'

I waved and nodded then chose what I wanted to eat. My food was brought to the table where I sat, squeezed in next to Arthur.

'Jason B. will be able to go home tomorrow but he's got strict instructions to take it easy,' I said.

'Mary'll see to that. Don't worry. She's a stickler for rules. He won't dare disobey her.' There was a general murmur of agreement.

'Arthur, changing the subject, is there a library here?'

'Yes, we couldn't manage without that, what with no television. It's in the church hall in a side room. Alice used to run it before she had her baby. She still comes in now and again to help Maggie. It's open until seven most nights, so if you eat up quickly you could skid in and get yourself a book.'

'Great, I'll do that, thanks.'

The library was a peaceful haven and I seemed to be the only visitor. Alice was sitting at a desk with Sandy asleep in a buggy. She looked up and smiled when she saw who it was.

'I did manage to sleep for nearly two hours before Sandy woke for her tea, so I told Maggie I would do this evening's shift.'

'That's good. I've been thinking about you, knowing you were coping alone. Now, I need something to read, to lose myself in. I like mysteries and who-done-its. Can you help?'

Alice stood up and beckoned me to follow. She led me to the farthest corner and gestured towards the shelves. 'You should be able to find something here.'

'Thank you,' I said, squeezing past her. As I did so our hands brushed. I felt a jolt of electricity. *Did she feel it too? This was dangerous. My mission was to escape back to my previous life, not to fall in love and want to stay.* The book titles blurred but came back into focus as I steadied my breathing. I chose one by Val McDermid and took it to the desk.

Alice took it from me, smiling. 'I forgot to say you can borrow two at a time. Do you want to fetch another?'

'No, this will do for now. Do I have to sign something?'

'I've already made you a borrower's sheet. I'll just jot down this title by the date.' She did so, handed the book back to me and said, 'You can keep it for two weeks, but I expect you'll be back before then.'

'Thanks, Alice. Bye.'

Chapter 7

2012

Eve waited for Adam to answer but he shook his head.

'I can't really explain this place, Eve. I found it by accident and have been camping here on weekends because I find it so peaceful. It's therapeutic, somehow. You'll feel it if you stay here.'

'I think I feel it already. I know why I was so desperate, I didn't want to live, but I feel safe here. It's as if all anxiety has dwindled into the background. If my clothes are dry, I'd like to go for a walk.' She got up, holding her blanket carefully around her, and felt the clothes by the stove.

'They're dry. Would you.... turn around?'

'I'll go and wash our dishes while you put your clothes on.' Adam left her. While he was scrubbing congealed egg off the pan, he wondered what he should do with Eve. *Should he invite her to stay? Should he show her the way out? Should he ask what had been so bad that she'd wanted to kill herself?* When everything was clean, he carried it back and called out. 'Are you decent?'

'Yes, you can come in.' He entered and noticed she had folded the blanket neatly and placed it back on the camp bed.

'Are you walking on your own or would you like company?'

She smiled and looked into his eyes. 'I'll stroll about on my own for a little while if you don't mind. I need to think.'

'Fine. I'll be here when you get back.'

She left him and he put some more wood on the fire before deciding to cut some more because his pile of logs, drying in one corner, was getting low. He enjoyed cutting down small trees and splitting logs. Sometimes he worried about deforestation but then realised that was silly when there was only him. It was hardly the same as logging companies pulling trees up by the roots with massive machinery, stripping them of branches and depositing them onto a trailer. Each tree taking just a few minutes, then on to the next one.

Eve was gone for about an hour and Adam was sitting in his camping chair reading when she returned. She had obviously done some thinking and had come to a decision.

'Adam, would you mind if I stayed here when you go back to work on Monday? I'll keep everything neat and tidy for you. If you agree, I have a favour to ask.'

'Ask your favour before I agree or not.'

'I will need a change of clothes. I can't keep wearing and washing these. If I give you my flat key, would you bring me something to wear, underwear, a washing kit and a towel? I do have a sleeping bag in the large cupboard in the hall, too. But I'll understand if you want to keep this lovely place to yourself.'

'That's a big favour. If I do it, I have a feeling you'll want to stay, sort of permanently.'

'I really don't know. If I'm here for a week on my own I might feel it's too basic, miss little luxuries, like a hot bath, and want to go back. Will you humour me, please?'

Adam nodded, then added, 'You might run out of food.'

He could see her giving that some thought then she smiled and said, 'If we can make a fishing rod tomorrow, I can catch my own. I'd love to do that. Have you got some strong, thin string and a safety pin?'

He laughed out loud and then she laughed too, but then she couldn't stop and began to cry. Adam went to comfort her, but she put up her hands to ward him off. She struggled to calm down and then looked at him, her eyes red and wet.

'Sorry,' she whispered, breathing heavily, 'I can't remember the last time I laughed.'

'It's not a problem. I'm going to fetch some water from the stream.' He left her to compose herself and thought about her request. She was damaged, vulnerable and he wanted to help her. When he came back, he agreed to everything she had asked.

'I could finish work early on say, Wednesday, and come then. I'd have to go back the same night, but it would make things more comfortable for you.'

Eve mustered a weak smile, 'Thank you. You're a kind man and I'm grateful.'

The following morning, having slept on the carpet, while Eve had the camp bed, Adam woke early. He put logs into the stove and went out to fetch water. He filled two pans so Eve could have a warm wash if she wanted it. She was still sound asleep when he got back, and he stood looking down at her. She looked so peaceful. He yearned to hold her and reassure her that everything would work out. Instead, he made two mugs of black tea and put hers on the floor beside her. Then he took his outside and looked at the trees nearby for suitable, slim branches to make a fishing rod.

After a simple breakfast of bread and jam, Adam showed Eve the branches he'd selected. She agreed and he chopped two down and trimmed them of twigs.

'Put a nick in the end to hold the string then we'll need the safety pins and some bait. If we take the shovel and dig in the sand, we'll find some shellfish or worms.'

Eve seemed to have taken charge and Adam was happy to let her. He had never been interested in fishing as a hobby, but this was different. They were fishing to eat.

Later that morning they took a section of seashore each, put worms on their pins, and threw out their lines. Adam needed help at first to make the baited end fly far enough, but he was a quick learner.

They stood quietly, each in their own thoughts. Adam found it a companionable pastime, even in their silence. His musings ceased when he felt a tug on his line. It surprised him and he almost dropped his rod.

'I think I've got one. What do I do now?'

'Pull in the line but not too quickly.' She didn't move towards him but watched, ready to help but just as Adam's fish appeared she got a tug on her own line.

Adam managed to get his hand around the wriggling creature and shouted, 'How do I kill it?'
'Bang it's head on that flat rock.'
He did it and felt a surge of elation. Now he understood what fishing had to offer.

An hour later they had caught three fish and decided that was plenty for lunch. Eve showed Adam how to gut them and while he worked, she fended off the wheeling gulls who eagerly sought the entrails.
'I was going to suggest we cooked them here on the beach, but I think the gulls are going to be too much of a nuisance. Let's take them back to the camp,' said Adam, 'By the way what sort of fish have we caught?'
'I think they're a type of perch.'

Adam left early on Monday morning while Eve was still asleep. When she opened her eyes and remembered where she was, she smiled with pleasure.
'Adam?'
There was no reply, so she half sat up, propping herself on one elbow and looked around. His rucksack was gone. He had gone. She felt a moment of panic. Was she capable of being on her own in this untamed place? The thought frightened her. She shivered and snuggled back under the blankets. As she huddled, she looked at the stove. It was glowing but needed logs. The stove was essential. It persuaded her to get out of bed and throw on some logs. Adam had left a pan of water, so she put that on to boil and made a mental note to leave a full pan that night. The cool box revealed little to eat so she would have to be frugal. Then a smile lit up her face as she remembered their fishing session. She would do that again this morning.
Eve pulled on her clothes, wrinkling her nose at her own body odour, then stepped outside. There was a strong wind blowing fine rain. The sky was grey. Darker clouds were rolling towards her ominously. She ducked back inside and looked around. Adam had left a cagoule on his seat. It had to be pulled

over the head. She had difficulty pulling it down, realising it was a least one size too small for her. Now, armed with a waterproof, she went outside again to use the hole in the ground that was their toilet. She had just finished when the fine rain changed into a heavy downpour. She ran back to the shelter. The weather sounded frightening outside as it battered the tarpaulin. The stove became her focus as she made herself a black tea, holding the mug in both hands for warmth and comfort.

When I said I'd like to stay here on my own I hadn't reckoned on a storm. She sat in Adam's camping chair and picked up his book. It was too dark to read. There was a torch. *I daren't use it in case I need it at night; just have to wait out the storm.*

'No,' she wailed out loud. Water was seeping under the door flap. She leapt up to fold the carpet back. Then she looked carefully around and saw water coming in at the back of the shelter. Now there was no time to lose if everything wasn't going to get wet. She picked up things from the floor and piled them on the camp bed until just the bed, carpet and stove were in contact with the ground sheet.

The storm became a roar. It was primeval, butting the tarpaulin like some beast. She had never experienced anything so frightening. The wind, water and sludge pushed at the bottom of the shelter until a tent peg gave up and flew into the air. The tarpaulin bucked against its bonds until the others pulled up and the wet canvas flapped with a cracking sound and then flew into the woods.

Eve cowed, her arms protecting her head. The mud sucked at her feet and her breath came in gasps as she stared in horror at the chaos. She watched the surge of mud topple over the stove and everything began to slide down the hillside. The bed fell over, the contents joined the rush downwards, and Eve felt herself going too. Was this it? Was she going to die in a sea of mud?

Chapter 8

2022

Olivia pushed open the door of Phil's flat, scattering the pile of post and circulars that had accumulated over three months. She picked it all up, went into the kitchen and opened the bin to drop in the circulars. The smell of rotten food made her step back and cover her mouth with her hand. She pulled out the plastic liner and tied it up before filling a bowl of water and cleaning the bin. *If the bin stank, then how disgusting would the fridge be?*

Olivia filled a plastic bag with the perished food then cleaned the fridge with bicarbonate of soda.

Her final, self-imposed task was to do his washing. She pulled the sheets off his bed and washed them along with whatever was in his dirty washing basket. While the machine was whirling around, she looked through the post and opened it all. Phil was a very organised person and most of the post contained statements showing his bank had paid standing orders or direct debits. There was nothing needing action from her. The washing was going to take a lot longer, so she made herself a black coffee and sat at his computer. She knew the password and then she waded through hundreds of e-mails. Where necessary, she answered saying Phil had gone on an extended holiday. She hoped, desperately, that was true. She missed him so much.

Tears dripped down her cheeks onto the keyboard, but she wiped them away and stood up. In her mind she could see her parents, so thin with worry. Dad had tried to joke, saying losing his son was the best diet he'd ever done. Was there anything she could do to find him?

An hour later, Olivia locked Phil's front door and went for a walk. She walked to the Metro Station and went to Newcastle. When she arrived, she walked to the quayside and went to look at the Tyne. It glinted in the sunlight as she leant on the rail watching its calm, relentless move towards the sea. It was somewhere near here that Phil jumped into a picture and fell, she thought. Turning around, she surveyed the area. Some people were crowding around something in the distance near the Gateshead Millennium Bridge. She strolled over to join them. It was another picture. Her heart did a flip. This time it was a narrow swing bridge with rope sides over a similar chasm. Could it take her to Phil, or was that stupid?

Olivia went home and, on the Metro, phoned Phil's friend, Rich.

When he answered she said, 'Hi, Rich. It's Olivia. Can we meet up and have a chat?'
'Yes, when?'
'Tonight?'
'Okay, when and where?' Before she could answer he added, 'Fancy a bite to eat?' He named a tapas bar, and they agreed on a time.

They had ordered their food and drinks before Rich said, 'So, what's this all about? I haven't seen you for ages and suddenly you want to chat. Have you heard from Phil?'
'No, but I had a stupid idea and wanted to tell you.' She looked at him and he raised an eyebrow but said nothing. She hunched her shoulders and said, 'There's another pavement picture of a river, in Newcastle. I think it's in the same place as last time. I wondered about going there late at night, as you did, and seeing what happens if I walk across it.'
'You must be crazy. I suppose you want me to come with you. Well, I can tell you now, I'll not watch another person disappear like Phil did, especially if I'm cold stone sober. What about your mum and dad? How could you put them through that

all over again?' Rich's harangue stopped abruptly as the waitress arrived with their food.

When she had gone Olivia said, 'Sorry. I told you it was a stupid idea. In fact, I wondered if we went across it together, holding hands, so if one fell, the other did too.'

'That's even dafter. I love Phil like a brother, but I'm not sure I want to risk my life and yours to find him, especially as he may well be...'

'Dead.'

Olivia had finished his sentence and the word hung between them like a fog. There was silence. She picked up her knife and fork. At first, she picked at her food but it was delicious and, as she had eaten nothing since breakfast, her dishes were soon cleared. She relaxed back in her chair and looked fondly at Rich. He looked up, saw her smile, and smiled back.

'Your stupid idea is growing on me,' he said. 'But not together. You can't give your parents any more grief. I could ask my company for an extended holiday and tell my parents the same. I'll do that tomorrow. If the picture fails to take me to Phil, I can always say my plans for a world trip failed. It's a big risk, though. Let me think about it.'

She stood up, went around the table and hugged him.

When they parted company to go home, they had agreed to meet at the Hard Rock Café on the quayside on Tuesday evening.

'If the picture's gone, then there's no harm done. If it's there I'll give it a go. I'm just a bit worried about you getting home afterwards, so late at night.'

'You're very sweet, Rich, but you don't know much about me. I've got a black belt in Judo and I'm very fit. I can take care of myself.'

'In that case, I'll be very careful not to annoy you, he said grinning. 'See you on Tuesday, bye.'

When Rich arrived at the Hard Rock Café it was noisy, as it always was, especially late in the evening. He was shown to a table and had just sat down when he saw Olivia looking around for him. He stood and waved. She reached his table, kissed him on the cheek, and said, 'I'll understand if you've changed your mind. We'll just have a drink and go home.'

'I'm good to have a go but might take the edge off with another whiskey.'

A waitress arrived and hunkered down, 'Can I get you guys anything, drinks, food?'

'I'd like a large glass of Merlot and another whiskey,' said Olivia. Rich was about to say which whisky he would like when the waitress looked at him. 'Same again?' He nodded, and she said, 'I'll be right back.'

There was a short silence when the waitress had gone. It seemed trite, somehow, to exchange the normal pleasantries when in an hour or so they were going to do something completely abnormal. It was Olivia that finally spoke.

'Have you told Mike?'

Rich shook his head, his smile wistful. 'Things have not been the same since Phil disappeared. Mike and I stopped going to rugby. It was as if Phil was the glue holding us together. Mike's started going to a gym, and I've taken up running. I want to build up my stamina and distance so I can have a go at the Great North Run. I'll still do that if tonight doesn't work.'

The waitress returned with their drinks, interrupting their conversation. They both sipped their drinks then Olivia said, 'I'm sorry your friendship with Mike has dwindled.'

It was after midnight when they walked across the quayside. There was no-one else around and a chill wind was blowing. As they looked down at the picture, the rope bridge appeared to swing in the breeze.

'That's strange, probably a trick of the light, a bulb flickering,' said Rich.

Olivia looked up at the lights and as she lowered her gaze back to the picture she glimpsed a man, in a brimmed hat, leaning against a bollard. He was not looking their way.

'I'm going to do it now,' Rich stepped onto the painted bridge. It swung violently under his weight, and he fell. His yell of surprise faded as he fell further and then she heard a distant splash.

'Rich! Rich!' shouted Olivia. The shock of seeing him disappear made her feel faint and she swayed. A strong pair of hands supported her, and a man's voice said, 'He'll be fine, I promise.' Olivia began to cry and scarcely noticed the man let go of her as she scrabbled in her bag for a tissue. When she finally dragged her eyes away from the picture, he was gone.

Chapter 9

2012

It was Tuesday night. Adam locked up and drove to Eve's flat. It was still drizzling with the remnants of yesterday's storm. *I mustn't forget a waterproof coat*, he thought. Her flat was in a Georgian building that must once have been elegant but was now almost derelict. He opened the front door and was met with peeling wallpaper and a smell of cooked cabbage and mould. *I might feel suicidal if I lived here.* He climbed the stairs looking carefully at his feet for fear the next step would crumble with dry rot. Eve's flat was at the top of the building. The cramped space felt worse because the ceiling slanted, so even he, with his diminutive stature, could only stand in the centre of the room. Her fridge door was ajar. He opened it and was surprised to see it clean and empty. She really had planned her suicide. Tears began to fall for Eve. He had to help her.

Her food cupboard held a few cans, so he packed those and then turned his attention to her clothes. There was a rucksack under her bed, so he put in sufficient clothing for four days along with two towels which filled it. He repacked and managed to add a cagoule. He remembered she had a sleeping bag and stuffed that in the same bag as the cans.

When Adam locked the door and stood in the street he breathed in deeply. It had felt so claustrophobic and insanitary he needed fresh air. He took everything back to his warehouse. He was going to leave them in his office but decided to take them down the stairs and leave them near the door. On Wednesday, he would have more food to bring down and it would save a journey if he did it now.

At the door to the other dimension, he couldn't resist opening it. *Why not take her things to her now?* She'd be surprised and he hoped she'd be pleased to see him so soon. It was not raining but droplets fell as he pushed his way through the bushes. He stopped and wiped his face before setting off for the shelter.

The devastation that met him was shocking. The stove lay on its side, half-buried in mud. The camp bed had been stopped in its slide by a tree and all his belongings were strewn everywhere. There was no sign of the tarpaulin or Eve.

'Eve, Eve, it's Adam. Where are you? Eve, Eve!'

There was no reply and Adam's heart hammered in his chest. He walked past the mess and where there was a clear place, just clean, damp grass, he began to go uphill. He toiled all the way to the top, stopping now and again to call her name, his breath rasping. It was flat at the top and the wind blew strongly, snatching away his calls.

What would I do if my shelter had been destroyed? I'd climb up to where it was safe from mudslides. I'd try to find a cave or if I had found the tarpaulin, I'd make a new camp deep in the trees as shelter from the wind.

Adam moved into the trees, his eyes darting all around. Then he heard a sound. It was bizarre. He heard singing. A few more steps and he saw her. She stopped singing as she heard him. Adam ran to her and took her in his arms.

'I thought you were dead. I'm so sorry I left you. Are you hurt?'

'Only a few cuts and bruises. I thought I was going to die when everything, including me, was swept down the hill by mud and water. So glad you're here. Is it Wednesday?'

She pulled away from him and looked ruefully at the state of her clothes, saying, 'I must stink.'

'You've set up a new camp. It's in a much better position than mine.'

She told him how she had struggled out of the mud and gone down to the river to try and clean herself. When the rain stopped, she had climbed up beside the landslide and found the tarpaulin caught in a tree. She had also found the cool box.

'The tarpaulin was too heavy. I had to drag it up here. I was exhausted and hungry, so I went back for the box. It was fine inside, and I ate just about everything. Kept telling myself to save some, but I was ravenous.' She looked up at the grey sky. 'Adam, you can't stay here, it's getting dark. Thanks for bringing my things.'

'Eve, everything's changed now. You've done brilliantly coping with such a disaster, but I can't leave you here. You must come back with me, now.' Adam couldn't read the expression on her face. Her eyes were filling, she frowned but then sighed. Was it relief or dismay? Then she nodded and turned away from her camp.

They went steadily downhill, holding hands, trying not to slip on the wet grass. Adam was still wearing her rucksack and carrying her bag. There was no conversation until Eve saw the door in the cliff.

'It's ancient.'

'It is and I'm afraid we've got to climb a lot of steps, 365 to be precise.'

She followed him along the corridor, and they climbed the steps. Adam paused when he heard her breathing becoming laboured and then, when they reached the top, he went through the hatch first and helped her up. He put down the hatch and moved the desk back over it.

'This must be your office.'

'It's my office and my warehouse,' he said, wanting her to be impressed. Then he looked at the state of her. 'Anyway, you need some TLC. I'm going to take you home.'

She shrank back to the desk.

'No, please Adam, not my flat. You've seen what it's like.'

'I didn't mean your flat, I meant my house. You can have a bath or shower and while you're doing that, I'll order a takeaway.'

He was rewarded with a smile, and she followed him to his car.

Eve was singing again, a folk song, as she showered. Adam's heart did a somersault. Was he falling for her or just felt sorry for her? It didn't matter.

He had plates warming in the oven, had laid the table and opened a bottle of red wine. The Chinese meal had just arrived when Eve emerged, looking clean and beautiful, her black, damp hair clinging to her head.

'That was heavenly. Thank you, Adam.'

He handed her a glass of wine, but she shook her head.

'No thanks. I'm an alcoholic and must never drink again. You go ahead and I'll have water. It smells delicious and I'm starving.'

'Help yourself while I get some water.'

He gathered up the wine bottle and glasses, pouring all of it away down the sink. When he was back with a jug of water and tumblers, she looked at him and said, 'That was partly why I felt suicidal. I was going to AA and managing well with their support but then my boyfriend dumped me and, as he was my boss, I lost my job. I couldn't afford my lovely flat and had to move to that dreadful one you saw. No money, nothing to eat. It was all too much.' Her voice cracked as she relived her despair.

'Don't think of that now, Eve. I hate to see you upset. Enjoy the food and then a good night's sleep will make you feel better.'

The following morning, Eve woke very late. The bedside clock said it was eleven o'clock. She stretched, revelling in the luxury of a clean, soft bed. Eventually, she managed to get up and went downstairs to the kitchen. Adam had left a note.

"I hope you slept well. Help yourself to anything you need. I will be home at 7pm.

Adam x"

Eve needed to show Adam her appreciation of everything he had done for her. She would have cleaned the house, but it was already perfect. Then she remembered her filthy clothes which she had left on the bathroom floor. His washing machine was in the kitchen, and she saw there were things in it. She opened the door to find her clothes. He had already washed them. She grinned. He probably couldn't bear the smell. At least she could dry them. The beautifully appointed kitchen had a door to the garden. Eve took a cup of coffee out there and looked around. It was small and neat. The patio had two metal chairs, a matching table and a rotary washing line standing in a tiny patch of grass. The garden had a high wooden fence that was softened by a few shrubs. A wisteria had large purple flowers and was supported on a trellis. There was a gentle breeze and Eve decided to hang her washing on the line.

By the time she was dressed and ready to go out, the washing was dry. She was enjoying this domesticity, but she was also feeling guilty. What could she do to show Adam how grateful she was? Perhaps she could cook dinner for tonight. She had no money, so she couldn't buy anything, so it would have to be whatever was in the fridge and freezer. It was quickly decided when she found pasta and mince. There were all the other ingredients to make a Spaghetti Bolognese.

Eve went for a walk and thought more about pleasing Adam. She knew he was attracted to her. Should she offer sex? Could she do it after ... In her mind, she saw Jack, strutting towards her undoing his belt, 'I know you're gagging for it and I'm just in the mood. Brace yourself sweetheart, this is gonna be hard and fast. Just as you like it, rough stuff.'

He had been cruel. He enjoyed slapping her, sometimes punching. Telling her a bit of pain would turn her on. She shook her head, sighed deeply, and dragged herself back from the mire of the past. Would Adam behave like Jack? She doubted it. Adam had shown her nothing but kindness. Sex with Adam would not be violent. Perhaps she didn't need to decide; she'd just wait and see how things developed.

Chapter 10

2022

When Adam was sure Olivia wasn't going to faint, he left her and ran quickly to his car. He drove as fast as he dared to the warehouse, parked in the yard, and ran inside to his office. He was so glad he didn't have to run down the steps. The industrial sized lift took him down in less than a minute.

The corridor was lit as he ran to the large vehicle-sized door now installed. There was a road enabling him to get to the river quickly and he leapt into his boat and started the engine. There was to be no hot drink or doughnuts for this man, if he survived the fall and the swim, because Adam had not been expecting him. He had stood by the picture that evening because he had a premonition. Sometimes he believed the other dimension communicated with him, but he couldn't prove it.

In silent cruising mode, Adam moved away from the jetty and then opened the throttle to full and put on the search light which he angled towards the shore. He knew nothing about the man he was trying to rescue but assumed he was friend of Phil's.

He must be brave because he had no idea what would happen if he fell into the picture. We can always use people like him. I wonder what skills he can offer. There he is!

Adam could see him standing on the pebbly beach. He was soaking wet, breathing hard and waving. Adam turned the boat and beached it.

'Hello, you look like you need rescuing.'

'I'm so glad to see you. Thought I was going to die when I fell.'

'Climb aboard.'

When he had reversed off the beach, Adam said, 'Take off your wet clothes. I can give you a towel and a blanket to wrap yourself in once you're dry.' He turned his attention to navigating the river and noticed that the sky was not quite as dark – a pre-dawn glow was discernible. 'It's not far now. I'm Adam. You are?'

'Rich. Do you know I fell through a picture?'

'Yes, but I don't know why or how it works.'

'My best friend, Phil, did the same thing back in the summer. Do you know him? Did he survive?'

'Yes, he's fine and I'll take you to his house as soon as we tie up. While I'm doing that, please collect your wet clothes and bring them with you.'

They walked up the hill to the flat area where Eve had put up the tarpaulin all those years ago. Then they walked the length of the village, passed the hospital, and reached Phil's house. Adam lifted the latch and walked in. People rarely locked their cabins.

He lowered his voice, not wanting to wake Phil. 'Here's the bathroom and that's the spare bedroom. Make yourself at home. I'll see you in the morning, bye.'

Rich used the bathroom and put his wet clothes in the bath, then went into the spare bedroom. The bed was not made but he had the blanket he had been wrapped in and there was another on the bed. He lay down and fell asleep immediately.

When I got up and went into the bathroom, I saw a pile of wet clothes in the bath. Whose were they?

'Hello, is there someone here?' There was a muffled grunt from the spare room. I opened the door. 'Rich! How did you get here?'

'Same way as you did. We thought you were dead. Why didn't you ring and let us know? Your mum, dad, Olivia, and Mike have been bereft since you disappeared.'

'The phones don't work here, there's no signal. Look, I've got to get ready for work. I'll give you some of my clothes and then I'll make a cup of tea. We can talk briefly over breakfast. I must shower and get ready now.'

Rich made short work of his scrambled eggs as he listened to my story of what had happened to me. It echoed his own to begin with but not when I described my quayside welcome.
  'It seemed I was expected as if I'd been head hunted for the job.'
  'What job?'
  'Chief surgeon and in charge of the hospital.'
  'Whew, that's quite a step up from being a junior surgeon. But even the most lucrative job in the world shouldn't stop you finding a way to contact your family or visiting once in a while. I still don't understand.'
  'I obviously tried to phone home but there's no signal here. I can't explain any more now, my surgery starts in five minutes. Make yourself at home, go for a walk. I'll see you at 1 pm at Diane's Diner.' I saw Rich frowning and laughed. 'It's not hard to find. See you there.'

Rich stood, feeling confused and irritable. He washed up the breakfast dishes and glanced at his digital watch. The face was blank. *Phil was right about that, anyway I'm so tired, I can't think straight. I'm going back to bed.*

Rich went to sleep immediately and when he woke, the large clock on the wall showed he had only twenty minutes to get ready to meet Phil. He felt anxious, not knowing where the diner was, but hurried out not wanting to be late. He stopped just outside the door and looked around. He turned right and began walking but could see the end of the village, the road going on between trees, so he turned around and went the other way, passed Phil's house, the hospital and it only took a few minutes to reach the shop and Diane's Diner. He didn't go straight in but paused, looking around at all the log cabins.
  This place is cute, more like Switzerland than England. He pushed the door open and saw Phil sitting with Adam. They waved him over.

'The system is you go to the counter, order your food and then sit down,' said Adam.

Rich nodded and ordered vegetable soup with a chunk of bread and butter then joined the others.

'Now can I have some explanations, please? I need to know what this place is and why Phil can't phone home to tell his mum he's safe?'

Adam put down his cup and said, 'I found this place about ten years ago and loved its unspoilt nature. No pollution, no plastics, no other people. After attempting to use it as a campsite, I decided I needed a more substantial place to live but I'm not a builder, so I had to have other people to help. My aim was to offer people who were out of work, or homeless, a job and a chance to make a new life here. I still live in the first cabin, closest to the river, and one of the men, Arthur, who built the cabins, still lives in his. Everyone here works for no wages. They have enough to eat and share their skills, so everyone benefits. This is a basic, simple life – no phones, no electronic tablets or computers.'

'Sounds a bit like the Amish communities in the States,' said Rich, 'That explains why Phil hasn't contacted his family, but it doesn't explain why he's still here.' He looked at Phil.

'I only found out recently that it was possible to go back to my old life. I thought I'd fallen through the picture to a different kind of life and was stuck in it. I like my job here and feel they need me. They could probably use your knowledge too if you opted to stay. You can think about that, but I must go back to work. Adam will answer any other questions you have.'

Rich sipped his water and said nothing. His brain was buzzing with excitement, fear and too many questions to process. Adam said nothing for a few moments. He watched Rich and wondered what his skills were and if he could be persuaded to stay. He was about to ask, when Rich spoke. 'If people don't get paid, what happens here in this café?'

'The farmers give their produce so Diane can make the food. It's all vegetarian but we do keep chickens so we can have eggs. Diane does make veggie sausages and burgers for those people that hanker after the food they're used to. We can all eat here. It costs nothing because we don't use money. Similarly, in the shop you take what you need if you prefer to cook at home.'

'There must be some things that you can't make yourselves. Phil had toilet paper, soap and shampoo.'

'You're right. Not many people worry about where these things come from. I'm not going to answer that, now, but I will if you decide to stay. Oh, I'd better add we don't have alcohol or any form of smoking. Now come with me and I'll show you our library, and our wind farm that gives us electricity, after a fashion.'

The wind farm, consisting of four turbines, was placed where the ruins of the priory stand in the normal dimension. It was a bleak position on top of a cliff, able to receive maximum wind from the sea or from inland.

'This is an excellent location,' said Rich, 'I don't suppose there are many quiet days when they're not turning.'

'No, but on the rare occasion when there's no wind, we use candles for light. To combat this, certain important places, like the diner and the hospital, have emergency generators. They run on diesel, another item that we can't make ourselves. You will have noticed there are no cars. We use tractors that run on electricity, and you'll now understand how frustrating it is when the power's down.'

'I might be able to help you by building a hydroelectric plant. There are so many hills here, you must have a stream or two running down to the main river.'

'Yes, it's our fresh water source. We've filtered and pumped it into every building. I was going to show you that next. It's more reliable than the wind and has never dried up in the years I've been here.'

'Let's go there next.'

That evening Rich talked to Phil about building a hydroelectric plant.

'I love the way everyone here is so mindful of the environment. It's like a tiny corner of Earth has been set aside for mankind to make a better job of things. I'm beginning to understand what keeps you here, now.'

It was great to hear the enthusiasm in his voice and I smiled.

'I see you've had the induction course 101 from Adam.'

'Yes, but it does make sense, no plastics, no pollution. People living in a healthy way.'

'True but the same people have had to give up alcohol, driving, mobile phones, the internet, games machines, television and cinemas. The evenings can be long and boring. Could you sustain a life as austere as this one?'

'I've no idea but I'm willing to try. I'll give it six months to a year.'

Chapter 11

2012

Adam parked his car in his drive and walked to his front door. He was smiling with anticipation. Eve was in his house and he could hardly wait to see her. When he opened the door, delicious smells wafted towards him. Music was coming from the kitchen, and he stood in the doorway, watching her. She was stirring something on the stove and gyrating at the same time. Adam wanted to take her into his arms.

'Hi Eve, I'm home.' She squealed with surprise. 'Shall we dance?' he asked, holding out a hand. She moved towards him, smiling broadly. They danced in the kitchen, bodies touching until the song finished. Eve stayed encircled by his arms and said, head on one side, 'Dinner's ready.'

Adam kissed her full on the mouth. He felt her respond.

She broke away from his lips, breathing quickly and whispered, 'Dinner can wait. Shall I turn off the heat?'

'Not completely,' he said raffishly.

She pulled away from his embrace to turn off the cooker. Without looking at him, she said, 'I'll race you upstairs.' She pushed past him, ducking his attempt to grab her and he chased her up the stairs, both of them giggling. She stopped at the top, 'Which bedroom?'

'Mine, the bed's bigger,' said Adam pulling his shirt off over his head. They undressed hurriedly, fingers fumbling in their haste. Adam swept Eve into his arms, and they tumbled onto the bed, their desire urgent.

It was all over too soon. They lay entwined and Eve said, 'Shall we have dinner and then try this again, a little slower?'

'Sounds wonderful,' said Adam. He got up, wrapping a dressing gown around him, while Eve put on her pyjamas, then they went downstairs.

'That was delicious, slightly spicy. What did you put in it?' asked Adam.

'A pinch of cayenne pepper.'

'I liked it. I'll clear up and make some tea.'

'No, you've been working all day. Let's do it together. I'll load the dishwasher and you make the tea.'

They took their mugs of tea into the lounge and sat on the sofa close together. Eve sighed with contentment.

'This is a lovely house and I'm grateful to you, for saving me, twice. I can't keep enjoying all these handouts though. I must get a job so I can contribute. It's not in my nature to be a parasite.'

'I never thought of you as being a parasite. You just needed help.' He thought for a moment and then said, 'Would you like to work for me? I can barely cope with the paperwork and have been thinking about employing someone. I'm also looking to buy a second warehouse, expanding big time. I can't then be in two places at once. What do you think?'

Adam had not anticipated Eve's reaction. She shuffled away from him along the sofa and looked down at her hands, twisting them together in her lap.

'Do you remember what drove me to suicide? Have you forgotten already? I worked for my boyfriend then he found someone else, dumped me and gave me the sack. I can't put myself in that position again.'

'So, is that it? You're just saying no?'

She squirmed and whispered, 'Can I think about it?'

Their second, slow lovemaking was abandoned. They went to bed in separate bedrooms.

Adam lay awake disappointed and annoyed with himself for not being more sensitive. Had he spoilt everything? Had he lost her now? Had he enjoyed his first and last intimate moment with her?

Eve lay awake. Adam was not like Jack. Adam was kind. She sighed, turned over, and thumped her pillow but was too tense to sleep. Finally, she got up and went downstairs to the kitchen. She warmed a cup of milk in the microwave and took it into the lounge then curled up on the sofa to drink it. She was holding the cup in both hands when Adam opened the door.

'Sorry, I didn't know you were in here. I couldn't sleep.'

'Me neither. I'm sorry, Adam, I spoilt our lovely evening.'

Adam knelt on the carpet and looked up at her.

'No, it wasn't your fault, it was mine. I was thoughtless and stupid. How can we sort this?'

Eve brought her bare feet down and sat up. She drank the rest of her milk and placed the cup on the side table. 'I think I must take the risk and say yes to the job.'

'Really? That's fantastic. Can you start tomorrow?'

She laughed and held up her hands. 'Slow down. There are things we must discuss. I don't even know if I can do it. What, exactly, will it entail? What will my hours be? What will my salary be?' She smiled at him.

'Why don't we have an induction day tomorrow, then if that goes well, a trial month. We'll know then if it's going to suit both of us.'

'Yes, that's a good idea,' said Eve, yawning 'Let's get some sleep.'

Adam stood up and held out his hand to Eve. She did not take it but stood, unaided and said, 'We'll sleep in our own beds, but I don't have an alarm clock or a phone, so will you wake me?'

'Course I will.'

The following day was hard for them both. It required concentration and the proximity of their bodies was distracting.

'I think I might do better now, Adam, if you made yourself scarce for an hour or two. Didn't you say there was a warehouse in South Shields you wanted to inspect?'

'Yes, but are you sure you'll be okay?'

'Don't worry. If the phone rings and I can't answer a question, I'll take a message. Now, go away, please.'

Adam went, feeling ambivalent. He felt he ought to stay in case she needed help but wanted to go. Once in the car, he focused on finding his way and thinking of all the parameters the new warehouse needed to have. It was currently being used by an animal feed company which meant it should have ticked the same boxes as one that can house human food. He needed to consider whether the animal feed company could still use it if there was sufficient space for other things. He did not want to rent this warehouse, he wanted to buy it, so all the profit would come to him.

While Adam was away, Eve continued to process goods and was beginning to believe she could cope with the job. She gave herself an afternoon tea break and sat thinking about everything. She was only feet away from the secret hatch. Did she ever want to go there again? That profound sense of peace she had experienced. Could she feel it again or had the storm whipped it all away? Her thoughts turned back to her current situation. *I must talk to Adam about wages and if he's happy for me to live with him. I must also go back to my previous hovel and collect the rest of my clothes. I have smart things to wear to work and I'll need them. I left my phone there and I must let the landlord know I'm not wanting to rent it any longer. Perhaps I should write a list!*

Eve was back at her desk, working, when Adam returned, looking pleased with himself. She looked at him. 'You liked the warehouse then?'

'I not only liked it. I made an offer and it's been accepted. This is something to celebrate.' He stopped smiling and looked seriously at her. 'Did you have any problems, messages?'

'No, it's been fine. It's been a good first day.'

'In that case, let's go out for dinner tonight and celebrate. Do you like tapas?'

'I eat almost anything. It's not a posh place, is it? Because I don't have any smart clothes.'

He smiled. 'Nobody dresses up there. Casual clothes are fine. We could go right now, I'm hungry.'

They went to the restaurant and Eve was pleased to see other people in jeans and T-shirts. She relaxed and ate everything.

'Sometimes, Adam, I think I'm dreaming. I'm so glad you pulled me out of the river.'

'So am I. They say mermaids used to lure sailors to their death, but my mermaid has brought me happiness.'

Eve smiled with pleasure and then frowned. 'I don't want to break this spell of mutual delight, but have you given any thought to the shelter? I've been thinking of it and wondering if we could build something more, erm, substantial to stay in. There're loads of trees. What about a log cabin? Having said that, I really have no idea how to build one.' She laughed but Adam looked interested.

'No, I hadn't thought of that, but I like the idea. I think I'd need someone with special skills to help and that would mean sharing our secret place. Let me think about it.'

They left the restaurant, went home and made love, slowly.

Chapter 12

2022

It was Sunday. Rich was in a deep sleep, lying on his back, snoring, so I decided to go for a walk. I set off down the hill and paused outside Alice's house, wondering if she'd like to come. I wouldn't know unless I asked. I knocked and could hear Sandy crying. The volume increased when Alice opened the door, looking harassed. Tendrils of fair hair had escaped her ponytail, and her T-shirt had a stain on it.

'Doctor Phil, come in. I'm in such a mess and Sandy's screaming because she's hungry. I had her breakfast ready and as I brought it to the highchair, she knocked it out of my hand. I had to clear it up and start all over again.'

I followed her inside and closed the front door then hovered in the hallway as she went into the kitchen. I heard her talking to the baby.

'Now then, Sandy. What's all this fuss about? I know you're hungry. Here we go, let's show Doctor Phil that you can be a lovely girl.' She came out of the kitchen carrying the shuddering and gulping, red-faced child. 'Come and sit down, Doctor, and while she's feeding you can tell me why you've come.'

Sandy was soon calmly eating as her mum fed her. Then Alice gave her a spouted cup and she sucked the warm milk, her little hands around the cup as her Mum steadied it.

'I just wondered if you two would like to come for a walk with me. I was thinking of the beach. It's a beautiful day, just a bit breezy and chill.'

'That sounds lovely, thank you. It'll take me half an hour to finish the feed, change Sandy and get ready.' She paused, obviously uncertain, then said, 'Would you make us a cup of tea? I haven't had anything to drink yet.'

'Have you had breakfast?'

'No, too busy trying to give Sandy hers.'

I went into the kitchen, filled the kettle, and then looked for mugs and tea. I found a loaf and toasted two slices. When it was ready, I brought it into the living room and was rewarded by a beautiful smile from Alice.

'Shall I take Sandy while you have your breakfast?'

'Yes please. It's lovely to have some help.' She stood up and passed the child to me and then sat down, took a bite of buttered toast, and sighed. I'm so glad you knocked this morning. I was feeling a bit down and now I've bounced back to the normal, positive me.'

'I'm glad I've helped but my motive was purely selfish. I didn't want to walk on my own.'

We both smiled and there was a companionable silence.

We walked down to the jetty and turned left. Alice had strapped Sandy to her front, so she had her hands free. I took one to help her down the steep grass bank to the beach. The wind buffeted as we pushed against it with seagulls wheeling and crying above us.

The tide was coming in and soon the beach would be submerged. We came level with the Black Midden Rocks, almost under water and stood watching two seals swimming, diving down and then resurfacing. I felt a surge of delight. *I love this place, so wild and natural. I want to stay here and get to know Alice and Sandy better – to become part of their lives. Could she feel the same way? It's probably too soon after her husband's death. It doesn't matter. I can wait.*

'If we don't want to get our feet wet, we'd better head inland,' said Alice, breaking into my thoughts.

'Come on, take my hand. It's very steep.'

I hauled her onto the grass and continued to hold her hand as we ducked between the trees, climbing steadily upwards. We paused for breath, turning around to look down through the trees to the estuary.

'It's such a beautiful place isn't it,' said Alice. 'Did you know it before you came here?'

'Yes. Apart from going to university, I've spent all my life here. I mean in the normal world. My parents and my sister live in North Shields. I miss them. What about you?'

'I was born in Sunderland and studied to be a pharmacist at the university there. That's where I met Dan, my husband. After my studies I worked in a local chemist shop. Dan was working in Newcastle. I don't have any relatives alive now. I miss my parents, but I miss Dan the most.' She hesitated and he thought she was going to cry but she said, 'You do know you can ask Adam to let you visit your family.'

'Yes. My friend, Rich, will be returning to gather materials to build a hydroelectric plant. He's promised to let them know I'm alive and well, but I'd like to see them myself. I ought to move my things out of my flat in Tynemouth and sell it. Then there's my job at the hospital. I don't know how to explain my absence for so many months. It's complicated in the "real" world.'

'It sounds as if you're committing to staying here. Are you wise to burn your bridges?'

I shrugged, 'I really don't know. I might feel different if I go back to see everyone. I won't be able to tell them where I'm living or how I disappeared.'

'No, Adam will ask you to keep our secret before he'll let you go.' Sandy stirred and whimpered. 'We're going to have to go back now, before she thinks it's lunchtime.'

'Okay. If we continue up, we should get to the road. Do you want a hand?'

'Yes, please, Sandy's getting heavy now.'

'I should've offered to carry her. I'll do that next time. Would you like to do this again?'

'I'd like that very much. Thank you for this morning, Phil.'

I left Alice at her front door and continued to my cabin. Rich was not there so I assumed he was at the diner. Usually, on a Sunday, I ate there and was sociable, but today, I wanted to be on my own. I made a simple lunch and sat down, thinking.

I should've asked Alice how she got here. Did Adam choose her because she was a pharmacist? Did she used to work in the hospital here before Sandy came along? Did she fall through a picture like Rich and me?

I'll ask Adam about going back when I see him. Perhaps I could go with Rich but I'm only free on Sundays. What happens to all the people here if I'm away for a week or I'm ill? There's still so much to find out. Alice was right. I must keep my flat in case everything here goes wrong.

Chapter 13

2012

The probationary month was up, and it was not necessary to discuss if it had worked out well. Adam was delighted to be able to concentrate on stocking his new warehouse. After just a few days, he realised he could trust Eve to make the right decisions. She was a natural.

She also managed the staff skilfully. When Bill's wife had her first baby, Eve sent flowers. She sent a card of condolence if someone's relative died. She was sympathetic when a person phoned in sick, but she was also astute, recognising when a malingerer thought she was a soft touch. In short, she had earned their respect.

Eve enjoyed the job, finding it interesting, sometimes challenging, but also satisfying. Her self-confidence had grown. She no longer worried about sponging on Adam. He loved her and she was sure, now, she loved him too.

They had finished their evening meal and Adam was about to put the television on when Eve asked him not to.

'What's up?'

Eve had been lounging but now sat up. 'We need to talk about the other dimension. In particular, the enormous amount of money you've been spending.'

Adam straightened his back but remained seated. 'How do you know what I've been spending? I haven't put it through the company. It's my own money.' He had been on the point of adding what he spent was not her business, but he held that in, not wanting to have an argument.

'I know that, but that lift being installed is going to be enormous. It must have cost thousands of pounds and it goes to a place that has nothing. You'll never recoup that money.'

Adam stood up, feeling irritated. He paced the room and then looked at her before speaking. Her face showed concern. She was not being critical, just worried.

'I'm careful with money, Eve, and I promise I'll never go into debt. This lift will enable us to take vehicles down – excavators, tractors, a generator. We talked about building a cabin for ourselves but, in my mind, I can see a street with lots of cabins, a whole village. Everyone living a healthy lifestyle, helping each other, and enjoying a simple way of life.' His eyes shined with enthusiasm. 'This is my dream, Eve, and the lift is the first step.' He laughed, 'It will mean the *end* of all those steps. It's my vision, my hobby. Other men might collect classic cars or renovate a stately home. The other dimension is mine.'

'That's quite a speech. I'm sorry. I really didn't mean to upset you. My office has been moved and I see all this activity going on. The workmen turning up when we're closing for the evening and going home when we open in the morning. They leave their equipment behind that wall you've had built and some of our workers have asked me about it.'

Adam frowned. 'What have you said?'

'You're exploring the possibility of more storage underground.'

'That's excellent, thank you.' Adam sat down again and smiled at her. 'Are we still friends?'

Eve's response was to get up and give him a hug. The hug led to a kiss and Adam pulled her to the floor.

Later, satisfied, and happy, Eve said, 'Making love on the living room floor is slightly decadent.'

'I hope we'll be able to make love in our own log cabin soon. Perhaps a couple of months.'

Eve grinned, 'That might not be so comfortable if there's no carpet. You even had carpet in the shelter.'

'Hmm, I'll think about that,' said Adam, lazily.

2013

It was a year since Adam had first gone down the steps. The cabin was finished. Adam called a meeting with the four men that had built it. They met in the cabin and looked at him expectantly.

'I picked you all very carefully to do this job. I needed to trust you not to talk about this place. You've not let me down. I also chose men who needed the work, for one reason or another. I have paid you a reasonable rate and you're free to leave. But.' He looked at their attentive faces and then continued. 'If you would like to live here, rather than go back to the rat race up above, I have a proposal. You can stay here and build a whole village of cabins, just like this one but I won't pay you anything.'

There were now frowns and murmurings, but Adam held up a hand.

'I will provide all the food you'll need, bedding and toiletries. Each of you will eventually have your own cabin, just like this one. My aim is to have a self-sufficient commune where people work for no money but eat what they produce. I know you probably think I'm crazy and you're free to go back now and never return. If you're interested, meet me at the warehouse tomorrow morning at 8 am. Thank you again for your excellent work.'

There was a bemused silence as they all rode the lift together and then left the warehouse. Adam hoped at least one or two of them might meet him tomorrow.

Eve was waiting at the top and when the men had left, Adam said, 'Are you ready?' She nodded and they both rode the lift back down.

'Oh, this is so different,' said Eve. 'I suppose you had to make a road to get the machines and generator to the site, but somehow, I was still expecting to fight my way through the bushes. The road went down towards the sea then curved left up the hill to the plateau at the top. As they reached the top, Eve saw the cabin for the first time.

'It's lovely, Adam, like something Heidi might have lived in.'

'Who's Heidi?'

'A little girl in one of my favourite children's books. She slept in the roof area and went up a little ladder to get there.'

'In that case, you're going to love it inside. Come on in.'

The large living space had a kitchen area at one end, with a fridge, a washing machine, an electric cooker and cupboards. There was no furniture. Eve moved into the hallway, and there was a door to a bedroom, another to a bathroom and at the far end, a ladder leading to the roof void. She turned and kissed Adam before climbing it.

'There's masses of space up here,' she shouted. 'It would make a child's bedroom and still have room for storage.'

She came down with a delighted grin on her face and hugged him. While his arms were still around her, she said, 'I was really nervous about coming back here. I imagined being crushed by scary memories and hating it, but it seems so different now. This cabin isn't going to be washed down the hill in a storm. It's strong and safe. When can we have our first night here?'

'Well, I think we'll need some furniture, so it'll be a while.'

'We didn't have much furniture in the shelter, but we managed. Let's come on the weekend and use sleeping bags on camp beds. It'll be fun. We could even go fishing again. I'd like that.'

'You're on, but I'll have to leave you to buy those things. I've got a lot to do before next Saturday.'

Chapter 14

2022

I finished my Saturday morning surgery and rushed home feeling excited because I was going to visit to my parents that afternoon. Adam told me to meet him at the diner, and he would show me the way to the lift. I was going to stay until Sunday evening and then come back, meeting Adam at 7 pm at the warehouse.

It was a dull, cold day, and I saw a sprinkling of snowflakes wafted by the light breeze before they melted as they touched the ground. I pulled my anorak hood over my head and hurried to the diner. Adam was sheltering in the doorway, waiting, and came towards me. 'You've chosen a miserable cold day for your weekend away. Come on.'

I said nothing but walked quickly, my hands in my pockets, barely keeping pace with Adam. When we got to the door, he pressed a button on a remote. The door was a large garage door and rolled up. As soon as the gap was big enough, we both ducked under to escape the snow that was now falling in earnest. Adam switched on the lights and pushed the button to close the heavy door.

'I had no idea the way out was so simple. Why did Rich and I fall into the river through a picture when we could've come this way?'

Adam didn't answer, but just pressed the button to make the lift rise. Then when we were at the top we went through a normal sized door into an office. Adam locked it behind us. I followed him as he locked the office door and then we walked through the warehouse brimming with goods. Forklift trucks were gliding around, and men were picking goods to be despatched. A lorry was half in the large entrance being unloaded.

'This is amazing, Adam. You're an entrepreneur. This is how so many goods find their way into our shop. You supply everything from toilet rolls to toothpaste. There's no money used so you must be giving us everything. Why?'

Adam frowned, obviously uncomfortable. 'I just want everything to work, back there; a clean lifestyle and others to enjoy it too. I can afford it. It's no different to giving to a charity, really. Oh, here comes Eve, my erm, partner. Eve, this is Doctor Phil.'

She smiled but made no attempt to shake hands. The Covid Pandemic had stopped that tradition. 'It's good to meet you. Adam was so pleased when you arrived and settled in so quickly. I do hope you're just on a visit and not leaving.'

'It's just a short visit to see my family. I don't want to be rude, Eve, but as it's such a short visit, I'd like to get on.'

Eve held up both her hands. 'Go, go. I don't want to hold you up.' She was smiling broadly, and I could see she had not taken offence. I smiled back and turned to leave.

I parted from Adam at the warehouse door. I knew where I was and walked, then began to jog the short distance to my parents' house.

When I arrived, I rang the bell and hopped impatiently from foot to foot. The door eventually opened, slowly and I was overwhelmed. Tears began to fall. Surely this frail old woman was not my mum. She gasped; tears threaded their way down the wrinkles on her cheeks as she gathered me into her arms.

'What happened? We thought you were dead. I can't believe you're here.'

I wanted to squeeze her hard to show how much I loved her, but I was scared of breaking a rib. 'I'm sorry Mum. I couldn't help it. I had an accident.'

Dad came to the door and hugged me too. He looked more robust than Mum but had also lost a lot of weight.

'I'll give Olivia a quick ring. She was coming anyway for lunch, but I'll tell her to come now.' He took his mobile from his pocket. Phil could hear Olivia's squeal of delight and Dad quickly ended the call.

'Come on through and sit down. I'll put the coffee pot on. How long are you stopping?'

Dad tossed this question out as he disappeared into the kitchen. Mum gave me another hug and then felt for my hand. 'I feel I must keep hold of you in case you disappear again.' She pulled me into the living room and sat on the settee close beside me. 'It's been so hard, losing you like that. I couldn't eat for weeks. I got so thin your dad made me go to the doctors.'

I squirmed with guilt, but she went on – twisting the knife.

'I had a lot of tests, and it seems my weight loss wasn't all grief. I've got bladder cancer. Next week I've got to start chemo.'

I bent over, my hands covering my head. 'You've been through all those tests, and I wasn't here to support you. I'm so sorry. Who's your oncologist?'

Mum leant her head on my shoulder, and I straightened to give her a hug. 'Mr G. Bates. Do you know him?'

Before I could reply, Dad came in carrying a tray and just as he put it down, Olivia let herself in. I stood up to give her a hug. She hugged me back and whispered, 'You met up with Rich then. It's so good to see you.'

I whispered back, 'I'm so glad you didn't go with Rich and were here to support Mum and Dad.

'Come on you two. Stop whispering, sit down, and have your coffee before it gets cold. We haven't got any homemade cake, but the baker's fruit loaf's pretty good.'

We did as we were told and dutifully drank coffee and ate cake. Then Mum asked the question I'd been dreading.

'You said you had an accident, Phil. Why didn't the police or the hospital let us know? And, when you were getting better, why didn't you ring?'

I hesitated a long time, wishing I'd rehearsed an answer.

'Well, if you're not going to tell them, I will,' said Olivia. 'He didn't have an accident. His injuries were deliberate. He was beaten up when he was kidnapped. Naturally, they took away his phone. He was kept in a basement, miles from here while the kidnappers decided what to do.'

Mum's hand was covering her mouth and her eyes glistened with tears. Dad was frowning and obviously thinking because he said, 'I don't understand why they would pick you. You're not famous and you don't have rich relatives. I'm quite certain the NHS wouldn't stump up ransom money for a junior surgeon. It doesn't make sense.'

I'd rallied now and embellished the story. 'I heard them talking one day. It seems they thought I was Johnny Flynn, the musician and film star.'

'Never heard of 'im,' said Dad.

'He played Mr Knightley in *Emma* and David Bowie in *Stardust*,' said Olivia. 'Come to think of it, you do look like him, Phil.'

Mum was alert now and asked, 'When they found out they'd made a mistake, why didn't they let you go?'

'They thought I'd go to the police. I was scared they might kill me to make sure I didn't.'

'So how did you get away?' asked Dad.

'They got careless. I managed to get free of my ropes and the next time food was brought in I was ready and waiting. I hid behind the door, hit him with my chair, then I ran. That was nearly a week ago. It was hard because I had no money, no phone and I didn't know where I was.' *That at least was true.* 'Anyway, I'm back now and so pleased to see you.'

'What's for lunch, Mum? Can I do anything?' asked Olivia, deftly changing the subject. 'I hope it's something warming. It's very cold outside.'

After lunch, Mum went for a lie down, so Olivia asked me to walk with her to the supermarket.

'Mum texts me her list and I usually get her groceries, so if we walk, you can help carry them.'

We set off and I said, 'Should we have asked Dad to come or if he wanted anything?'

'No, as soon as the door shut behind us, he'll have settled into his chair and will sleep until we get back. He's finding Mum's illness very stressful.'

'You must be too. I'm sorry to have left you to cope on your own.'

'None of this has been your fault, Phil. I was just so glad Rich managed to meet up with you. He came to see me in the middle of the week. He explained your position and was very enthusiastic about building a hydroelectric plant. What I don't understand is why you've only just managed to get leave to visit.'

'It's because Adam wanted me to become committed to the job and to the community. Even then *he* didn't tell me returning was a possibility. It was Alice.'

'So, Alice, middle-aged, greying hair?' Olivia was teasing, smiling as she looked sideways at me.

'No, Alice is twenty-nine, curly fair hair, blue eyes and has a beautiful baby girl called Sandy.'

'She's married?'

I shook my head. 'A fairly recent widow.'

Our conversation ceased as we entered the supermarket. I pushed the trolley and followed Olivia around the shop. She knew her way round and it was soon done. On the way home, she asked if I was able to stay overnight and see Mum and Dad tomorrow.

'Yes, I'll stay as long as I can, but I have to take surgery on Monday. What I can do is show you the warehouse. That's the civilised way in. The woman that works there is called Eve and she would be able to get a message to me if you need to before next weekend.

Tonight, after dinner, I must go to my flat and do some sorting out. I'll sleep there and come back in the morning.'

'There's not much to sort out. I've cleaned out the fridge, emptied the bin, washed your bedding and tidied.'

I stopped walking, put down the bags and gave her a hug. 'What a star. The best sister a man could ever have. Thank you. I should also thank you for daring to ask Rich to go through the picture.'

'That was Rich's idea. I told him I was going to try. He thought of Mum and Dad and said he would go instead.'

'He's the best.'

Chapter 15

2013

Petro

Petro said goodbye to the other men, without discussing Adam's strange offer. The new life Adam was suggesting sounded exciting. Once inside his bedsit, he went straight to the chest of drawers, pulling out clothes that he'd need and placing them neatly on the bed. Then he got a holdall and put them in, adding a towel and some slippers. When that was done, he heated a ready meal in the microwave, ate it, then went online to check his bank account. He was very careful with money and knew there was enough to pay the rent and other bills for six months, but he had to check. After that, he played on his games machine. He would miss playing so he wanted to make the most of the evening.

When his eyes were drooping, he went to bed but lay there thinking. *I like Adam but I don't feel confident to ask him about the place. It was so odd going so far down in the lift and coming out into unspoilt countryside. At least it was unspoilt until we built the road and the cabin and there will be more, even if I have to build them on my own. How can Adam be sure the people he gets to live in them will be respectful of the nature around them and take care of it?*

The next morning, Petro poured away the unused milk, emptied the rubbish bin and cleaned the sink. Then he looked around, to make sure everything was neat and tidy for his return in a few days. Then he picked up the holdall, locked the door behind him and walked briskly to the bus stop, whistling quietly.

Arthur

Arthur set off for his bedsit, pondering on the offer Adam had made. When he opened the door, a waft of stale air met him. The bin needed emptying in the kitchen area. He sighed, grabbed the offending bag, and bent to tie it up. As he did so the stench pushed into his face, and he looked away with disgust. *Why am I such a slob? I'll take it straight out to the Biffa bin.* As he lifted the lid and swung the bag into it, he thought of an analogy. *This bag is me and the Biffa bin is where I was heading when Adam spoke to me in the pub.*

Arthur realised how close he had come to destitution and resolved to go back and work for just his board and lodging. He had enjoyed the camaraderie of the other men and hoped some of them would also go back. But more than that, he had learned new skills and become fitter and stronger in the process. While working for Adam, he had also found his self-respect.

Now, he grabbed a rucksack and threw in changes of clothes and other essentials then left the bedsit for his favourite Italian restaurant.

The waiter asked Arthur what he would like to drink.

'A large bottle of sparkling water please. Do you want my order too?' The waiter nodded and he said, 'I'd like garlic bread followed by a pepperoni pizza.'

The waiter made a note and walked away, returning quickly with the water, so cold the outside of the jug was misted with condensation. Arthur filled a glass and drank all of it in one long glug. He let out a satisfied breath. *I thought only several pints of beer could slake my thirst but that was almost as good.*

Arthur still found it hard to be in a restaurant on his own. He looked at his phone, but there were no messages. *I should've got the numbers of the other men then we could've texted our decisions. I really don't want to be the only one to turn up tomorrow.* His eyes roved around the restaurant and alighted on an elderly woman. She cut a slice of pizza, folded it in half and ate it with her fingers. He smiled, looked away and saw the waiter bringing his garlic bread, dripping with melted butter.

When his meal was finished, Arthur paid and went back to his bedsit. He really hated living there. It was far too cramped for a large man. He went to bed, looking forward to the next day with more than a little trepidation.

It was 7.45 am and Adam waited at the warehouse entrance in the hope that one or two workmen might be interested in his proposal to build more cabins for no pay. It was a fine sunny morning with a chill in the wind, and he rocked forward and backward on his heels, feeling anxious and impatient.

He was about to go inside when Petro arrived, quickly followed by Arthur. Adam's smile stretched from ear to ear. He went forward to greet them. 'I can't tell you how delighted I am to see you. Come on, let's go down and we'll talk about accommodation and such like.'

They threaded their way through the shelving stacked from floor to ceiling with goods and Adam unlocked the door to the room that held the lift. Once outside, they all walked to the finished cabin and went in.

'I consider this to be my cabin but as it's the only one, you two must share it while you work on the next one. I know there's no furniture, and it will be primitive with camp beds and camping chairs, but it will be warm. As I said, I will provide food and any extra tools you might need. You can toss a coin as to who owns the next cabin you finish. Either way, when two new cabins are finished, you can both have one each. Any questions before you start work?'

'Yes,' said Arthur, half raising a hand. 'If you expect us to start work now, I don't see any food, or other essentials and how can we sleep here tonight without the camp beds?' Adam nodded. 'Good questions, Arthur. When I said you'll start work I didn't mean clearing a space for the next cabin. I'll need your help to get everything down here and get you settled in. It's the middle of the week so I am also happy for you to spend the weekend up above if you want to. In fact, if you have somewhere to go, I'd appreciate it if you left the cabin for me to use this weekend.'

The next few hours were spent collecting goods from the warehouse and taking them down. By lunchtime everything was in place and Adam told the men to use anything they wanted from the cool box and to let Eve know if they were short of anything.

'I know I've said this before, but I must impress on you the importance of keeping this place a secret. You must not invite anyone one here to come and see it and there must be no smoking or drinking of alcoholic drinks. I'll come back on Friday evening, about 5 pm, to see how far you've got.'

When Adam had left, Arthur looked at Petro.
'Will no smoking or alcohol bother you, Petro?'
'No. I've not had enough money to drink or smoke so it's no problem. What about you?'
'I'll find the no drinking hard because when Adam found me, I was almost an alcoholic, but this job has helped. I've only thought of booze in the evenings and then I was anxious not to waste money. At least if I'm living here, there's no temptation. Come on, let's get cracking and fell some trees.'

Later that evening, tired from the active work, Petro and Arthur sat in the late sunshine and chatted.
'Where do you come from, Petro? You've almost no foreign accent, but your name isn't English.'
'Until 1991, I lived with my parents in Croatia. Serbia tried to invade our country and we left to travel to England. My uncle lived here, in the north of England, so we made our way to be with him. It took a month, and we were not sure the immigration authorities would let us in. It helped that we had relatives and soon we were living in Newcastle. I was ten years old. My father found work and I went to school. Now I feel I'm English. I wanted to come back and work here because this place has something special.'
Arthur nodded. 'I feel the same. It's peaceful, just the sounds and smells that nature makes. I was in a bad way, when Adam found me, propping up a bar. Before that, I had a wife, my own house and I thought life was perfect. We had some savings, and I made an unwise investment. I believed all the spiel that I would get five per cent return on my money. They were crooks. After a year my wife suggested we went on a cruise, so I needed some of the money to pay for it. The company had quietly disappeared, and all my savings went with them. I asked for

help from the police, and they investigated but I got no money back.

'I'm sorry that happened to you, Arthur.'

'Thanks, but the story gets worse. My wife was so incensed at my stupidity, she left me. Then she demanded her share of the house. I had to sell it and my half was not enough to buy another. I rented a bedsit and was depressed, lonely and started drinking. There was just one good thing.'

'What was that?'

'We had no children.' As he said this Arthur stood up to stretch his legs. He was a well-built man, with long legs and the camping chairs were too low. There was silence as he walked about, then Petro spoke.

'I was living in a bedsit too. I had a job making furniture. Good quality, expensive to buy, furniture. Then my boss became bankrupt. He was a superb craftsman but didn't have a head for business. So, I was out of work. Jasmine, my girlfriend, wanted to go out for meals, go to clubs and dance. I had no income, couldn't give her the things she wanted, so she found another man that would. You and I are a pair. I was also lonely and desperate when Adam found me, but I was not drinking. He found me at the Job Centre.'

Petro and Arthur worked well together. Petro had the skill, Arthur the strength. When Adam came on Friday, he was delighted with their progress.

'I thought, now that there were only two of you, that little would have been achieved, but you've cleared a space big enough for two cabins and all the logs neatly stacked. Well done.'

Both men smiled with pleasure and rode the lift for their weekend break. Adam stayed below, checking the cabin and making a list of the things he and Eve would need for their fishing weekend.

When he arrived at the top of the lift she was waiting, her arms filled with sleeping bags and pillows. 'I thought I'd stack everything in the lift. I've got food shopping and bought two proper fishing rods.' She looked excited and happy. 'Are we going to sleep there tonight and tomorrow?'

Adam took the bedding from her and kissed her. 'Yes. I want to make the most of our mini holiday. It's also a lot of effort for just one night.' He grimaced before adding, 'We'll also have to clear our stuff out so the men can use the cabin on Monday. I'd like to go home first to change into something more casual.'

'Yes, we'll have to because I haven't packed any clothes yet.'

Their weekend was wonderful. They caught plenty of fish on Saturday, enough to put in the cool box to cook on Sunday too.

'I've just one complaint,' said Adam, wiping bread around his plate. 'There were no chips to go with the fish.' He was smiling, his eyes twinkling, and Eve threw a pillow at him. He caught it deftly, laughing and then became more serious. 'Let's decide what sort of furniture we should have in here.'

'It seems to me, it ought to be cottagey, you know, flowery cushions and curtains, with saucepans hanging on the wall and maybe a dresser. A wooden table and simple chairs, a wooden double bed, and a set of drawers for the bedroom. How does that sound?'

'Good, I can see it when you describe it, but I didn't have a clue. So, what do you think to Petro making the furniture? Did I tell you that was what he did before his job ended?'

Eve nodded, frowned, and thought, before replying.

'I don't see how he can do all that as well as building more cabins. It means this won't be a comfortable, furnished cabin for years.'

'You're right. He's working for free, at the moment, but I could offer to pay him to make furniture on a weekend or see if I can get more men. I'll think about it.'

Petro loved working with wood and preferred making furniture to building cabins, so he happily agreed to Adam's suggestion. He would be paid for the furniture he made, providing he did it in his own time. He became a workaholic and in the evenings Arthur resented Petro's happy concentration as he shaped and sanded the wood.

'Okay, Petro. I've had enough of sitting on my own every evening while you work. What about giving me something I can do to help.'

Petro hesitated, 'I told you Adam's paying me for this work. If you help me, I'll have to share my earnings.'

'No, you won't. It's good for me to be penniless then when I go up top, I have no money to spend on drink. I'll just help for the sake of companionship.'

'In that case, I'll show you how to fix these chair legs into the lathe and sand them as they turn.'

Petro demonstrated and watched Arthur do the first one. He nodded in satisfaction and went back to making a kitchen table. By the end of that evening Arthur had sanded a dozen chair legs and graduated to hand sanding the seats. As they worked, they chatted about many things including music.

'I've been playing fiddle for as long as I can remember,' said Petro. 'My father played and put a tiny one under my chin when I was a small boy. I never learnt to read music, but I can play any tune once I've heard it a few times. Let's finish work now and I'll play you some folk tunes from Croatia.'

Arthur was soon tapping his feet to the catchy rhythms and then began to dance. Petro sang to his music in his own language and when the song ended, they both laughed with delight.

'Let's do this again, Petro but I'm shattered now and must sleep.'

Petro put his fiddle carefully back in its case and they both went to bed.

Arthur and Petro were the only workers for three months before Adam managed to recruit some more. Petro then returned to his bedsit for a weekend and did some organising. He phoned his landlord and gave notice to quit. Then he looked at his bank account. Adam had been paying him by transfer and now he could see there was a total of ten thousand pounds. There would be no more because he no longer had to build cabins, only advise here and there. He would be working full time on furniture and would not be paid. Petro sold the contents of his bedsit and returned to the other dimension with bags of clothes and other possessions he wanted.

He had no regrets. He had never felt more valued or happier working for Adam with Arthur.

Chapter 16

2022

I was sitting on the sofa in Alice's cabin, holding a sleeping Sandy on my lap and crying. I'd just told her about Mum's cancer, then I was unable to say any more.

'Oh, Phil, I'm so sorry.' Alice squeezed onto the sofa and put her arms around me. I felt her warmth and comfort spread through me. We were silent, together, and then I sat upright, wiped my eyes, and blew my nose.

'I'm sorry to have burdened you with my worries.'

'No, I understand you wanting to be with your family. Such a conflict of loyalties! I'd like to say go, go home, and support them, but we do need a doctor. Have you spoken to Adam? He might be able to find someone to stand in while you're away.'

'No, I did my surgery and then came to see you.'

'So, you've had nothing to eat.' He shook his head. 'Let's go to the diner, take advantage of Sandy's deep sleep. Adam might be there.' She collected the pushchair, carefully lifted Sandy into it, then gently pulled her little arms through the straps. She tucked a blanket around her and fetched her own coat. There had been no more snow, but the wind was icy cold.

Adam was at the diner, sitting with Arthur. I ordered our food while Alice went over to Adam.

'Hello, I hope you don't mind if I take Adam away from you for a few moments. We have a problem that we hope he can solve.'

Few men could resist Alice's beautiful smile and Adam stood up and came to where I was now sitting with the pushchair.

When he had sat down, I explained, finishing with, 'I love working and living here, Adam, but I need some time off to be with my family.'

Adam nodded and thought before saying, 'Is there enough work for two doctors?'

'Not really, but I'd struggle to cope if there was another virus like Covid 19.'

'Do you know any young doctors who might like the experience of being a GP?'

Suddenly I thought of Steph. She had been infatuated with me at medical school and was in her first year when I was in my final one. We'd had a short fling, but neither of us was ready for a steady relationship. I might still have her telephone number. 'I could try Steph, but I'd need to go up to use my phone.'

'If you use the lift now, there'll be no people in the warehouse. You could phone from there,' said Adam. 'I'll come with you to unlock the doors.'

They both stood up, just as Diane arrived carrying two dinners.

'Sorry, I've got to go, but I won't be long.' I said to Diane.

'No problem, I'll keep it hot for you.'

'Thanks, see you soon, Alice.'

'Good luck,' I heard her say as we left the diner.

'Hello, Steph. Do you remember me, Phil from med school?'

'Phil, of course I remember you. How are you? Did you get to be a surgeon?'

'Yes, but at the moment I'm a GP doing surgery when necessary. What about you, GP or did you specialise?' There was an awkward pause. 'Was that a difficult question? If so, I'm sorry.'

'No, Phil. I just wasn't sure where this was going and why you're ringing after so many years.'

'Okay, here's the truth. I'm working in a rather special commune, in the North of England. I'm the GP and surgeon in their tiny, but well-equipped hospital. I'm the only doctor but my Mum's battling cancer and I need to be with her. In short, I need a locum, like now, and I thought of you.'

'Oh. I'm sorry about your mum, Phil. How long would you need me?'

'I'm not sure. Say, two weeks initially and then I'll know more. During that time, I'll be able to come and see you. I just can't leave all those people without a doctor.'

'What about accommodation?'

I began to feel a tingle of excitement. She hadn't made excuses. 'My cabin has two bedrooms. You can use the spare room. My friend, Rich, uses it sometimes but he can use mine if he turns up. What do you think?'

'What about pay?'

Now it was my turn to hesitate. 'There's no pay. It's a commune. We all eat for free and work for our keep. I'll give you a glowing reference if that'll help. Where are you? Could I show you the place? I think you'd like it.'

It seemed she was currently living in Newcastle. We agreed to meet the following day, after surgery at 6 pm, at a pub near the warehouse. Adam had been waiting for me to finish my conversation and now he looked at me, eyebrows raised.

'Well, she didn't say no but I need to find out more about her. Would you mind waiting while I look her up?'

'No, but I'm cold. You can do that from Eve's office.'

We went inside, Adam locking up behind us. I sat in Eve's office chair, using her computer to find out what qualifications Steph had and, if possible, where she was working. While I was doing that Adam made us a coffee and produced two jam doughnuts. I suddenly realised I was ravenous and ate both before looking at Adam, embarrassed.

'Sorry, Adam. I don't suppose they were both for me.'

His face creased with a smile. 'They were both for you. I know you've had no evening meal.'

'Adam, this is fantastic. Steph specialised in eye surgery and has just come back from working in Africa in one of those travelling eye clinics. She took a year out from her job in a private hospital in Newcastle to do it. I've promised to meet her at the pub round the corner tomorrow at six, so will Eve still be here to let me out and then, hopefully, to let us both in?'

'I'll talk to her tonight. If she can't do it, then I will. Shall we go down?'

I went back to the diner to see if Alice was still there and felt a twinge of jealousy to see her talking to Arthur. She hadn't seen me arrive but then Diane shouted, 'Doctor Phil. I can microwave your dinner. I kept it for you.'

Everyone then looked at me. I smiled and nodded. 'Yes please.'

Alice patted the seat beside her, and Arthur stood saying, 'I'm going home now. Alice has been telling me about your mum. I'm sorry. I hope her treatment works quickly.'

'Thank you,' I said as I sat and looked at Alice. 'Keep your fingers crossed. I'm meeting a Doctor Steph tomorrow and she's interested.'

'That's brilliant, Phil, but Sandy and I will miss you. You will come back, won't you?'

'Yes. I'll be able to visit to see how Steph is doing sometimes too.'

Alice waited, having another cup of tea, while I ate my late meal, then we walked back to her cabin together. 'Do you want to come in? I feel I want to make the most of the time with you before you leave.'

'I'd like that, thank you.'

Once inside, Alice lifted the sleeping Sandy into her cot and watched as she snuggled down with a sigh. Then she closed the bedroom door and walked over to me. She held out her hand and I took it but didn't move, unsure what she meant.

'Please Phil, make love to me. I really need it and I think I'm falling for you.'

I stood up, kissed her, then lifted her up in my arms and carried her to bed.

Later, just before I fell asleep, I said, 'I didn't say it before, too eager to comply with your request, but I love you.' Alice's breathing was slow, she was asleep and hadn't heard me.

I spent the hours at work the next day feeling elated and grateful. I'm sure I welcomed all the patients with a broader smile than usual, then listened, was sympathetic, prescribed where necessary and enjoyed my day.

After work I went to the lift, found the door unlocked and went up to the 'real' world. Eve was in her office, and she asked me when I'd be coming back.

'I should think it could be an hour, no more. If Steph isn't interested, it could be even quicker. Will you be here?'

'I'll go home and get dinner ready. Should be back in an hour.'

We walked out together, and I left her locking the door.

When I entered the pub, I saw Steph chatting easily to the barman. She was tall, her red hair cascading over the shoulders of her denim dress. As a nod to the cold weather, she also wore thick black tights, Doc Marten boots and a faux fur was on the stool beside her. Steph had a glass of wine in her hand, and I wondered if she'd be able to cope living in a dry commune. I went up to her, kissed her cheek and looked at the barman, who raised his eyebrows enquiringly.

'A pint of lager please. Would you like another?'

Steph shook her head. While the drink was being poured, I said, 'How are you? You look great with that tan, as if you've been on a sun-drenched beach.'

'Well, not exactly, Phil. I've been working abroad, Africa, on a mobile eye clinic. I've done so many cataract operations I can almost do them with my own eyes closed.' She laughed but added. 'It was very rewarding but exhausting. I've been back two weeks and not due to return to work here for two months. So, I could help you out. I'm sorry about your mum. I hope she responds to treatment.'

'There are some things you ought to know before you agree. This commune is in a secret location, and I need you to promise not to talk about it.'

She laughed. 'Really? Now I'm intrigued.'

'It's also a no smoking, no drinking place. That's why I'm really enjoying this lager. If you're still interested, would you like to come and see it now? I know it's dark, but you'll get the feel of things. We can have a meal at the diner. The food's excellent.'

Steph nodded, we finished our drinks and slid off the stools.

When we emerged from the lift Steph paused, 'Where are we?'

'We call it the other dimension. Let's walk up to the hospital first. You need to see if you want to work there.' As we walked past, the diner looked inviting, brightly lit with delicious smells wafting into the night.

'That smells good. I'm hungry.'

I ignored her comment and pushed on. 'This is it.' I unlocked the door, put the lights on and she followed me as I showed her around.

'It's really cute and lovely but there's no computer in either consulting room.'

'No computers anywhere and your phone doesn't work.'

She immediately took her own out of her pocket and looked at it.

'We keep patient records on cards as in the olden days. Anyway, come and look at the operating theatre. It's well equipped, and we have a nurse and an anaesthetist on call.'

'How do you call with no phone?'

'You send a runner. If you decide to do the job for a couple of weeks, I'll introduce you to everyone. It's a small community, not unlike the villages you've been visiting in Africa.'

'No, Phil, this is much more sophisticated. If we've seen it all, I'd like to visit that diner.'

'I'll just show you my cabin because that's where you'll be staying. My friend Rich may be there. He comes and goes building a hydroelectric plant.'

Rich was there. Introductions were made. Phil showed Steph his bedroom where she could sleep.

'Have you eaten, Rich? If not, you can join us at the diner.'

'Thanks, but I'm full. You go ahead. Are you sleeping here tonight?' He saw Phil nod. 'I'll see you later then.'

At the diner there were greetings from nearly everyone. I looked around, smiled, and nodded before taking Steph to the counter.

'You're popular,' said Steph. She turned to the young lad behind the counter. 'What's your favourite meal here?'

The boy went red but replied without hesitating, 'The meat loaf. It's scrummy.'

'I'll have one of those please and just tap water to drink.'

'The same for me, please, Justin.'

Justin nodded and said, 'It won't be long, Doctor Phil.'

We went to a vacant table and sat down.

'It's nice the way he called you "Doctor Phil". Does everyone use first names here?'

'Yes, unless they're duplicated. We have a Jason A. and a Jason B. for instance.'

'So, I'll be Doctor Steph.'

'Is that a subtle way of saying you'll do it?' asked Phil.

'Yes.'

I leapt out of my chair, nearly knocking the plated meals out of Justin's hands. I went around the table, kissed Steph on the cheek and said, 'Thank you. That's lifted a load off me.' I sat down and added. 'When can you start?'

Chapter 17

August 2014

The pavement artist had just finished his summer creation and a small crowd had gathered watching him work. The rail of a wooden ship seemed to rise out of the ground and a plank hung over the side above shark infested waters, waiting for anyone who dared to walk it. Nobody moved to try it and the artist grinned. He knew it was because he was there, but he also wanted his picture to dry or it would smudge, so he sat down in the sunshine. People looked, commented, and threw coins into his tin. Later, when the sun was going down, he was packing up his things when a woman walked up to the picture.

'Not a nice death,' she said. 'I wouldn't mind the water closing over my head and sinking, but I'd not want to be eaten alive by sharks.'

The artist nodded. 'I agree but it's only a bit of fun. Now the sun's gone in, I'm feeling a bit chilly so I'm going home. What about you?' He looked at her, shoes worn down at the heel, faded jeans with holes that weren't designer. His eyes travelled up to a pink, thin T-shirt and one arm clutching a large bag with a brown jacket slung between the handles. Her hair was brown, unkempt, and her young face was smudged with dirt and care worn.

She shrugged in answer to his question and turned away.

'Would you like a cup of tea? No strings. You look like you could do with it and a square meal.'

Now she looked at him, uncertain but obviously tempted.

'I've not got to sleep with you, or give you a wank?'

He held up his hands, shaking his head. 'I promise. Come on.'

She trailed after him as he led the way to a small café. Once inside he said, 'Tea, sandwich?'

'Yes please. I like milk but no sugar.'

He gestured her to sit at an empty table while he ordered. He came back with two teas, a cheese and pickle sandwich and two pieces of rocky road. He watched, smiling, as she ate half of the sandwich in moments, started on the second and then looked up at him. She sighed and sat up. 'Sorry, I'm being a pig, but I was so hungry. I'll try to slow down and be a bit more ladylike.'

She smiled, just a glimmer, and then it was gone as she concentrated on eating. The artist put down his cup and took a piece of rocky road, pushing the plate with the other piece towards her. She took it and screwed up her face as she tasted the sweetness.

'This is heaven, thank you.'

It was drizzling and chilly as they were leaving the café. The artist turned up the collar to his coat and placed his hat on his head.

'What's your name?' he asked.

'Diane.'

'I'm glad you enjoyed your sandwich, Diane. I'm Leo. Tell me, can you swim?'

She grinned, 'Yeah, pretty good. Why?'

'If you're looking for a new life. Take a chance, walk the plank.'

Diane looked at him quizzically, but he said no more, just turned and walked away. She stood still and breathed in deeply.

When you have nothing, such a small thing as a full tummy can make such a huge difference, she thought. She had nowhere to go, having been evicted for non-payment of rent a week ago. Sleeping in doorways was not only cold but dangerous. A woman she'd met, pushing all her goods in a shopping trolley, had told her horror stories of rape and theft. Aimlessly she walked back to the picture and looked at it in the fading light.

Leo had been kind. *Perhaps I should take his advice.* The light drizzle was becoming a little heavier, so she pulled her jacket out of her bag and put it on. She looked around to make sure she was alone before stepping onto the side of the boat. It rocked slightly so she waited until it was still, then walked along the plank and jumped, attempting to miss the shark filled water. It did not go to plan. The plank bent under her weight. She fell, down, down, down, hitting the cold water with a splash and snatching a quick breath as the momentum pulled her under. She was still holding her bag. It was weighing her down. She let it go and swam strongly to the surface, gasping with the cold and shock.

The rain thudded onto her head, and it was inky dark as Diane trod water, looking for land. There were no lights. She wondered if she was in open sea and licked her lips. They were not salty. It was a lake or a river. Could it be the Tyne?

I must conserve my energy. I'll float on my back and let the currant take me. Must not panic. The artist promised a new life, not death. Must believe this.

As Diane floated, she remembered swimming lessons as a child. They had put pyjamas over their swimming costumes and were told to tread water and remove their trousers. Then they tied a knot in each leg, scrunched up the top and blew into it, making a float. It had worked.

I can't do that my jeans are full of holes. Her thoughts were halted when a log bumped against her. She turned and held onto it, tight. The sky was lightening, the rain had stopped, and she thought she could see the shadowy outline of land. She kicked her legs, propelling herself and the log in that direction.

The log suddenly hit something hard and rolled out of her grasp. Diane floundered then put her foot down. She felt a rock. Another step and she sank below the water. This was not the shore but isolated rocks. Swimming and testing for rocks as she went, Diane finally reached the beach. It was much lighter now and she could see trees and bushes on a hillside. She stood up, heavy in her sodden clothes, staggered onto the grass and collapsed.

The artist and Adam met for the first time beside the pirate ship. Adam stood looking down at it, and the artist stood up and walked round to stand beside him.

'We need to talk,' he said.

'Why must we?' asked Adam, looking at him. The artist was not tall or remarkable in any obvious way. He had brown hair pulled into a ponytail, a beard of the same colour, thin lips, and pale blue eyes.

'We both want the same thing. To create a Utopia, a Nirvana, a place where people can live in harmony with each other and nature.' He paused and was encouraged by Adam's nod of agreement and continued. 'You have found such a place, but I discovered it long before you. I thought I had been chosen, by God, to use my find to benefit the world, to create an Eden that humans wouldn't spoil. But I lacked the courage to begin. I didn't have enough faith in myself and, I suppose, too little faith in God.'

Adam's eyes opened wide. 'I had no idea anyone else was aware of the existence of the other dimension. I thought it was my vision, my discovery. How did you find it?'

'I bought a lockup to store some of my pictures. I liked painting large canvases then. The floor of the lockup was filthy with dust and debris, so I swept and washed it with a view to sealing it. I didn't want my paintings gathering dust. I expect you can guess the rest.'

'You found a trap door with steps going down. You must have been gutted when I bought the warehouse.'

The artist grimaced. 'I was frightened. I thought someone else would find it and not have the same ethos. I'm so grateful you feel the same. Then again, perhaps you were chosen, as I believe I was, by God.'

'I'm not really a religious man.'

'Perhaps that's not important to God. What is important is the desire to share a beautiful place with likeminded people.'

The artist paused, took a deep breath and as Adam said nothing, he continued. 'I want to contribute in some way. The men that are working now building cabins are a good choice. They have all been at the bottom of the social scale, some homeless, all out of work. They needed a new start. What would happen if you wanted someone with a skill who has work and a comfortable lifestyle? How could you persuade them to give up what they have, to help in your commune?'

'I don't know. I've not really thought that far ahead. Anyway, how do you know what I've been doing? Do you have another door to the other dimension?'

'The other door comes when I do a pavement picture like this. People play at walking the plank. If I concentrate really hard, the water liquifies and anyone that falls in, if they are a good swimmer, will arrive at your other dimension.'

'Yeah?' said Adam. It was obvious by his grin he thought it highly unlikely. 'You must think I'm so gullible.'

'Believe what you like but I'm not lying. I did it last night with a desperate young woman called Diane. She'll have arrived by now, unless she drowned. If I'm going to help you, "kidnap," the right sort of person, you'll need to get a boat. They may not all be good swimmers.'

'I'd better go and see if this Diane's alive then,' said Adam, beginning to walk away. Then he stopped and turned back. 'Just in case what you're saying is true, how can I get in touch with you? I don't even know your name.'

'My name's Leonard. Friends call me Leo and here's my card. I do these paintings three times a year. Christmas, Easter and during the school summer holiday.'

Adam looked at the card and put it in his pocket. 'Okay, Leo, I may be in touch.'

Chapter 18

2014

It was mid-morning when Arthur came down to the river with his fishing rod. He was hoping to catch enough for a meal that night. As he came towards his usual spot, he saw what looked like a large bundle of rags washed up on the beach. He was curious, so he put down his rod and tackle and went closer. A body. His heart began to thump in his chest and part of him wanted to run away. The other part pushed him to look closer. He had heard people say that a dead person looked like they were asleep. This woman's eyes were closed, but he could see movement. She was breathing.

'Hello, er Miss, can you hear me?' She sighed, her eyes still closed. Arthur bent down onto one knee and touched her arm. It was very cold and her sleeve was wet. He took off his jumper and placed it over her then spoke louder. 'Hello, you must wake up now. I need to get you warm. Please wake up.' Now he shook her shoulder and her eyes flickered open, then shut, against the brightness of the sun. He moved, placing her in shadow, and her eyes opened fully, then she scrambled to get up and away from this stranger.

'I'll not harm you. There's nothing to fear. But you're cold and wet. You need to come with me to my cabin. I can get you a hot drink and something to eat.' These were the magic words and at last, she nodded.

'Yes, please.'

Arthur helped her to her feet and steadied her as she swayed. He left his fishing things and walked with her, slowly, through the woods to the road.

'Where am I?'

'We call it the other dimension. We're building a village where everyone can make a new start.' They reached the third cabin and then Arthur stopped. 'This is my cabin. Come in and I'll fetch you a towel, then you can have a shower to warm yourself up.'

'Can I trust you?'

'You can. My name's Arthur. What's yours?'

'Diane. Thank you, Arthur, for being so kind.'

They went inside, a clean towel was given to her, and Arthur showed her the bathroom. While she was in there, he went next door to find Petro. He was a much slimmer man than Arthur and he hoped he'd have some clothes that might fit Diane, but Petro was not there. He went behind the cabin to an extension where there was a large workshop and found him sanding a table.

'Don't you ever rest? This is our lunch hour and you're working.'

Petro grinned. 'I've had a sandwich and I wanted to do this before we started building again.'

'You're going to have to stop because I went fishing and caught a young woman, asleep and soaking wet. She's having a shower now and I've no suitable clothes to give her. Can you help?'

As he was speaking Petro was already moving towards the door that led into his cabin from the workshop. Arthur followed and Petro found some clean shorts, a T-shirt, then added a pair of pants. They both went out of the front door and knocked on Arthur's door.

A voice said, 'Come in, Arthur. The shower was lovely.' Then she saw Petro, 'Oh, hello.'

'I'm Petro and I've got some clean clothes that might fit you better than Arthur's.'

'Thank you.' She took them from him and went back into the bathroom.

'She looks good in just a towel, doesn't she?' said Arthur.

'Yes, very, but maybe instead of drooling you should put the kettle on.' Arthur grinned and did as he suggested, then buttered some bread and made a vegan cheese sandwich.

'I'll just see her settled and then I'll come back to work,' he called as Petro went out.

A few moments later, Diane emerged looking fresh and boyish in Petro's clothes.

'Is that tea and sandwich for me?' she asked.

'Yes. Please make yourself comfortable. I can't stay any longer because Petro's gone back to work, and I should too. I'll see you later, bye.'

Diane watched him go and then ate her sandwich as slowly as a ravenous person could. *The last time I ate anything was when I was with the artist, she thought. He was right to tell me to walk the plank. I think I've found my new life, but I don't know what I can do here. Arthur seems lovely, a proper gentleman. I'm not sure about Petro, yet, but he did lend me some clothes. That reminds me. I must wash my clothes. I wonder if there's a washing machine.*

She stood up, went to the sink, and washed her cup and plate, then dried them, and put them away.

There was a machine, but she was not sure if Arthur would mind her using it. She used a bar of soap and washed everything by hand. Leaving the clean, rinsed clothes in a heap on the draining board, she went outside to see if there was a clothesline. She expected to see a rotary one, but between Arthur's cabin and Petro's was a line stretching diagonally attached at each end to a jutting log end. Pegs were dangling on the line, so Diane retrieved her wet clothes and hung them up.

Her jobs were done so she decided to explore. She began by walking down the hill, past another cabin and she wondered who owned that one. So, there were just three cabins. Hardly a thriving village. There were sounds of men working, voices and laughter that drew her uphill and she found them working on the fourth cabin. Arthur was helping to lift a log into place. Petro was supervising and there were three other men she had not met. They were busy and did not notice her, so she sat on a tree stump in the sunshine and watched.

Chapter 19

2022

It was Steph's first day at work, so I changed the sheets on my bed, cleaned the cabin and met Adam to go up in the lift. I was anxious to see Mum and Dad and tell them I could stay for two weeks, but first I needed to go to my flat.

I unlocked the door and stood for a moment in the doorway remembering how this had once seemed like home. Now it felt cold and unwelcoming. My first task was to pack some clothes. I pulled out a favourite sweater and smiled. It was fine being clothed for work by Adam, but I was looking forward to socialising while wearing something different. I imagined wearing it as Alice snuggled against me on the settee. I was missing her already.

When I'd finished packing, I went through my post, paid some bills and checked when the lease on my flat ended. It was next month. I immediately rang the landlord and said I didn't want to renew it. I was supposed to give more than one month's notice, but the landlord had someone desperate to have a flat, so he agreed. This galvanised me into action and I packed everything small enough to go into plastic sacks. Finally, I phoned a house clearance company to get rid of the furniture. It took several journeys carrying things down to my car, but then I locked the door of my flat, feeling a sense of satisfaction.

As I drove to my parents' house, I decided to use this time to sell my car too. I had no income. Soon I would have no flat and no car. My commitment to my new life was total but I had to keep some money in the bank, as a contingency.

Dad opened the door and his face creased into a smile. 'Phil, I'm so glad to see you.' Then his expression changed to a frown. 'I can't let you in, though. Mum's just had some chemo, she's not very well and the doctor said she mustn't meet other people. You know, in case they give her something, like Covid.'

'Dad, I'm a doctor but where I work is totally free from those sorts of viruses. I tested myself this morning for Covid, so I promise I'll be no threat to Mum, and I really want to help.'

I saw Dad's face screw up as he tried to fight the tears of relief. I stepped forward and hugged him. His voice was muffled in my shoulder.

'I can't bear to see her so weak and so brave. It breaks my heart and I'm so tired of doing everything and worrying.' He gave a shuddering sigh, pulled away from me and wiped his eyes on a tissue. 'The only good thing is I'm becoming a fair cook. How long can you stay, Phil? I'll put the kettle on.'

'Slow down, Dad. I've got two weeks off work and might be able to have more if you still need me. Now let's go into the kitchen, then you can sit down while I make the tea.'

Dad sat on a wooden chair at the kitchen table and watched me put the kettle on and get out three mugs.

'Mum has to have a plastic beaker with a lid and a spout and put plenty of milk in or it's too hot for her.' I nodded and found the beaker. When it was ready, I gave Dad his cup and then picked up my own and Mum's.

'I'll take this up to her while you drink yours - if that's okay?'

'That's fine, Son. She'll be so pleased to see you.'

I steeled myself to enter the bedroom with a smile, trying to think of her as a patient, not as Mum. She had her eyes closed. Her face was white, and she had lost so much hair I could see her pink scalp through it. I scarcely recognised her. A sob escaped my throat, and she opened her eyes, saw me, and smiled. Now she was Mum, but I couldn't suppress my tears. I put the cups down as she lifted a hand, then sat on the bed and held it.

'I've brought you a cup of tea. Shall I help you sit up?'

'Yes, please. I'm a bit weak.'

'I know. Chemo saps your energy.' I picked up the beaker and she took it from me, sipping gingerly.

'That's lovely, not too hot.'

I drank some of my tea and then said, 'I've got a couple of weeks off work so I'm going to move back into my old room and give Dad a hand.'

'That's the best news I've heard in ages. Dad's exhausted looking after me and I feel so guilty.' She held up a hand as I was about to speak. 'I want to tell you about my treatment before I get too tired.'

I listened and when she told me the date of her next hospital visit, I said I would take her and talk to her oncologist. I would have to put the idea of selling my car on hold for a while.

'Now pet, I've drunk my tea, talked too much and I need to sleep. Go downstairs and help Dad.' I picked up the cups and went down, feeling like I was a little boy again, doing as my mother asked.

Dad was still sitting at the kitchen table. He was slouched forward, his head resting on his folded arms, sound asleep. I put down the cups quietly, went into the living room and phoned Olivia.

'I can't tell you how pleased I am you're going to stay at Mum's. I'll pop over tonight after work and stay for a meal if there's enough.'

'We haven't discussed tonight's meal, but I'll fetch a takeaway if nothing's organised. Mum and Dad are both asleep so I can't ask now.'

'When I come over, I usually collect a shopping list, but you can do it now, or perhaps Dad could do it himself. I don't think he's been out of the house, apart from hospital visits, for weeks.'

'I was thinking of showing him how to order online. What do you think?'

'He can probably manage it but while you're there suggest he does the shopping himself. He'll enjoy doing it and will come back with all kinds of things Mum usually avoids like pies, cakes and biscuits. Anyway, I've got to go. Thanks for ringing, see you tonight, bye.'

Dad wandered bleary eyed into the living room. 'Was that Olivia? I thought I heard voices. Must've dozed off.'

95

'Yes. I wanted to tell her I was here, so she didn't feel she had to come over to get your shopping list but she's coming anyway to see us.'

'That'll be grand, both of you at once. Perhaps Mum might feel like coming down for an hour. Now, lad, tell me all about your life. I want to know about your job and if you have a girlfriend.'

The rest of the morning passed quickly as I described my little hospital and recounted some of my cases, such as Jason B.'s accident. Dad listened intently, frowning sometimes, smiling at others, and then said, 'It seems to me you really like being a GP with a bit of surgery here and there to keep your hand in.' He smiled, his eyes twinkling. 'I know there's a girl somewhere too. Come on, tell me everything.'

'She's lovely Dad, in every way and has a daughter about fifteen months old called Sandy.'

'A daughter. So, is she married, divorced? You didn't tell me her name.'

I held up my hands. 'You haven't given me a chance. Her name's Alice and she's a widow. I love them both very much.'

'Is Alice one of these modern, skinny women that're always watching their weight?

'No, she's shapely. I know you'd like her.'

'Will you bring them here so we can meet them? When Mum's feeling low she often says she wants to see you and Olivia settled, before she dies.'

I frowned. 'I don't like her thinking like that. It's morbid. She's got every chance of a full recovery. Anyway, I will bring Alice and Sandy to meet you when Mum's able to cope with visitors.'

'That'll be grand. Now, let's have some lunch and then, as you're here, I might have a little snooze.'

I nodded and stood up. 'You make a start and I'll see if Mum fancies anything.'

A few moments later I went into the kitchen where Dad was buttering bread and said, 'Mum says she fancies an egg sandwich and a cup of tea. I'll put a couple of eggs on to boil.'

Dad smiled, happily. 'That's good, she's eaten next to nothing recently. I was going to make ham sandwiches but put another couple of eggs on, Phil. Let's all have egg sarnies.'

The days passed quickly, and Mum began to get stronger. She was now getting dressed every morning and able to do small things like making a cup of tea. The atmosphere in the house was much calmer as Dad began to relax. I felt more confident about leaving them on Sunday to go home. I wanted to see Steph and make sure she was happy to work the second week and I was desperate to see Alice.

It was Saturday afternoon and Olivia had joined us for lunch. It was a simple meal of sandwiches and cake, but Olivia nearly choked on her piece of Battenburg when Mum said, 'Phil's got a lovely girl called Alice. He's going to bring her and her little one to see us soon. So, when are you going to bring a young man to see us?'

Olivia shook her head. 'I don't have anyone special, Mum. I have lots of friends and mostly go out with several of them.'

'I thought you might be interested in Rich,' said Phil. 'You know he's been building a hydroelectric plant?' She nodded.

'Well, it'll soon be finished, and I think he's planning to come back to live in this area. I got the impression from him that the attraction here was you.'

Olivia squirmed as Mum smiled and said, 'There, Rich is a lovely choice. He's clever and will never be out of work with his qualifications. It's high time you settled down and had a family. Your biological clock is ticking.'

'Thanks a lot, Phil. And you, Mum, must not try to run my life. There's nothing romantic between Rich and me. I like him but that's it. Talk about something else and I'll go and make some tea.'

We watched her flounce from the room and heard her making unnecessary noise getting out cups and filling the kettle then banging it down on the worktop.

'Do you get the impression we've upset her?' said Dad, grinning.

Chapter 20

2022

Doctor Steph was proving a great success particularly with the female patients. She was kept busy with smear tests and mammograms, as well as treating haemorrhoids and cases of thrush. She giggled inwardly thinking she had examined more private parts of women in a week than she had in a year in Africa. That was obvious anyway because she had been treating eyes, not nether regions. On the other hand, she had seen few male patients for anything more embarrassing than a cut finger needing sutures or a scalded arm.

Steph had kept meticulous records but found it irksome to write by hand. Everything was so much quicker and easier with a computer. She was looking forward to seeing Phil who was coming tomorrow. She picked up her medical bag and strolled the short distance to Phil's cabin, hoping Rich would not be there.

'Hi Rich,' she called, as she opened the door. There was an answering grunt, and she made a wry face. Rich may be a great engineer, but she thought he was a slob. He just dropped his dirty clothes on the floor and behaved as if she was his skivvy. She knew she should just step around his mess and leave it to him, but she was a neat person and hated living in a muddle.

Steph made two cups of tea. 'There's tea here, Rich.'

'Thanks,' he said, coming into the kitchen and taking a noisy slurp. She resisted pulling a disapproving face.

'How's the hydro plant going?'

'Good,' he nodded. 'We're nearly ready for a test run. If it works, the wind turbines will become the back up and our electricity should be more reliable. The aim is to negate the need for diesel generators. We don't want any dependence on fossil fuels.'

'You're really committed to this place. What are you going to do when everything is working fine? Are you going to stay here or go back?'

Rich scratched his head. His facial expression told her he had no idea. Finally, he shrugged. 'Have you anything to go back to? A job, a girlfriend?'

He grinned. 'Don't tell Phil but I really miss seeing his sister, Olivia. I've met her a few times, she's lovely. I don't just mean her soft brown hair, big brown eyes, and a figure to die for.' He gestured the shape with his hands. 'She's strong and brave. You know, she was willing to jump into the picture, risk her own life? Amazing girl.'

'Jump into the picture?'

He grinned. 'It's a totally bizarre and dangerous way of getting here. No doubt you came into a warehouse and down a lift.'

'Yes. It was very civilised.'

'A few times a year a pavement artist paints a superb picture on the quayside. It always involves something dangerous, like a broken bridge over a chasm. It tempts people to walk onto it and jump the gap. I don't know how it differentiates who ends up falling in the water, but Phil did. It was so scary. He just seemed to disappear into the chasm and then we heard a splash. So, when I wanted to find Phil for the sake of his family, the only way I knew was to jump into the picture. I did it and, as you can see, I survived but it's definitely not for the fainthearted or for a non-swimmer.'

Steph grinned and shook her head. 'This is some kind of elaborate wind up. There's no way I'm going to fall for that. I'm going to the diner for something to eat.'

As Steph went out of the door, she heard Rich say, 'If you don't believe me, ask Phil tomorrow.'

When Steph pushed open the door to the diner, she saw Alice sitting alone, eating a meal one-handed while holding a boisterous Sandy on her knee.

'Hello, Alice, Sandy's looking well, lively and into everything. Would you like me to hold her while you finish your meal?'

'That would be great, Doctor Steph, but go and order yours first.'

'Okay, I won't be long. I think I'll have the pasta, same as you. It looks delicious.' She gave her order and brought a jug of water and a glass back with her. She placed them well into the centre of the table and then took Sandy and sat down with her. Sandy settled on her knee and Alice picked up her knife and fork.

'Thank you,' she said. 'This is so much easier than one-handed.' She took another mouthful, swallowed and said, 'Phil's coming tomorrow. I'm really looking forward to seeing him.'

'Yes, he said he'll pop in to see me, to see how things have gone this week. I'm pleased to say it's gone well. But I think the men here are shy of a woman doctor. My surgery has been almost all females.'

'I can relate to that. It's not easy for a woman to be examined in her private places by a man.'

'What's the ratio of men to women here, roughly?'

'It's probably two-thirds' men and one-third women. I think there are just fifteen families with children, so the teacher has to be versatile, teaching all ages at once.'

'I haven't met the teacher. Male or female?'

'Male, Martin, but I forgot, there is also a play group nursery thing run by Sandra. The children go there until they're five then move on to the school. They try to keep abreast of the National Curriculum so if the youngsters leave here, they won't be at a disadvantage.'

'But I assume they won't be taking national examinations, so they'll have no qualifications to offer. That will make it impossible for them to get into a university. Does that worry you about Sandy's future?'

'I haven't really thought that far ahead. Now, talking to you, I do feel a bit anxious.'

'I'm sorry. That looks like my dinner coming. Can I give Sandy back?'

'Of course.' Alice stood and took Sandy then put her into the buggy. 'She needs to go to bed now. Thanks for helping and the chat. Enjoy your lunch, bye.'

Steph watched her go. *This place is far from perfect even though it's a lovely community.* She sighed and began eating.

Chapter 21

2016

Diane had been sharing Arthur's Cabin and cooking for all the builders for two years. She made a shopping list and gave it to Adam once a week. He bought everything and delivered it. The system had worked well up until now, when there were twenty-five men and women wanting three meals a day and snacks. It wasn't the work but the size of Arthur's kitchen that was the problem. There weren't enough worktops, his pans were too small, and when Adam got her some catering saucepans the cooker was not big enough.

Adam arrived to collect her shopping list and she decided to tell him her idea.

'Can I talk to you Adam? I know you're always in a hurry, but this is important.'

Adam nodded, glancing down at the list in his hand.

'I think you should put a team of men onto building a café. It needs proper stainless-steel worktops, a catering cooker with at least five rings and a big oven. I've got suitable pans, but the café will need a counter, furniture, cutlery, plates and so on. I can't feed all these people using Arthur's kitchen. It's just too small.'

Adam sat down, frowning, his elbows on his knees, tapping his lips with his first two fingers. She thought he was going to shake his head and say it wasn't possible. He was quiet for so long that Diane turned away and began to get out ingredients for making scones. They were the most popular cakes. She made them every day, half with dried fruit and half without. She also put the kettle on to make some tea, and still Adam was silent.

Finally, he spoke. 'That's an excellent idea, Diane, and I realise, watching you starting to bake, that this kitchen is far too small. I'm going to take all the men off what they're doing and make this a priority. I'll get a catering brochure and you can choose what you need. I'm going to speak to the men now.' He stood up and then said, 'What sort of size building, do you think? Two cabins, three?'

'I think two cabins would be big enough. One with no internal walls for the sitting space. The other needs half for sitting and half for the kitchen and counter.'

'But if we made it three cabins then we could have a meeting room, perhaps a snooker table, dart board, board games, table tennis.' He was almost gabbling in his enthusiasm. 'What about a library and an indoor play area for toddlers?'

Diane laughed. 'Slow down Adam, we haven't any children here. But I think an extra room for leisure activities would be brilliant. Tell that to the men and they'll be working overtime to get it up and running.'

Adam left quickly to call his meeting and Diane mixed her dough feeling excited. She wondered how long it would take to build. The area was expanding quickly as the builders became more efficient. There were now twenty-three cabins. It seemed the right time to build some facilities for all these people.

She had just put the scones in the oven when Arthur came in smiling, his eyes shining with the news. 'Have you heard what Adam's planning?'

'Yes. The café was my idea. I can hardly wait.' Arthur put his arms around her waist and hugged her from behind.

'You're the best fish I've ever caught out of the Tyne.' She twisted around so she was facing him. They kissed. Then they kissed again but before things got out of hand Diane stopped and pulled away, breathless and laughing.

'I've got to get the scones out and you've got to get back to work. I'll see you at lunchtime.'

Arthur made a rueful face then went towards the door. Before he opened it, he turned, seeing Diane with her oven gloves on, holding a tray of scones. 'They look good. You look good enough to eat too.' She put the tray onto the cooker top and Arthur said, 'Will you marry me?'

Diane's smile got broader, and she removed her gloves before going up to him. 'You know I will, but do we have to build a church first?'

'Good point. I hadn't thought of that. Perhaps we can just jump the broomstick like people did long ago in America. A church. It's a long time since I've even thought of it. Did I ever tell you I was once a keen church goer and became a lay preacher? I couldn't marry people, but I did take other services. It all went wrong when I became dependent on drink. I lost everything including my faith.'

Diane reached up and put her hands around his face. 'You're a good man that made a mistake. You paid a heavy price for that mistake but now you've got your life back. I believe you could get your faith back too. We can have a wedding without a church, but I would like to have God included in it. I'd like hymns, prayers and then dancing afterwards.' She went on tiptoe and kissed his lips before letting go of his face. Then she stepped back and said, 'Now go back to work or Adam will dock your pay.'

'What pay?' Arthur was still laughing as he closed the door behind him.

Diane continued to cook, a large pan of vegetable soup was nearly ready and there would be crusty bread she had made earlier that morning. The people would arrive at Arthur's door with their own bowls, plates and cutlery. She would serve them, and they would take it back to their own cabin to eat it or if the weather was fine, sit on a pile of logs where they'd been working. They would wash up their own things ready for the evening meal. It occurred to Diane as she thought about the café that she would have to do all the washing up too. She frowned and decided she would have to get some help if the village was going to get bigger. A dishwasher would be helpful too. There were far more men than women, and the women that were there worked in the kitchen garden. They were all either married or living with one of the builders.

Everything was ready and she heard a group of people approaching, all talking excitedly. There was a rap on the door. She opened it, smiling her welcome. Then it was very hectic as she ladled soup and people helped themselves to as much bread as they wanted. Everyone wanted to talk to her about the café.

'We're clearing the site right now.'

'I've been trimming the logs for it. There's a huge pile already.'

'My cabin's on hold while we do this but I don't mind. It's such a brilliant idea.'

'I can't wait for the games room.'

It was a pleasant day outside so most people gathered, sitting wherever they could. When the clanking of spoons lessened, Arthur stood up. He was an imposing figure, tall and broad but a gentle giant that had earned the respect of everyone.

'If you'll just listen for a minute, I'd like to tell you all something.' There were a few interested murmurs and then silence, only broken by the wheeling seagulls hoping for breadcrumbs. Arthur looked around at his friends and said, 'You've all just eaten Diane's delicious soup and her bread. I want you to know that I'm the happiest man here today because Diane has just agreed to marry me.' There were cheers and whistles.

'She should be here, Arthur. I'll go and fetch her,' said Petro. He got up and went quickly to Arthur's cabin and knocked.

'Hello, Petro, have you come for seconds?'

'No, I've come for you.'

He took her hand and led her to the building site. She was overwhelmed when everyone clapped and cheered her. She walked to Arthur who was holding out his hands. 'I've just told them we're going to be married.'

'When's the happy day, Diane?' asked Petro.

'We haven't really discussed it but perhaps it should coincide with the grand opening of the café you're building. What do you think, Arthur?'

She did not hear his reply because of all the cheering, which increased when Arthur kissed her. It was a long, hard kiss.

Six Months Later

Eve arrived for the wedding in a brightly patterned dress that flowed from her shoulders to just below her knees. She had pink sandals on her feet and carried a matching, small handbag. Adam was wearing a light grey suit with a blue T-shirt underneath, and he held Eve's hand as they arrived at the entrance to the café. There was a piece of ribbon across the door and Petro greeted them, holding a variety of tools. He held the ceremonial scissors to cut the ribbon, but there was also an electric drill on the floor, and he had some screws in his pocket. A step ladder leant against the wall. Everybody else had arrived, dressed as smartly as they could for the big occasion.

Arthur arrived a few minutes later looking impressively grand in a dress suit with a white shirt and a bow tie finishing the effect. When Diane arrived, dressed in a cream dress with embroidered pink roses on it, everyone clapped. She was carrying a bouquet of wildflowers as she stood next to Arthur. It became quiet as Adam held up a hand.

'We have two special ceremonies here today. The first is the grand opening of our café. It just needs Petro to nip up the ladder and put up the sign. It will not be referred to as our café anymore, but Diane's Diner.' Everyone waited while Petro screwed the name sign above the door. When he had done it and come down the ladders, he moved them aside and Adam and Eve stepped forward.

Petro handed Eve the scissors and she said in a loud, clear voice. 'I declare Diane's Diner, open.' Then she cut the ribbon. Everyone cheered as they made their way inside.

The interior had been decorated with bunting and the wedding cake with two tiers stood on the countertop.

When everyone was inside, and the chattering had ceased, a retired priest stepped forward.

'Hello everyone. My name is Father Gallagher and Adam asked me here today to officiate at the wedding of Arthur and Diane. We will begin with Diane's favourite hymn, *Lead Us, Heavenly Father, Lead Us.*

Petro lifted his violin and led the singing. Father Gallagher then went through the ceremony finishing with, 'I now pronounce you, man and wife.' There was an eruption of cheering as they kissed. Adam shook the priest's hand and elderflower cordial drinks were handed round. A buffet was on the counter and, for once, Diane was not helping. She had cooked much of the food and made the cake, but today she was off duty. Several of the kitchen garden ladies had insisted that

Diane enjoyed her day while they did the honours. It was a happy sociable occasion, and the buffet plates were soon empty. There was a ceremonial cake cutting and that provided everyone with a sweet course.

When the eating was over, Petro picked up his fiddle and started to play lively music. The table and chairs were pushed back, and everyone danced. It was the first celebration of any kind that had happened in the other dimension and Adam glowed with delight as he twirled Eve around until she had to call a halt for a breather. She pulled him outside.

'I haven't danced for years and I'm definitely not fit. Just give me a moment and I'll be back in there.'

'Let's wait for a slower one, then we can dance closer, cheek to cheek, body to body. You're so lovely Eve. I'll never stop wanting you.'

'Well, you'd better make a bit of room in your heart for someone else because in seven months' time, you're going to be a dad.'

Adam's face was incredulous. He picked her up, whooping and swinging her around, then placed her carefully down.

'I didn't think today could get any better and it just has. Can I tell anyone? Should you see a doctor?'

Eve shook her head. 'I'll wait another month, just to be sure, then I'll see a doctor. Let's not tell anyone until it's confirmed.'

'What about doing a pregnancy test? I think you can get those at a chemist.'

'I did a test this morning, but we had so much to do, getting ready for the ceremony and the wedding, so I decided to tell you later.' She smiled happily. 'So now, you know.' He kissed her and then led her back into the diner to smooch in a slow dance.

Chapter 22

2022

I walked up the lane towards Alice's cabin. I knew I should visit Steph, but I'd been thinking about Alice all week. I knocked on the door and went in. Toys littered the floor. There were dirty plates on the kitchen work surface, but I barely noticed the mess because Sandy was screaming. Where was Alice? Something was very wrong. I pushed open her bedroom door and she appeared to be sleeping – impossible with Sandy's wails.

I felt a wave of fear as I rushed to the bed and felt for a pulse in her neck. It was there, just. Was she in a coma? Her skin felt clammy and hot. She was too hot. A high temperature. I yanked back all the covers, gathered her in my arms and took her into the bathroom. I lowered her gently in the bath then ran the water, tepid. As the water crept around her body, Alice moaned. 'I'm cold, freezing. I must get to Sandy.' She tried to sit up, but the effort was too much.

'I'll sort Sandy out while you stay here. The water will bring your temperature down.'

I was reluctant to leave her shivering in the bath but did so anyway, knowing that she would relax if Sandy stopped crying.

I went into the baby's bedroom and the smell told me she needed a nappy change. She made it difficult, wriggling and crying but when it was done, I picked her up and took her into the kitchen. Her crying reduced to shuddering gasps as I put her into her highchair and gave her a cup of milk. She picked it up and drank thirstily.

Now she was quiet I looked through the cupboards and found some baby cereal, mixed it with milk and sat down to feed her. I gave her a spoon too. She dug it into the bowl but most of it fell off before it reached her mouth. In between her efforts, I put a spoonful to her lips. She opened her mouth like a baby sparrow.

When her cereal was finished, I cleaned Sandy's hands and face and then the highchair. She was safe in there, so I gave her what was left in her cup and a toy, then went back into the bathroom.

Alice was sitting up and she looked at me. 'Thank you for seeing to Sandy. I want to get out but I'm too weak. I'll need help.'

'Right. I'll just get some clean pyjamas and your dressing gown.'

When I returned, I put my arms under her and lifted her out, carefully putting her feet on the floor. 'Can you stand?'

'Yes.' I helped her out of her dripping pyjamas and rubbed her with a towel. She was still shivering as I helped her into the clean night clothes. 'What's wrong with me?'

'You have a fever. When did you start to feel ill?'

'Yesterday.'

'You should've gone straight to the hospital.'

'I couldn't make the effort – I thought I'd feel better in the morning.'

'What you needed was a phone. Then you could've called for help. I don't know what would've happened to you and Sandy if I hadn't come today.' I was angry and struggled to control it. I breathed deeply and said calmly, 'Let's get you into the kitchen.'

'Mum, Mum, up,' said Sandy, lifting her arms.

'I can't pick you up. I'm not well enough.' Alice sank onto one of the dining chairs as tears ran down her face.

I put a glass of water in front of her. 'Try and drink this. You'll be dehydrated. I need to get you into hospital where they can find the problem and treat you.'

'What about Sandy?'

'I'll look after her. I'm going to pack a few things into a bag for you. Will you be okay for a few minutes?' She nodded. I rushed into her bedroom, opening drawers looking for more pyjamas, slippers and underwear. I stopped, briefly, to take another deep breath, trying to think clearly. I was no use to her in a state of panic. Then I went into the bathroom and filled a sponge bag. There was a rucksack under the bed, so I put everything in there, then returned to the kitchen.

Alice looked up at me and gave me a wan smile. I managed to smile back and said, 'I'm going to take Sandy to the hospital and collect a wheelchair for you. Then we can get you there quickly and safely.'

She nodded. I picked up Sandy, swaddled her in a blanket from the pram and left the house. I wanted to run up the lane to the hospital but curbed my speed, aware I was carrying a precious bundle.

Steph smiled when she saw me but raised an eyebrow at Sandy in my arms. I didn't smile back, and she said, 'Is there something wrong with Sandy or is it Alice?'

'Alice, I found her unconscious with a high fever. I need a wheelchair to bring her here. Have you got a spare bed?'

Steph took Sandy into her own arms. 'Yes, don't worry. It'll be ready for her when you get back.'

'Thank you.' I let off the wheelchair brakes and left.

Alice was exactly where I'd left her. I shrugged her rucksack onto my back and then went to her and felt her pulse. It was better than it had been, but her forehead was hot and clammy. I noticed she had drunk all the water.

'Alice I'm going to help you into the wheelchair. I'm going to lift you but see if you can take some weight on your feet.' I lifted her under her arms, and she managed to stand but I couldn't let go of her, knowing she'd fall. 'Well done. I'm going to carry you now and sit you in the wheelchair. Here we go.' She slumped in the chair and I used the waist strap to stop her falling out. It was very cold outside, so I put her fleece over her legs then pushed her to the hospital.

I went through reception, where I saw Sandy playing on the floor surrounded by toys. Helen, the receptionist, was watching her. She smiled at me as I rushed past. I managed to smile back, despite my anxiety. In the ward I found Steph waiting, with a drip ready, and the bed covers turned back. I lifted Alice onto the bed, and she sighed, her eyes flickering partially open.

'Now, Phil, step back and let us look after her. Your job now is to take care of Sandy.' Steph's tone was firm, but I hesitated before nodding and going back to reception. I knew I should pick Sandy up and take her home, but I sat down instead, my feet almost touching her. I leant towards her, my elbows on my knees and my hands supporting my head. She looked up at me and smiled, showing me a toy train. It clattered when pushed along and gave an occasional whistle. 'That's a train, Sandy. You are being a good girl.'

'Are you okay, Doctor Phil? You look exhausted. Would you like a cup of tea?' asked Helen.

'That would be great, thank you.' I saw her go into the little kitchen area and when she returned, she carried a mug of tea and a plate of buttered toast with marmalade. 'I know you don't like sugar in your tea, but I thought you could do with a few calories,' she said.

I took it from her and smiled. 'That was very thoughtful, Helen, thank you.' When I bit into the toast, I realised how much I needed it. The plate was quickly cleared, then I drank the tea and sat back with a sigh. 'That was delicious. I know I should take Sandy home but would you mind looking after her a bit longer so I can check on Alice and have a chat to Steph?'

'She's not causing me any problem. You go.'

'Thanks. I'll just pop my cup and plate into the kitchen. If you need me, I'll be in the ward.'

Alice was on a drip that Steph was adjusting as I walked in. 'Good timing, Phil. We X-rayed her, and she has a chest infection, so I'm filling her with antibiotics, and she's sleeping. That's all we can do for now. We've just got time before morning surgery to talk about last week. Let's go into consulting room one.'

We walked through reception and Sandy now had a companion, a little boy about the same age. His young mother smiled at us, and Steph glanced at the large clock on the wall. 'I won't be long, May.'

'It's no problem, Doctor Steph. I'm early.'

In the consulting room Steph went quickly through the cases she had treated that week. I listened, adding a comment or two.

It was clear to me that she was not only enjoying herself but doing an excellent job. When we'd finished, we both stood up.

'Are you still able to cover next week for me?'

'Yes. What are you going to do about helping your parents now you've got Sandy to look after? Alice will need at least a week to get her strength back.'

'I don't know, I've scarcely had time to think about that.' I ran my hands through my hair.

'Well, you could take Sandy with you to your parents. It will be logistically complicated but not impossible.'

'Yes, but babies need so much stuff and I'm not sure where she could sleep. I'll give it some thought. I'd better go now and let you start surgery. See you later.' I went back into reception and Steph called May to come into the consulting room. Sandy was still clutching the train and when I tried to take it from her, she began to cry.

'Let her take it, Phil. We've loads of toys here and I personally won't miss that one. The noise drives me crazy.'

'Thank you.' I carried Sandy out into the crisp fresh air and chatted to her on the way back to Alice's house. 'We're going to have some fun today, Sandy. I'm going to take you to the play group and after that, we'll go home and pack for a visit to your grandparents. They'll really love you. Then later this afternoon we'll go back and see Mummy.'

'Mummy,' said Sandy. I was pleased she wasn't upset and missing her mum because I could do nothing about that.

The playgroup began at ten, so I went straight there. Sandy wriggled and said, 'Down.' I obliged and she toddled to a sit-on train. I helped her sit astride it then she proceeded to play with the little train in her hand as she rocked the big one forwards and backwards. One of the young mothers said, 'I think Sandy will want to be a train driver when she grows up, but she'll have to move away from here, unless Adam plans to build a railway.'

'Does it worry you, what the children are missing?' I asked.

'No. I don't want my child to spend his time staring at a screen. I want him to understand nature, make a life here, farming like his dad does. This is real living. Our previous life was just an existence.'

'What about education? We can't offer good quality secondary schools and there's no university or agricultural college for your son to go to.'

'Huh. A fat lot of use college would be here. He can learn everything he needs to know from his dad. All you learn at college is how to comply with the hundreds of rules and regulations. Even without the EU, there are loads of issues, and don't get me started on Health and bloody Safety.'

I was beginning to wish I hadn't begun this conversation but then it was snack time and parents got tea and biscuits as well as the children. I moved to my tea and got accosted by another mother who wanted to discuss her ailments. I was pleased when it was time to go home for lunch.

Sandy had her afternoon nap and while she was sleeping, I packed a rucksack with baby essentials. I knew I could buy anything I'd forgotten but my funds were limited.

When Sandy woke, I gave her a drink, changed her nappy, and then put her into her pushchair. 'We're going to see how Mum is and then we'll go and visit Grandma and Grandad.'

At the hospital we went straight to the ward. I was pleased to see Alice was awake. She smiled and tried to sit up. I helped her, being careful to avoid touching the drip in her arm. Once she was propped on pillows, she could see Sandy, who, still in her pushchair, said, 'Mum, Mum up.'

I released the straps holding her into the pushchair and lifted her onto the bed so Alice could put an arm around her.

'I have missed you, Sandy but it looks like Phil has taken good care of you. What have you done today?'

'Train,' said Sandy.

'Yes,' I said. 'You acquired a toy train here and then you sat on a big one at playgroup. Then we had lunch, and you had a nap. Now we've come to see you, and you seem brighter already.'

'It's seeing you and knowing Sandy's fine. Thank you for bringing her. I'm so tired. Before I fall asleep, tell me what you're going to do about your mum and dad.'

'I do need to go there and stay this week, so I'm taking Sandy with me. It's going to be hard for you, but I promise we'll both be back on Friday evening and then you'll probably be well enough to come home.'

I expected Alice to object, perhaps be frightened that I'd take Sandy and not come back, but she just sighed and said, 'Thank you.' As her eyes closed, she whispered, 'Did I tell you Dan died of pneumonia?' Seconds later she was asleep. I prayed silently that she would recover as I carefully picked up Sandy and placed her back in the pushchair.

'Mummy's gone to sleep, and we must go to see Grandma.'

Chapter 23

2017

Eve was feeling fat and uncomfortable. She had been so pleased, all those months ago, to tell Adam she was pregnant, but carrying a baby, now it had grown so much, was an effort. Every night Adam insisted she put her feet up and he would cook the meal. She would then look at her feet, just visible beyond her bump, and see the swollen ankles. Adam still told her how beautiful she looked but that was not how she felt. There was just one month to go, and she had arranged to have the baby in hospital. They were no longer living in the other dimension because there were no medical facilities there. Several people had first aid training and there was a first aid box, but there was no-one with knowledge of midwifery.

Adam had engaged a young man, Keith, to take over Eve's job while she was on maternity leave, so when she turned up for work, she was just there in an advisory capacity. Keith was in his twenties and had just finished university with a degree in business studies. He was able to do the admin part of the work but had a lot to learn about managing the staff. Eve knew she could leave him to do it but found it hard to let go. So, she arrived every morning in time for coffee and went home mid-afternoon. It gave her something to do to keep her mind off the approaching due date.

It was Adam's 40th birthday and he wanted to celebrate it in the other dimension. Diane had made him a large fruit cake and decorated it with little log cabins and a large forty candle. This had been carefully hidden from him so it would be a surprise. Diane had also had some help stringing bunting around the diner in between organising a special birthday meal. Adam was keen on spicy food, so she had made a vegetable curry, naan bread and poppadoms with dips. Everyone had been invited so it would be a proper party. Petro had been asked to play for the dancing, but Eve, with her constant backache, would have to sit out.

As it was Adam's birthday, Eve had told Keith she would not be in. It was time to give herself some pampering. It began mid-morning with having her hair cut and blow dried. That was followed by a manicure. She might be extremely fat, but she was going to look as good as she could that evening, for herself and Adam.

By the time Adam arrived home at 5:30, Eve looked beautiful in a long dress that shimmered, seeming to change colour as she moved and fitted under the bust, then flowed to her low-heeled silver shoes.

'Wow, Eve, you look magnificent! I'll have a quick shower and get dressed. I can't wait to go to the party with you on my arm.' He gave her a quick kiss and ran upstairs shouting, 'Have I told you recently that I love you?'

'Just this morning,' she shouted back but he was already in the shower, and she knew he could not hear her. 'Oh,' she gasped as a pain forced her to sit down. She sat very still, both hands on her bump until it subsided. *I hope that doesn't mean the baby's coming.* She grinned, thinking. *I'll just have to keep my legs crossed tonight.* She stood as Adam came down the stairs, his shaven head gleaming, dressed in a light grey suit with a black T-shirt under it. He came towards her, his arms out, and they hugged then kissed.

'You smell wonderful. The perfume I gave you this morning, I think,' said Eve. 'You look good too. No wonder I married you. Come on or the main man of the evening will be late for his party.'

Adam drove them to the warehouse. He opened the big doors and then drove his car inside. Eve walked slowly to her office and unlocked it while Adam closed the big doors. They used the lift and then Adam held her hand to help her up the hill to Diane's Diner.

It was dark now and the fairy lights Arthur had strung along the front twinkled a welcome. There were balloons over the door that flapped and bounced as Adam opened it, and warm air enveloped them, along with cheers. The room was full and as Adam gazed around, everyone was smiling. He turned to Eve, put his arm around her waist, and they moved to the seats of honour Arthur was indicating.

Arthur continued to stand. The room quietened, everyone waiting for him to speak.

'We're all here to celebrate Adam's special birthday. I know dinner's ready so let the party begin.' There were claps and cheers, then plated meals were brought out. Adam and Eve were served first. Adam looked at it, a broad grin on his face and shouted, 'Who told Diane I love curry?' There was laughter and chatter as other people received their plates and ate with enjoyment. The atmosphere was warm and happy. Adam smiled at Eve. 'We're surrounded by all our friends. Who could ask for more on his birthday?' His face creased with concern as he saw Eve grimace with pain. 'Eve, darling, what's up?'

'Adam, you might be getting a baby for your birthday. That's the second pain I've had this evening.'

'Oh my God. Should we be getting you to the hospital?'

'Not yet. Let's not break up the party, you haven't even cut your cake. Everyone's finished eating and cake is our pudding. Diane will be bringing it out soon.'

'I don't care about cake, my birthday or anything. You are my world. Are you sure there's no rush?'

Eve nodded and then Arthur shouted above the hubbub. 'Make way for the cake. Come on, Adam, you've got to make the first cut.' Diane placed the cake on a small table in front of the counter. Adam put on a big smile and moved towards it. He looked down at the decoration and had to wipe away a tear. Then he leant over and kissed Diane on the cheek. It had gone very quiet, so Adam thanked Diane so everyone could hear. 'That's a wonderful cake. It's got little cabins on it. Before I cut it, you should take it round so everyone can see how perfect it is.'

'I think everyone else has seen it already, Adam. I just kept it hidden from you, so go ahead and put the knife in the middle.

You might need to press hard because it's royal icing.' Adam cut the cake then Petro played *Happy Birthday*, and everyone sang. Everyone that is, except Eve. His smile dropped as he saw her face grimacing again.

'What's the matter, Adam?' asked Diane.

'It's Eve. I think the baby's coming.' They both watched as Eve struggled up to the toilet.

'I'll see if she's okay,' said Diane. 'Arthur, take the cake into the kitchen to be cut up. Eve's not so good.'

When she got into the ladies' toilet, Eve was sitting on the pan groaning. 'The pains are coming quicker. My waters have broken. I can feel something between my legs.'

'It's not the most hygienic place to have a baby but I think you should lie on the floor. Let me help you down, then I'll get Jason B.' He was an arable farmer now, but she knew he had once worked with sheep. She threaded her way through the tables and spoke, her mouth close to his ear. He looked scared, then told his wife. They both stood up and joined Adam in the smallest room of the building. Jason took charge.

'Adam, will you move and sit your legs on either side of Eve and lift her so she's leaning against you. Diane, leave us and put a note on the toilet door telling everyone to use the gents. Then bring us lots of towels and a pan of warm water.' When Diane had gone, Eve cried out in pain.

'Don't try to fight it, relax when it's over. I'm going to have to look at what's happening so Mary will take off your underwear.'

'I know what you're going through, pet, I helped me mam when she had her fifth.' Mary removed Eve's wet pants, balling them up and putting them to one side. 'Now lift your bottom and I'll slip this towel under you.' Mary arranged the full dress as a kind of tent over Eve's spread knees and Jason peered under it.

'I can see the top of his head. When the next pain comes, start pushing as if you're going to the loo.' Eve cried out, bore down and Jason said, 'Keep pushing. Stop when the pain goes. Well done, I can see more of the head now. This is the hardest bit. Once the head's out, the rest's easy.' Mary dampened a towel and gave it to Adam to mop Eve's face. She managed to say, 'Thank you,' before the next pain waved in. Jason had his hands ready to catch the head and with one more pain, the baby was born. There was no doubt because he protested loudly at being ejected so forcibly.

There were smiles and congratulations as Jason said, 'It's a boy and he's perfect.'

The new family emerged from the ladies' toilet about an hour later, Adam holding his son, swaddled in yet another towel and Eve walking carefully, supported by Mary. Jason said he would stay behind and clear up the mess, but Adam shook his head.

'You must come out with us. What would we have done without you? I want to thank you, in front of everyone. Come on.'

The noise of cheers from everyone in the diner was deafening but the baby did not stir, sound asleep after his ordeal. Adam looked around, grinning at everyone and they went quiet.

'Eve's just given me the best birthday present ever. It's a boy.' He was going to say more but the cheers and applause began again. They waited until it was quiet and then Adam said, 'Jason was brilliant. He behaved so calm and efficient, as good as any doctor. Where did you learn all that, Jason?'

Jason squirmed and said, 'I've never brought a human baby into the world, but I've brought many a lamb.' This provoked an outburst of laughter as the group made their way out of the diner to Adam's cabin. Eve had a shower and then went to bed while Mary and Jason stayed with Adam.

'I see you've got a cot already. Shall I put him in it? Then, perhaps we could all have a cup of tea?' said Mary.

Adam nodded and when the baby was taken from him, he got up to boil the kettle. 'What a day. I can hardly believe I'm a dad.'

'You will when he gets hungry and screams his head off. We've already heard he's got a good pair of lungs. What are you going to call him?' Jason looked at Adam, his question hanging in the air. Adam brought cups of tea on a tray, sat, and said, 'I don't know. We discussed it but nothing seemed quite right.'

Mary giggled. 'He was born in a loo so you could call him Louis. That poor kid will never live it down. Everyone knows about his unexpected arrival.'

'I think I can do better than that. If Eve agrees I'd like to call him Able, Abe for short. If we follow the Bible, he should be called Cain, the first born, but I think we'll go for his brother.'

Mary and Jason lifted their cups and clinked them together. 'Here's to Abe.'

Chapter 24

2022

I arrived at my parents' house feeling excited and anxious. Could Mum cope with a baby in the house? I rang the bell, then let myself in. They rarely locked the front door during the day.

'Hello, you've got visitors.' I was pleased to see Mum coming to the door. When she saw us, her hand went to her mouth with surprise and delight.

'Have you brought Sandy? Where's Alice?' She stepped back as she spoke, allowing me to move the pushchair into the entrance hall. Mum bent to see Sandy, smiling as she spoke to her.

'You've come to see us at last, Sandy. You really are a beautiful girl. Will Daddy get you out of your harness and then I can see you properly?'

'Alice is in hospital with pneumonia, so I had to bring Sandy with me if I wanted to be here with you this week. I hope she won't be too much for you.'

'No, Dad and I will be only too pleased to help. Dad's gone shopping, just to the Co-Op, to get some milk and a few bits. Bring Sandy into the kitchen while I make us some coffee. She can sit on the floor and I'll give her some pans and a wooden spoon.'

The noise of the kettle coming to the boil was almost drowned out by Sandy's enthusiastic efforts at drumming and we smiled and said nothing until the coffee was ready.

'Let's sit here, while she's enjoying herself,' said Mum. 'Does she eat normal food, mashed up?'

'Yes, but she's never eaten meat. Her Mum's vegetarian.'

'Oh, well that shouldn't be a problem. We always have several vegetables with our meat so she can eat those.'

'She also drinks oat milk, so I'll need to get some. She's never had cow's milk and that might upset her stomach.'

Mum reached for her mobile and sent a text. 'Your Dad only left a few minutes before you came. He might still be in the shop, especially if he's stopped to chat to someone.' Her phone beeped a few minutes later. 'He's going to buy oat milk and put an emoji with a surprised expression.' She laughed. 'I didn't tell him about Sandy. Thought I'd let him enjoy the surprise.'

'Up, up,' said Sandy looking at her grandma.

'Oh, you gorgeous girl. I'd love to pick you up, but I don't think I'm strong enough. Daddy will pick you up and perhaps you could sit on my lap.' I picked up Sandy, then rummaged in a bag for a baby cup with two handles. I gave it to Sandy and when Mum sat in an armchair and raised her arms, I placed Sandy on her lap. 'It's a long time since I've felt the soft warmth of a child on my knee. Thank you for bringing her.'

I smiled. 'I didn't have much choice, but I'm glad you're well enough to do this.'

'The chemo knocks me out for a few days. Then I gradually feel better and I'm almost well in time for the next dose.' She grimaced. 'I'm like a swing boat, up and down. I just say to Dad, it'll be worth it in the end.'

I hugged her, being careful not to squash Sandy. Dad returned from shopping at that moment and I went into the hall to meet him. His broad smile showed how pleased he was to see me. Then he had to sidestep to pass the pushchair and said, 'Have we got visitors?'

Later that evening, when Sandy was deep asleep in my bed, Olivia arrived.

'Sorry I'm so late. I really wanted to see Sandy, but I had a deadline at work. Are you staying all week?' I nodded and she said, 'Good then I'll invite myself for tea tomorrow and leave work early in time to meet my niece. Will that be okay, Mum, Dad?'

'You know it'll be fine,' said Mum. 'I'll make a stew with mustard dumplings. We haven't had that for ages.'

'Yea, I love your stews,' said Olivia. 'Do you want me to get any shopping?'

'No, thank you pet. Phil can get it.'

We all went to bed early and Sandy woke at seven. I took off her nappy and sat her on the potty giving her the noisy toy engine to play with. I was ridiculously pleased to see her move onto her hands and knees to get off the potty and she'd used it. 'There's a good girl. Shall we try you on the potty after breakfast?'

I washed and dressed her, then we went quietly downstairs to find Dad cooking bacon. 'Good morning. I heard you two talking, thought you'd be down soon. Mum's still asleep. Would you prefer a bacon sandwich or egg and bacon?'

'A bacon sarnie would be great, thanks. I'll get Sandy a drink of oat milk and she can have bread, honey and a banana.' I stood Sandy on the floor. She plopped onto her bottom and then began to whimper. Dad turned off the cooker and picked her up and sat at the table with her on his knee. Sandy stopped whimpering and watched me. I gave her the cup of oat milk which she drank thirstily as I buttered some bread and put a thin smear of honey on it. I looked around the kitchen and picked up the tea towel and draped it around her as a makeshift bib. Sandy ate the bread as I sliced a banana into thick chunks.

'She's doing well feeding herself, isn't she? Perhaps we should buy a highchair. It would be worth it if you're staying all week. We might even run to a cot. There's room beside the bed in your room.'

'That would make life here easier and I'm sure Alice will want to come and see you when she's well. Thanks, Dad. Shall we do that this morning? Mum might feel strong enough to come with us.'

'She can't walk far without having to sit and rest but you've got the car. Why don't you take some tea up to her and ask if she'd like that?'

We all went shopping for baby essentials, Dad insisting on paying for them.

While we were browsing, Mum suggested they bought Christmas presents for Sandy and Alice. 'We might not be able to see them at Christmas, but it would be lovely to know they had something to open from us.'

They bought Sandy a doll and a warm winter coat. I wanted to say she liked cars and trains more than dolls, but I didn't want to spoil Mum's day. I made a mental note to buy Alice a warm jumper while I had access to shops but not then – Mum was too tired to do any more.

By the time Olivia arrived, the stew was nearly ready, and Sandy had been fed, bathed and was in her pyjamas. Olivia was smitten at first glance. 'Oh, you're so beautiful. Are you really as angelic as you look?'

Sandy held up the toy she was holding and said, 'Train, ah, ah.' Her voice was singing the train's horn.

Olivia sat on the floor beside her and said, 'Trains have to stop at the station so the people can get on. Let's make a station.' She picked up some cardboard boxes Mum had given Sandy to play with and built a structure. 'There. Will your train fit inside the station?' Sandy pushed the train under but was reluctant to let go so her arm knocked the structure down. Olivia laughed and that became the game. Whatever Olivia built, the train knocked it down.

When Mum declared the meal was ready, I picked Sandy up and took her, the train and a cup of warm milk upstairs. In just ten minutes she was ready and snuggling down, eyes closed. I came down to enjoy a hearty, meat-filled dinner.

Chapter 25

2018

Petro met Adam coming out of his cabin. He could hear Abe crying and Adam grimaced at the sound. 'Morning Petro, Abe's walking quite well now but he just fell over and banged his head. It's nothing serious but he thinks it is.' He laughed and Petro smiled. Petro had no wife, no children and was filled with envy at Adam's happiness.

'I wanted to ask you something, Adam. I've been here for six years and I'd like a holiday. I want to have two weeks up top. There are some things I would like to buy, like violin strings and I'd like to look at buying some tools if there are any new ones on the market.'

Adam's face showed surprise and concern. 'You will come back?' He saw Petro nod and added, 'I will pay you for any tools you buy to use here.' He thought for a moment and said, 'Where will you stay? Do you have relatives?'

'No, I was going to find a bed and breakfast somewhere.'

'You could use my house. Since Abe was born, we've hardly used it. But perhaps you planned to travel abroad or go somewhere else in the UK.'

'No, no plans like that. I'd be grateful to use your house, thank you.'

'In that case, stay there while I get my keys.' Adam went back inside and Petro realised the crying had stopped. Adam returned and asked, 'When are you planning to go?'

'Today, if that's okay? I'm up to date with my work.'

'I'm sorry, Petro, if I seem to be awkward. I've no problem with you having a holiday. It's just the first time anyone has asked. You go and enjoy yourself.'

'Thank you.' Petro almost ran the few steps back to his cabin. He felt excited and a little anxious. He wondered how he'd cope with the frantic noise and bustle of Tynemouth, after the quiet life he'd been living. He packed, in his usual neat fashion, and then emptied the contents of his fridge into a bag and carried it next door to Arthur and Diane's house. Diane opened the door in her dressing gown and he noticed the bulge of her tummy.

Before he explained what he was doing he blurted out, 'You're pregnant.'

Diane pulled her dressing gown closer and smiled. 'Yes, I suppose we can't keep it secret for ever. Anyway, come in, Petro. What's in the bag?'

Petro told her he was going away for two weeks and her eyes opened wide. 'You're a dark horse. You haven't told Arthur, have you?'

'Well, I was about to. Is he still in bed?'

'No, he's gone to help the farmers erect another greenhouse. He'll be shocked when I tell him. You will come back?'

'Yes. Is there anything I can get you?'

'No, thank you. I've no money to pay for anything.'

'Sorry, it was silly of me to ask. I'd better go now. See you later?'

She reached up and kissed him on the cheek. 'Bye Petro, have a lovely time.'

He collected his holdall from his cabin and set off to meet Adam at the door to the lift.

The directions to Adam's house were easy to follow and Petro unlocked the front door feeling almost like a burglar. He expected a neighbour to accost him and ask what business he had to be there. But nothing like that happened and he explored the house. There was very little in the fridge and as there was a shopping list pad and pen on the worktop, he wrote down milk, suddenly realising it could be cow's milk. Then he added pork sausages, bacon and steak. He was unsure what all that would cost and added a question mark to the steak.

He left the kitchen and went upstairs. The spare bedroom was obvious because the bed was unmade but Adam had explained where he could find sheets and a duvet cover. He decided to make the bed immediately. Ten minutes later he was back downstairs and sat in the lounge with the remote in his hand. The television blared out, but the controls were new and complicated. Adam and Eve had Sky and Petro had never been able to afford such a luxury. The programme was about cooking, and he found himself engrossed until the adverts appeared, too loud and frenetic. It was shocking so he turned the television off. In another corner, there was a games machine. This was quite old and Petro recognised it. It was tempting to turn it on and play but he decided to save that treat for later and go food shopping.

Petro began by going to the bank. He explained he had been abroad, his debit card had expired, so would they issue him with a new card. It seemed they wouldn't do that over the counter, but after a lot of discussion he was allowed some cash, and he gave Adam's address for them to send his new card to him. He entered a small supermarket and picked up a basket. As he put things in, he added up the cost, not wanting to spend all his money on his first day. He did not buy the steak but bought burgers instead. He promised himself a steak when he had a debit card.

The two bags of groceries were hefty, so he went back to the house and unpacked them. He was about to make a coffee then thought he could have a frothy one if he walked back to the town. It was only a ten-minute walk.

He went into a shop he had not seen before but they only did coffee to take out, there were no tables or seats. Petro fancied the bustle of a coffee shop, so he went to one on a corner, the ruined priory just beyond it. He had been to this café before and knew the décor was all wood. The walls were crudely panelled, and the centre table was a long, refectory type with benches instead of individual seats. He had intended to sit at a table on his own, but the café was very busy. He ordered his coffee and treated himself to a piece of cake. He was then shocked to find it cost him £6.50. The barista said she would bring it to him so he looked around but there was just the long table left with an elderly couple sitting at one end. He sat at the other. As he waited, Petro noticed nearly everyone had a phone on the table or in their hands. There was some face-to-face chatting, but many couples were ignoring each other and texting.

Petro was wishing he had brought a phone when his coffee arrived. It was frothy with real dark chocolate curls on top. It was heaven in a sip. His enjoyment was spoiled by an influx of young mothers with babies in pushchairs. The noise of them talking to each other, talking to their children, and laughing seemed too much. The room felt stifling as they all crowded onto the long bench seats, one mother accidentally elbowing Petro as she attempted to climb over the bench to sit on it.

'Sorry,' she laughed. 'There's not much room today. We come here every Monday. The coffee's excellent.' Petro could bear it no longer and slid off the bench.

'There you are, you've got a bit more space now.' As he stood, he noticed the elderly couple were also vacating. The three of them stepped into the fresh air and breathed deeply.

'It was a bit hectic in there. I didn't even finish my coffee. Couldn't cope with the noise,' said Petro.

'We felt the same,' said the woman. 'We thought we'd walk down to the car park where there's a van that sells good coffee. There are benches nearby and you can watch the sea. Sometimes we see seals or even a dolphin. Would you like to join us?'

'Yes, thank you. If you show me the way, I can find it next time.'

'She's not there every day, but I think she'll be there today. If not, we'll walk down to the Fish Quay.' It was not far to the car park that overlooked the Tyne estuary, and they were soon in the queue to buy coffee. Petro asked for a cappuccino and moved away holding the hot cup in both hands as the wind from the sea blew chill. When the others were served, they all walked to a bench seat with a perfect view. They sat, sipping, looking at the boats and searching for wildlife.

'Are you on holiday here?' asked the old man.

'Yes, but I used to live not far away, in North Shields.'

'Then all this will be familiar to you.'

'I didn't come to the seaside very often in those days because I worked very hard, only had Sundays off and I spent that time shopping and doing basic chores. This is lovely.'

The conversation ceased for a while and Petro half closed his eyes imagining all the trees that hid this view in the other dimension. It was only possible to see the estuary if you walked down to the shore. There was nowhere with a view as expansive as this. He breathed in deeply. Did the air feel any different? Could he taste or smell the pollution? No. The air felt great, and the view made him feel as free as the seagulls that whirled and screeched above and below him. Was the austerity of his present life necessary? Would he feel differently if he had a wife and family?

The couple rose, breaking into his reverie. 'We're going now, nice to have met you. I hope you enjoy the rest of your holiday.'

Petro rose too, 'Bye, thanks for showing me the coffee van and this glorious view.' They set off back to the car park, but Petro wanted to walk down the hill with the sea on his left, heading for the Fish Quay. He remembered there used to be lots of cafés and bars there. Could his funds run to lunch out?

As he walked, Petro decided to keep an open mind. It was impossible not to compare his two life choices when trying to decide which he preferred. He had not forgotten his promise to Adam and Arthur to return but he had not committed himself for life in the other dimension.

Petro walked by a fish and chip shop and found the smell irresistible. It would be cheaper than having a meal in a café. That was the case, but when he walked out with his polystyrene box, he was surprised how much it had cost. There were empty tables and chairs across the road and other people were eating there too, so he joined them. The taste matched the smell, with the added tang of vinegar and tomato sauce. What a treat. He savoured every mouthful, then wished he had bought a drink too because now he was thirsty.

The Fish Quay smelled of fish as well as fish and chips. Petro explored further and discovered the source. There were six or seven fishing boats moored by a large shed. Lobster pots and fishing nets were piled in areas and in-between the fishing gear were parked cars. It was obviously a very busy place but not in the afternoon. The boats bobbed and swayed with the wind and the waves but there were no people in the area. He walked further along the Tyne and saw men fishing with rods. They did not seem to have caught any, but Petro knew some fishermen threw them back into the water.

Petro had gone fishing with Arthur in the other dimension. They either shared them out for their own consumption or gave them to Diane to use in the diner. She often made them into fish cakes or her superb fish pie.

The sun had gone behind a cloud and Petro shivered. He walked briskly back up the hill to Tynemouth and back to Adam's house.

That night, after playing for three hours on the games machine, he snuggled down under the duvet feeling delighted with the first day of his holiday.

Chapter 26

2022

At the end of the week, I took Mum for her chemo session. She was remarkably cheerful considering her knowledge of how weak and ill she would feel following the treatment.

'I've always been a positive person and, somehow, being with Sandy this week has made me want to live even more than I did before. I want to be a small part of her life and watch her grow. I hope Alice likes us and will come to see us often.'

'Alice will love you and Dad. Her parents are dead, and you'll be excellent substitutes.'

'That poor girl, no parents and then her husband died too. I'm so glad she's got you to love her. Oh dear, we're here. Drop me at the entrance and you can then find a parking space.' Mum got out of the car and I moved off. As I drove around, eventually finding a space, I prayed that the treatment would be successful, and she would get her wish to see Sandy grow up.

I took Mum home after her treatment and then I started to pack to go back to the other dimension. Sandy and I were going to leave first thing tomorrow – Saturday. It was hard when Mum cried as I put Sandy in the pushchair. I knew the reaction to Chemo had kicked in and she was feeling rough. It was also because I couldn't even tell her when I'd be back because I'd have to go back to work. Steph only agreed to a fortnight, and she had to get on with her own life.

I met Eve at the warehouse with Abe. She let us in, and they came down with us in the lift. Abe and Eve spent the week in Tynemouth so he could go to school. At the weekends, they returned to their cabin. As we went down in the lift, I asked Abe if he enjoyed school.

'It was hard at first because the other children had all been to nursery school. I went straight into year one. I didn't know any of the other children and I wasn't used to the system. Now I love it. The work's not difficult and I've lots of friends.'

This made me think about Sandy. I wanted her to have a good education and choices which she would not have if she stayed in the other dimension all the time. I felt Eve had got things right and I decided to talk to Alice about it.

Alice. As I thought of her, my heart did a flip. I had every faith in Steph and antibiotics but now I couldn't wait to see her, hoping she'd be at home, worried she might still be in hospital. I said goodbye to Eve and Abe at their cabin and walked quicker, pushing the pushchair and then I began to jog. Sandy giggled and shouted, 'faster, faster.' She was kicking her legs with excitement. I slowed down, aware how selfish I was being and how careless. If I should trip, Sandy could tumble. She was strapped in but the thought that I could hurt her was sobering.

At her cabin I went in without even knocking. Sandy called, 'Mum.'

And there was Alice smiling at us both. She was in her pyjamas and dressing gown, so I knew she was still not well.

'Did we wake you? Are you well enough to be at home?'

'No and yes,' laughed Alice as she bent to undo the pushchair clips. She lifted Sandy and puffed out her cheeks with a grunt. 'What has Grandma been feeding you on? You've grown so big.'

'She's had a proper veggie diet so don't worry. Mum and Dad loved her and really want to meet you. I had to promise to take you to see them as soon as you were properly well. So, tell me, as I make us a cup of tea, how have you been?' We all moved into the kitchen and Alice put Sandy on the floor and gave her some toys.

'I barely remember when you took me into hospital but after twenty-four hours of antibiotics, I began to feel better and found I was hungry. When I first tried to get out of bed to go to the toilet, I felt shaky and had to have Nurse Jane with me, in case I fainted, but after that I got stronger and then I wanted to come home. They said I had to prove I was fit enough to look after myself, so I had to make a cup of tea and carry it to a table. I passed the test and they let me out yesterday. I slept and slept last night. Even a little hospital like ours can be noisy at night and I found it difficult to sleep. That's why I'm not dressed. Give me ten minutes to shower and then you can go to the hospital to see Steph. She's great, by the way, and you can tell her I said so.'

I stood as she did and said, 'I'll give you ten minutes if you'll give me a kiss first.' I took her in my arms and felt I'd come home. 'I've missed you,' I said, my hand at the back of her head feeling her soft hair.

Steph was busy taking surgery, so I said hello to everyone and walked into the ward to see who was there. I was surprised to see Arthur. He was on his side, snoring, so I quietly picked up his notes. He'd had a minor heart attack, but tests showed no damage. He would probably go home today. At that moment Arthur turned over, opened his eyes, and saw me.

'Hello, Phil. Good to see you. But you're not as attractive as Doctor Steph.'

'No, I'm sorry to see you've had a problem. But it's good you've done no damage to your heart. Has Steph given you any instructions?'

'Yes. She says I'm going to have to take soluble aspirin every day and go easy on the cakes and biscuits.' He groaned and continued, 'How can I do that when my wife is the best cook in town?' He put his head on one side, grinned and said, 'She didn't say I couldn't have a scone.'

I laughed. 'Unfortunately, that's also on the list but she couldn't mention every sweet treat. I could let you go home now but that's not ethical. Steph will be along when she's finished surgery. I think she should release you as you've been her patient.'

'No problem. I'll just enjoy this time in bed, while I can.' He shut his eyes.

After my visit to the ward, I went back to the waiting room, and seeing five people there I opened the second consulting room and began work. Helen brought a cup of tea when my first patient had left and said she'd taken Steph one and told her I was here and helping.

By lunchtime the last patient had been seen and Steph and I had a chance to chat. I filed my notes on the patients I'd seen and told her I'd visited Arthur. I also thanked her for looking after Alice and allowing me to go home.

'So, how's your Mum standing up to her chemo?'

'She's amazing. I took her to the hospital to have another dose of chemo yesterday so she's not that well this morning. She loved Sandy and can't wait to meet Alice. I just don't know when I'll get back to see her.' I saw Steph frown and added, 'That doesn't mean I want you to stay on. I'm so grateful for this fortnight off.'

'I've loved being here and I can see why you've stayed, although Alice and Sandy are a big pull. It's made me think I'd enjoy being a GP and I'm going to look for local vacancies when I go back. Would you write me a reference?'

'I'm happy to but it may not be worth much because I can't reveal where I work.'

'You could just put it as a small cottage hospital in Tyneside. Let me see what type of references are needed when I find a job. How can I get in touch with you?'

'Address an e-mail to me, care of Eve's work address, which is where the lift is. I'll write it down for you. Are you going back today?'

'Yes, but I'll have to pack. I'll go after lunch. I can't resist just one more meal at the diner before I go. By the way, I'm happy to come and do another stint here but you'll have to have a word with Rich. He's such a slob and you can tell him I said that.'

'Yes, I've been meaning to tackle him about his messiness. Now I can tell him you'll only return if he changes his ways.'

Chapter 27

2018

Petro woke up to a dull, wet day and gave himself permission to snuggle back under the duvet and go back to sleep. He never did this but now he could because he was on holiday. The bedside clock said it was nearly eleven o'clock when he woke again. He threw back the duvet and went downstairs and put the kettle on. There was a fancy coffee machine, but he wasn't sure how to work it. While the kettle was boiling, he made toast and then ate his breakfast in front of the television.

The sound and pictures were not engaging his attention and he found himself thinking about going to the job centre. Guilt washed over him but then he pushed it away. Supposing there was a job that suited him. Perhaps he could commute, going home to his cabin on weekends and then he could still do repairs and make furniture as he did now. The thought excited him, so he put his breakfast dishes in the dishwasher and went out.

He walked to North Shields, deciding to see what was on offer there but had a plan to use the Metro to go into Newcastle where there would be a bigger selection. He knew he could also look online but his phone was not a smart one. There was an iPad and computer at Adam's house, but he didn't think it was right to use it. The walk to North Shields Job Centre took about fifteen minutes, then he queued to talk to a person. There were a few people using computers, but he didn't feel confident.

He felt even less confident when he walked out an hour later. There were no jobs in the area for someone with his skill – a craftsman. He could get a job fitting kitchens or on a building site but this was not what he wanted.

'You look like you've lost a fiver and found a penny. I assume you had no luck in there. Can I buy you a coffee?' The voice came from a young woman who was very thin with black braided hair. She was chewing gum. She grinned at his startled face and said, 'Don't worry, I'm not after your body. You just looked so miserable I wanted to cheer you up. Come on.'

She set off without looking back and he followed, amused. He'd never been propositioned before, but it was only a coffee. She led him into a coffee shop and began to queue before asking him how he liked his coffee.

'A cappuccino please.'

'I'll make that two. Why don't you find us a table with comfy chairs.' It was busy and most tables were taken but then a couple rose from a settee beside a low table, so he slid into the space, still warm from their bodies, and pushed their cups and plates to one end. He waited, glancing at the girl who was paying by card, and wondered if she was just being kind or if she had some other agenda.

She arrived a few minutes later carrying a tray with two cups of frothy coffee with chocolate sprinkled on top. She put the tray down, smiled at him and said, 'Hi, I'm Angie.'

'Thank you, Angie, for the coffee. I'm Petro.'

'That's an unusual name, not English then. But I'm not English either. I'm Scottish.'

She took a sip of her coffee then used the spoon and creamed off some of the sweet froth and ate it. 'What sort of job were you looking for?'

Petro put down his cup and said, 'I want to make bespoke furniture, you know, by hand. I love working with wood, but they said they hadn't anything like that on their books.'

'I'm not surprised, especially here. It's not exactly the wealthiest town and only rich people buy handmade furniture.'

'I realise that, now, so I'm going to try Newcastle next. I might have more luck there. What about you? Do you have a job?'

She nodded. 'I'm a primary school teacher and, as you can probably tell by the number of children around, it's half-term holiday. Well, I've finished my coffee so I'd better do some work. '

'But I thought you said it was half-term so you're on holiday, right?'

'That's the theory but in fact, most conscientious teachers do their planning during the holidays and that's what I'm going home to do. Good luck with your job hunting, see you. Bye.'

Petro stood up, not wanting her to go. 'Thank you for the coffee.' He watched her wave an acknowledgement as she left the café. Suddenly he felt lonely. He stood to go, annoyed that he'd been too shy to ask for her phone number. Then he thought she might not be interested in a man who was out of work. In the other dimension he had friends and was highly respected for his skill and his violin playing. Here, he was not much better than a tramp – no fixed abode, no job, no friends. He sighed and walked to the Metro station.

The journey on the train felt novel. It had been so long since he had travelled on any form of public transport. He looked out of the window, remembering his excitement as a child to be on a train. He got off at Monument and walked through Fenwick Department Store to use their toilet and then emerged into the dull day outside. Everywhere was busy with families and once again the feeling of loneliness washed over him.

He knew where the job centre was and strode towards it using energy to eradicate his bleak mood. It was important to feel positive if he was going to find a job.

This time he went straight to a computer, as there were a lot of people queuing. He typed in furniture making. Immediately, he saw a possibility. There was a vacancy for a skilled woodworker in Moore handmade furniture – the owl man. He'd heard of the mouse man in Yorkshire. Every table, chair, sideboard had a tiny mouse carved on a leg. He wondered if all Mr Moore's pieces had a tiny owl on each one. He printed the advertisement and queued to find out if the job was still there and if they would make him an appointment to go for an interview. It seemed the workshop was in Tynemouth so that would be perfect. He felt excited and anxious that the lady behind the glass screen would tell him the job had gone.

It had not gone but there was another person interested. Mr Moore was doing interviews tomorrow and would like applicants to be prepared to demonstrate their skill.

'Do I have to bring my own tools?' he asked. She shrugged.

'He didn't say. It's up to you.'

Petro walked back towards the Metro station but realised he was very hungry. It was two o'clock and his coffee seemed ages ago. He looked around for a sandwich bar or a McDonalds but most of the places were restaurants. Then he remembered he was on holiday and treated himself to a hot dinner and a glass of beer.

While he ate, he thought about the day. It had been an emotional rollercoaster. He thought about Angie, with regret, and his job interview tomorrow with excitement. It was more than enough for one day. He paid his bill and walked to the Metro station, anticipating being back at Adam's house and playing on the PlayStation.

The following morning, he was up early, breakfast was soon over, and he headed out for his interview. He had not attempted to wear smart clothes, he didn't have any, but he was clean and hopeful.

Mr Moore was about fifty-five years old, medium height, broad in the body with iron-grey hair and a short, clipped beard. He held out his hand to Petro in welcome and Petro took it smiling.

'Come into the workshop and I'll show you around.'

There were lathes, tools of every sort hanging neatly on racks. The floor had recently been swept but curls of wood shavings sat in piles. The air smelled of wood and Petro breathed it in. The guided tour didn't take long and Petro was then led into an office with a computer and telephone on the oak desk. Filing cabinets stood against one wall and there was a table with a coffee machine on it, a kettle, and a fridge, presumably for milk.

'Take a seat, Petro and I'll make us a drink. Coffee or tea?'

'Coffee please with milk, no sugar.' They said no more until they were both sat with coffee and a plate of biscuits between them.

'Now, tell me where you've worked before and what experience you've had.' Petro talked about his job and being made redundant.

'I knew him,' said Mr Moore. 'A real craftsman but no business sense. He sold his beautiful work too cheap. But that was seven or eight years ago. Surely you haven't been out of work all this time?'

'No, Sir.' He took a deep breath. 'I've been working in a commune, building log cabins and furniture. It's been enjoyable but now I want to leave and start earning money again.'

'I've heard of places like that, religious, is it?'

Petro shook his head. 'Not religious but very...erm ...green. You know, wasting nothing, eating only what can be grown, no plastics used. Wind power only and no television, radio or mobile phones.'

'Interesting but now you want a change?'

Petro nodded, realising how much he wanted to work for Mr Moore.

'Well then, let's go back into the workshop and my son, Frank will put you on making a chair.'

Three hours later, Petro was sanding the last part of a kitchen chair, prior to putting it all together. He had been given a chair to copy and worked as quickly and carefully as he could. He knew if Mr Moore wasn't satisfied then there was nothing he could do because he'd given all he could give. He held his breath as each part was carefully examined and then there was a snort of laughter as he found the tiny carved owl. He looked up and smiled at Petro. 'Your work is superb. When can you start?'

Petro let out a whoosh of air, grinned and said, 'Monday.' That would give him a few days more holiday and time to find somewhere to live. They shook hands and Mr Moore said, 'Let's go into the office and we'll talk about wages.'

Petro was reeling when he left the workshop. He wanted to tell someone, Arthur, or Adam, but knew they would not give him the wholehearted congratulations he was looking for. He had started to walk back to Adam's house but veered off and went to the coffee shop where he had met Angie. He ordered a frothy coffee and treated himself to a chocolate muffin. He took his tray to the table they had sat at the day before and wished she was there.

He bit into the muffin and found himself disappointed. It was sweet and moist, but the chocolate was insipid. Diane made much tastier ones. He was going to miss the camaraderie of the other dimension if Adam refused to allow him to commute. He was sipping his coffee gingerly in case it was too hot when a voice made him almost drop the cup.

'We must stop meeting like this. Hello again, Petro.'

He stood up and grinned. 'I didn't expect to see you, Angie. Let me buy you a coffee.'

'Thank you. I'd like exactly what you have, including a muffin but not chocolate, lemon if they have one.' She sat at his table while he went to the counter. There was no queue, so he was back quickly, well as quickly as was possible in a coffee shop.

'Thank you,' said Angie. 'So how was your day? Any luck on the job front? You're smiling like the cat that's got the cream. Tell me all about it.'

Petro did and she was so pleased for him she stood up, went around the table, bent down and kissed him on the cheek, saying, 'Congratulations, fantastic news.' She sat down and added, 'When do you start?'

'Monday.'

'So, you can relax now and enjoy your holiday.'

Petro shook his head. 'No, I've got to find somewhere to live. I'm staying at a friend's house at the moment.'

They chatted about what sort of accommodation Petro would look for and Angie described where she had seen some flats with signs up saying vacancy. The cake and coffee were finished but there was a reluctance to leave. It was Angie who made the move.

'Look, I've got to go now but I'd like to see you again. If you're not married or anything, I mean. Give me your number. God, that's presumptuous of me.'

'No, I'd really like to see you again.' They exchanged numbers, both stood up and walked out of the café together.

Chapter 28

2022

It was Christmas Day and I sat happily on the floor, amidst the chaos of discarded wrapping paper, playing with Sandy. Delectable smells came from the oven as Alice checked the roast potatoes and parsnips. I had thought everyone would go to the diner for Christmas dinner, but it was closed for the two days of the holiday. It really didn't matter to me. I was happy wherever I was if Alice and Sandy were there.

Sandy had opened her doll from her grandparents and had not let go of it. I had bought her a wooden train track and engine with trucks to push around it. Sandy had watched as I built it. When I'd finished, I offered her the engine. She put the doll down and tried to put the engine on the track, but she couldn't align the wheels.

'Look at the wheels, Sandy. They have a groove, and that groove must fit on the rails. You try it.' I was delighted to see her succeed and the train glided easily around the circle.

'Metro,' she said. 'Train's going to Newcastle.'

'We went on the Metro to go Christmas shopping. Do you remember?'

She nodded her head.

Alice brought us a drink, tea for me and orange juice for Sandy. Then she opened the chocolates and we all indulged. Sandy had never eaten any sweets before, but Christmas time was special. She was not happy, however, when Alice put the lid back on the box.

'More chocolate, more,' and when that didn't work, she shouted, 'Please!' We both laughed.

'You can have one more after dinner. It'll be ready soon.'

'What are you going to call your doll?' I asked, trying to distract her from chocolate.

'Baby,' she said.

'Yes, she is a baby, but she needs a name, like Sandy, Alice, Diane.' I watched Sandy thinking about this and finally she said, 'Annie, baby Annie.'

'That's a great name. Is Annie going to sit at the table with us for Christmas dinner?' She nodded and with perfect timing, Alice shouted, 'It's ready.'

We sat at the table, and I looked at the festive centrepiece made of holly and pinecones and the paperchains we had all made the day before. A feeling of wonder and gratefulness almost made me cry. How lucky was I to have this moment with the two people I loved so much.

'This looks wonderful, Alice. I think we should have a toast.' We picked up our glasses of grape juice and I said, 'Here's to many more lovely Christmases together.' We clinked our glasses and Sandy held up her plastic beaker.

There were no Christmas crackers and no turkey, but the food was tasty with lots of vegetables and a rich gravy.

The pudding was traditional, but we couldn't set it alight without alcohol. Sandy had never seen that done before and I felt a frisson of regret that I couldn't show her those bluish dancing flames. Perhaps when she was bigger, we could have Christmas Day at my parents' house where she could enjoy all the little extras that I felt she was missing. Then I realised, I was missing them.

After lunch was cleared and everything tidied, we went for a winter walk. It was bitterly cold. 'I think it might snow,' I said and then we laughed as a few flakes drifted down. We were not the only ones enjoying the fresh air. We knew everyone. 'Merry Christmas' greetings echoed around. It was too cold to stop and chat and Sandy's ability to walk any distance was limited so when we reached the end of the village, now way beyond my cabin, we turned around and walked back. We were nearly there when Arthur opened his door and beckoned us in. We spent the afternoon with them playing silly games. Arthur and Diane had a little boy of four and a girl almost the same age as Sandy. They didn't really play much together but they laughed a lot, as did the adults and it was delightful. I was enjoying the company and could have stayed longer but when Sandy was wilting, quiet and sucking her thumb on my knee, Alice said we had to go home, give her a snack, and put her to bed.

Later that night, when we were in bed, I asked Alice to marry me. She rolled on top of me, held my face in her hands and kissed me tenderly. 'I thought you'd never ask,' she said with a broad smile. 'I'll marry you as soon as we can organise it.'

It was two days before New Year's Eve and Alice was rushing around the cabin packing the last-minute things that we needed to spend three nights at my parents' house. I had asked permission from Adam and had left details of how I could be contacted with the people on duty at the hospital. The tray under the pushchair was laden, and we both had rucksacks.

'The shops will be open if there's anything we've forgotten,' I said.

'Yes, but that requires money and I have none. Do you have any?'

'You know I do. Are you feeling nervous about meeting my family?'

'Not nervous, terrified. I'm scared they won't like me. They might think I've hooked you and lumbered you with a child that's not yours.'

I laughed. 'They already adore Sandy, and they'll love you too. Stop worrying and let's go. Adam will be waiting now at the lift.'

It was very cold. A bitter wind was blowing. The ground, slushy yesterday, was hard with ice and tricky to walk on. The going was slow and unpleasant. We met Adam and he went up in the lift with us.

'You'll be surprised when you go outside,' he said. 'It's warm and dry. That's global warming for you.'

He was right. It was probably ten degrees warmer than where we lived and there was no sign of snow, slush or ice. We walked quicker than before and soon reached Mum and Dad's front door. I rang the bell and noticed Alice biting her lip. 'It'll be fine,' I said as the door opened.

Fifteen minutes later we were all sat in the living room. Dad brought in a tray laden with cups of coffee and homemade mince pies.

'Are those made with orange in the pastry?' I asked. When Dad smiled and nodded, I added, 'The best mince pies ever. You must have one Alice.'

'I will.' The tray was now on the coffee table, and she leant forward and took one. She didn't bite into it as I had done then I realised she was looking for a plate or serviette.

'We don't stand on ceremony, don't worry if a few crumbs escape.' She grinned and used her other hand to catch any stray bits that should drop.

'Can I have a mince pie please?' asked Sandy.

'You can have a bite of mine to see if you like it.' Alice held what was left of hers towards Sandy who bit a piece off and chewed. 'Yummy, yummy in my tummy. Can I have a whole one, please?'

I pushed the plate towards the edge of the table so she could get one for herself. Mum was watching, had said very little, but hadn't stopped smiling. Now she leaned towards Alice and said, 'She's such a poppet. I can hardly believe you're all here. I seem to have been waiting to meet you for ages.'

Alice responded with one of her heart-stopping smiles and said, 'I've been terrified of meeting you, in case you didn't like me. Sandy's obviously broken the ice for me.'

'Terrified!' said Mum. 'You'd really no need to worry. We won't bite.'

'I can see that now and I'm really pleased to meet you both.' She hesitated, drew in a deep breath, and went on, 'I know you've been ill with cancer. How are you now?'

Mum's smile grew wider as she said, 'I've finished the chemo and so far, it's all clear. I must go back for a check-up in three months and if it's still fine, six-monthly appointments. I feel so well now and, of course, relieved of all that anxiety. So, we can celebrate a new year with enthusiasm.'

That evening, we sat down to dinner together. Mum had made a vegetarian lasagne and Dad opened a bottle of red wine. There was a jug of iced water on the table and Sandy had that, but shivered as she drank it, making everyone laugh. I accepted wine and so did Alice saying, 'I haven't had a glass of wine for many years so I might get tipsy on one glass. But I always feel it makes an occasion like this extra special. Where we live there's no alcohol and apart from eggs, everyone eats vegetarian.'

'So, what happens to the male chicks and the chickens that are too old to lay?' asked Dad.

'I don't know. To be honest, I've not thought about it. I suppose the male chicks could be grown to a size when they're big enough to eat and sold outside. There are a lot of things we have to buy from outside because we can't grow them or make them ourselves so perhaps the chickens pay some of that back.'

Dad looked at me for confirmation and I just nodded.

When Sandy was ready for bed, I let Alice take her upstairs, so I had a time with Mum and Dad.

'Alice is lovely,' said Mum. 'She's intelligent and friendly. Just the sort of girl I would've chosen for you if I could.' Dad and I laughed and then he topped up our glasses. 'Don't drink it all yet,' I said. 'You must save some for a toast when Alice comes down.'

We sipped and were so quiet I could hear the minute hand of the kitchen clock ticking round. We felt full of good food and contentment. There was no need for conversation. Alice's slipper shod feet made little sound on the stair carpet, but we all heard it and looked up as she came in.

'She only heard about a page of the story and fell straight off to sleep. It was lovely of you to buy the cot and the highchair. It makes such a difference, and I could tell Sandy felt at home as she snuggled down.'

I stood up and handed her the glass of wine. 'Don't sit for a minute, we've got an announcement to make. I just want to tell you that I asked Alice to marry me, and she said yes. We're officially engaged but I haven't bought a ring yet.'

Mum clapped her hands together and her eyes were shining with tears. Dad stood up and shook my hand and then hugged Alice. 'Congratulations. We must have a toast.' He raised his glass, 'Here's to Alice and Phil.' Mum echoed him, and we all clinked our glasses and drank.

Chapter 29

2018

Petro went to bed and dreamt of Angie. In the morning he got out of bed quickly, made tea and toast and was ready to go out well before nine o'clock. His plan was to go to the estate agents to find a flat to rent, but it was far too early. He thought of going for a walk or even trying a run along the coast but then realised he could look online for flats. He hesitated to use Adam's computer. It was probably protected by a password. Still, there was no harm done if he just switched it on.

The screen lit and when all the icons and apps appeared he looked for one he recognised – Google. It seemed there was no password, so he began to search for flats. There were a lot of new ones on the Fish Quay at North Shields, but the rent was prohibitive. He needed something older, inland. There were two that caught his eye and he thought he might be able to walk to work from them or perhaps, cycle. He grinned at that thought because he hadn't ridden a bicycle since he was a child.

It was now after nine, the estate agents would be open, so he noted the address of the flats and the agent renting them, then set off.

The first flat he saw was spacious but that was probably because there was no furniture. It was on the second floor. There was no lift and he immediately saw the difficulty of getting what furniture he could afford up the stairs.

The second one he saw was on the ground floor. It was empty of furniture, but it had a kitchen with built-in appliances including a washing machine. That's better value for money, he thought, as he moved through the lounge and looked at the back garden. He was not sure if that was his responsibility, but it had French windows that lead out onto a small patio. There were two bedrooms and one bathroom. It was exactly what he wanted. He agreed on the spot and went back to the estate agents to sort out the paperwork. By lunchtime he had the keys but was much poorer, having to pay the first month's rent in advance. His next step was to look at his bank account, but the branch of his bank had closed. He found a cash machine and discovered he had enough money to feed himself for a few weeks but not enough to buy furniture.

He thought about all the things he'd made for the other dimension and wondered if Adam would let him take his bed. He could put that in the living room to start with, so he'd have somewhere to sit as well as somewhere to sleep. It now seemed imperative that he returned to the other dimension and spoke to Adam.

At the warehouse he asked if he could speak to Adam or Eve and the man there asked him to wait. Eventually Adam appeared and looked quizzically at Petro but indicated they shouldn't speak.

'Nice to see you Petro, come into my office.' When they were alone, Adam raised an eyebrow and Petro blurted out everything. There was a short silence and Petro watched Adam shake his head. Then he put a hand on Petro's shoulder and said, sadly, 'Oh dear. I've never had to make such a hard decision. I think of you as a friend, Petro. You've been with us since the beginning and now you want to go back into the rat race. Is there a girl somewhere in all this?'

Petro smiled, shyly. 'I have met someone, Angie, but obviously its early days. I've only known her a week. The main attraction is the job. So, what do you think about me commuting?'

'I don't think it'll work. If you do it, other people will follow and then the community will not stay a secret. You'll want to bring Angie to meet everyone and then we'd have to swear her to secrecy too. I think it could be the collapse of all we've worked for.' He sighed. 'I have to say no. If you move away from us, it must be permanent. But I'm happy for you to take your bed, bedding and anything else you need to get you started. That's the least I can do after all the furniture you've made for us. If we go down now, you can do some packing and

I'll help you, once the warehouse is shut, to move whatever furniture you want.'

As they went down in the lift, Petro's heart felt as if it would burst with misery. Was he doing the right thing? Giving up all he'd helped to build, moving away from his friends? It was too late, he reasoned. He'd rented the flat, was starting work on Monday, and he was seeing Angie tomorrow.

Adam left him and went back to work, promising to return at 7 pm to help with the lifting. Petro went home and tears fell as he packed his clothes into a rucksack and tied his bedding into a huge bundle. In the past he would have used plastic sacks, but these were none in this dimension. He added a saucepan and a frying pan to the pile and then looked around as if trying to remember every detail. With a jolt he realised he had not packed his tools.

The toolbox was under the bench. He filled it, handling them thoughtfully, remembering when he'd bought and used them. He had to be selective and ignored those that were for tree felling including a huge saw with a handle at each end for two people to use. It was poignant thinking about them, but he could only take tools he would need in the new job.

Everything was ready and now Petro realised he was hungry and went to the diner. He ordered lasagne, feeling the need for filling food. When he'd ordered, Arthur walked in.

'Hello Petro. I didn't expect to see you today. You still have a day or two's holiday, don't you? I'll just give my order and you can tell me all about it.'

Petro sat down and sipped some water, feeling agitated. They'd been friends since the beginning. Six years of working together, eating together and socialising. A wave of misery assailed him as he realised he would never know if Diane's baby was a boy or girl. Arthur sat down heavily and smiled at him, but the smile faded when it was not reciprocated.

'What's wrong? Has something awful happened? Someone died?'

Petro managed a glimmer of a smile as he shook his head. 'None of those but I'm feeling desperately sad because I'm leaving tonight.'

'What do you mean, leaving? Why? I thought you were happy here with us. You can't leave. You're my best friend.'

'When I went on holiday I met a lovely woman, Angie. She's a teacher and we seemed to just click...'

'Now I get it. I really understand the pull of romance. Sorry, to interrupt. I can see there's more.' Their dinners arrived and Petro kept quiet until the waitress had gone. Everyone would know soon but he just needed to talk to Arthur.

'That's not all. I looked for a job and found one making bespoke furniture. As soon as I talked to the owner, Mr Moore, and looked around the workshop, I knew I wanted it. I start on Monday. I also found a flat and I'm taking Angie to see it tomorrow.'

'Phew. You don't let the grass grow under your feet. I assume Adam knows.'

'Yes. I asked him if I could stay, living here and working in the other world, but he refused. I'm going to miss everyone, but I have to go.'

Arthur nodded and they said no more as they ate. When he'd finished, Arthur leaned back in his chair and sighed. 'I can't believe it. Diane will be upset too. Anyway, what time are you moving out? I'd like to help.'

'Adam's coming at seven to unlock everything.'

'Okay, I'll see you then.' He stood up abruptly and walked out of the diner. Petro felt drained of all energy. He got up more slowly, walked back to his cabin and curled up on the bare mattress, his head cushioned on the bundle of bedding. He fell asleep and only woke when Adam walked in.

'Are you ready, Petro? I've brought a tractor and trailer and there's a van waiting outside the warehouse. Let's go.' Petro began to dismantle the bed and Adam helped. Arthur arrived and carried things out to the trailer. The weather was windy but not raining so nothing was going to get wet. When everything was aboard, Petro climbed into the trailer and Adam drove to the lift. When the doors were open, he backed the trailer into it, but it was not quite large enough to take the tractor too. He jumped out of the cab and unhitched the trailer. Arthur stood, ready to shut the doors and waved until he could no longer see Petro.

They were silent as they rode up in the lift. The warehouse was empty.

'Stay here, Petro, I'm going to bring the van right up to the office door so we've less distance to manhandle everything.' Petro nodded, too full of emotion to speak. The activity of filling the van helped calm him and he managed to say. 'I appreciate the help, Adam. Are you coming with me or am I to drive the van and return it?'

'I'm coming to help you unload. Then I'll know where you live, should we need you.'

They were driving now with Petro giving directions. 'This is a big step you're taking, leaving all your friends behind. I'll be happy to keep you in touch, by letter, if you'd like that.'

Petro smiled. 'Thank you, I would like that. Now it's just round this corner on the right. That's it. Stop.' They unloaded everything and Adam admired the flat.

'You should've bought more furniture. You can't manage with just a bed and these few things. I'll go back and fetch some chairs and a table, at least.'

Petro held up his hands. 'No, I've thought about this. You'll want to use my cabin for someone else and then you'll have to go and buy a new bed but that's all. We all knew you spent a lot of your own money helping us to be comfortable. I didn't want to add to your expense any more than I could help. Thank you for all you've done for me, including lending me your house for my holiday. Go back now and give my love to Eve and everyone.' He held out his hand and saw tears glistening in Adam's eyes as he shook it.

Chapter 30

2022

I felt New Year's Eve would be something of an anti-climax after last night when I'd announced our engagement, but Mum had plans. She seemed to have regained most of her old energy and was busy baking for the occasion. It was a good time for Alice and me to go into Newcastle and buy a ring. Dad was playing on the living room carpet with Sandy, and I tentatively asked if we could leave her with him.

He looked up at us, smiling. 'That's what grandparents are for, isn't it? You go out and enjoy yourselves. We'll be fine.'

'Thank you. I rarely get the chance to go out without Sandy,' said Alice.

'No problem. Go, but wrap up warm. It's bitter out there.' We wasted no more time and did as instructed, swaddled in thick coats, hats, scarves and gloves. We walked briskly to the Metro station and by the time we'd bought our tickets, a train was rolling in. We sat together, holding hands, and said little as the train stopped at various stations then moved on. It seemed everyone was getting off at the same stop as us – Monument Station. We moved along, stepped off the train and walked through Fenwick Department Store. Alice slowed and seemed to need to touch nearly every garment.

'Your Mum's organising this party and I've nothing to wear.'

'Ah,' I said. 'Let's look in some other shops once we've bought the ring. I promise then I'll be patient and let you try on every dress in the shop.' She nodded and moved away from the extremely expensive, beautiful dresses. The centre of town was thronged with shoppers hoping to get a bargain in the sales. I held Alice's hand, because I liked doing it but also to stop us getting forcibly separated.

Within moments I'd spotted Berys, and we both peered at the engagement rings in the window. The prices were frightening.

'They're all gorgeous, Phil, but far too expensive. Let's see if we can find somewhere cheaper.' Now I was the one moving reluctantly away. I wanted to buy her the best, but she had other ideas. I didn't know where to go next so I used my phone to search.

'Right, follow me. I think it's just around the next corner.'

The next jeweller's shop was not so plush, but the rings still looked lovely.

'Does anything catch your eye, Alice? Don't go by price. Please chose something you'll be proud to wear.'

'I'd prefer something simple, like a single solitaire but there are several in different settings.'

'Let's go in and ask to try some on.'

We stood at the counter while several trays of rings were brought out. Alice had her finger measured and then each ring was tried on the measure to make sure it was going to fit. There were eventually just two that fit well but she couldn't decide between them. Alice looked up at me. 'Help me out. Which one shall I have?'

'I like the one set into a heart. It seems to say how I feel.'

'That's lovely,' said the woman serving us. 'It's nice to meet a romantic man.'

Alice smiled and nodded. 'That's the one then.'

A little box was fetched, and the ring was put into it, then the box was put into a tiny carrier bag. I paid and we went outside. Alice took my hand then pulled me to her and kissed me. 'Thank you. It's a beautiful ring. I'm looking forward to showing it to your mum and dad when we get back. Now, shall we get a cup of coffee before we go dress shopping? I want to make the most of this trip.'

We sat with our frothy coffees, both enjoying the luxury. The diner served mostly tea and the coffee was instant. Alice took her ring out of the box and put it on, moving her hand to see it catch the light and sparkle. 'It's beautiful. I can wear it, can't I? We're officially engaged.'

I nodded. 'The ring is beautiful and so are you.' I leaned over and kissed her.

Clothes shopping took much longer than ring buying. I began to worry about my bank balance as Alice chose a dress then needed underwear and finally, pretty shoes. When I was laden with bags and boxes, we walked towards the nearest Metro station and then I saw a cash machine. I interrogated it and saw I was still solvent but from now on, we needed to be careful. It made me seriously think about where I worked, earning nothing but bed and board.

As we sat on the train, I talked to Alice about it.

'I've been thinking about it too', she said. 'While Sandy is young, we need very little, and I know where we live is a healthy environment. There's no air pollution, we eat sensibly and there are no sweets to rot her teeth. There are children for her to play with and we all have the same ethos. In the big wide world, she won't be so safe. But later, when she needs to go to school, I think it will be different.'

'So, you're saying let's give it two or three years?'

'I think it should be just two. You need to get a job and we can't be sure you'll get one locally. Newcastle Infirmary might have its full quota of surgeons.'

'I'll also need to retrain because there will have been new procedures while I've been away.' I paused, took a deep breath and added, 'By then, I might have decided I want to be a GP. I do enjoy what I do now.'

She took my hand, squeezed it, and said, 'You don't have to make that decision now. There's plenty of time.'

New Year's Eve was hectic. Mum wanted the house cleaned from top to bottom and last-minute food preparation had to be done. Then it was eight o'clock and Olivia and Rich arrived clutching a bottle of wine each.

There was lots of kissing and hugging then the party began. I filled everyone's glasses, but Mum still seemed uneasy, on edge. She stood in the kitchen, her arms hugging herself as if she was cold.

'What's up, Mum? You don't seem relaxed. Are you cold?'

She shook her head.

'What can I do to help?' She patted my arm.

'Don't worry, there's nothing you can do. I invited Mike and told him to bring a friend. I didn't get a reply so perhaps he's not coming. I wanted it to be a lovely surprise.'

I felt a surge of anxiety. *How can Rich and I explain what happened when I fell into the picture? He's bound to ask where I've been all this time and why I haven't got in touch now I'm back. Mum didn't know. She thought it would please me to have both my best friends here. I must tell Rich.*

I took a deep breath and said calmly, 'I seem to remember Mike was never that good on time keeping. Give him another ten minutes then serve the food.' I saw her nod and went to find Rich, my heart pounding.

'What's up?' he said when I approached. He and Olivia were sitting close together on the settee. I told him quietly and Olivia leant in to catch my words. Both their faces paled. Dad had gone upstairs to check that Sandy was asleep, and Alice had gone into the kitchen to get a glass of water. We needed an idea quickly.

'What about the abduction story we told your parents?'

'That won't do. He saw me fall and I was away for months. Why, when I appeared again, didn't I ring him?'

'I think we should tell him a version of the truth. You did fall through the picture into another dimension where there was a commune and you didn't know how to get away,' said Rich.

'I think that's better but if Mum and Dad hear that, they'll not understand, having already told them a lie,' I said, feeling panic rising. The doorbell rang and we all looked at each other in alarm. I went towards the door, but Dad got there first.

'Mike, how lovely to see you and this is?'

'Hello, Mr Clarkson. This is my fiancée, Fiona.'

'Welcome, let me take your coats,' and then 'Oh, thank you. We love Prosecco, chocolates too.'

I decided it was time to face the problem and went out into the hall.

'Mike! It's been a long time. Lovely to meet you, Fiona, oh and this is my fiancée, Alice.'

Alice had appeared from the kitchen and there was a general bubble of congratulations. Alice suggested we all went into the living room where the greetings were continued with Rich and Olivia.

'Are you two engaged too?' asked Fiona.

If there had been room, they would have sprung apart but Fiona had settled beside Olivia.

'No,' said Olivia, smiling. 'We came together but we're just friends. Phil is my brother and we've all known each other for years.'

Alice had noticed Fiona's ring and said, 'Your ring is beautiful. Have you had it long?'

Fiona held her hand out, admiring her ring. 'A week. We got engaged on Christmas Day. How long have you had yours?'

So far everything was going well and then Mum shouted that the food was ready.

The dining room table was only just big enough for eight people and it looked beautiful, glasses gleaming, tureens steaming and Mum holding a pile of warm plates. I stood up to help and soon everyone was eating, and the conversation turned from engagements to appreciation of the food. I noticed Mum was eating very little and her face looked grey. She was exhausted. We had managed the main course with no talking about my weird disappearance. Alice and I helped Mum clear the plates and bring in the pudding. I stacked plates in the dishwasher and asked Mum how she was.

'I'm delighted it's all going well but I'm exhausted. I could really do with going to bed now, not in...' she looked at the clock on the wall, 'In an hour and a half.'

'Why don't you slip away, quietly and I'll explain you've been ill?'

She put a hand on my arm and leant in for a hug. 'I'll do that, thank you. Oh, Alice, don't forget the cream in the fridge.'

I made the explanations and began to serve the pudding. Dad went upstairs to see if Mum needed anything. There were just six of us left in the room.

'Now then,' said Mike. 'When your Mum rang and invited us, I was so shocked, and angry, I just thanked her and said yes. I saw you fall into that picture and now you're here, with a fiancée and you never thought to tell me. Are you going to explain how you disappeared and then arrived back and never got in touch?'

Chapter 31

2018

The flat felt chill when Adam had gone. It seemed a big, empty space and Petro felt bereft. This was his second new start. He wanted to feel positive and excited but at that moment, he just felt sad.

A text from Angie helped raise his mood. 'Can I come and see your flat?' He sent a reply with the address. Her reply was, 'Coming now.' This sent him into tidying mode which just meant making the bed. As he did so, he imagined Angie on it striking a sexy pose, inviting him to have sex with her. He wanted that very much but was scared to suggest it in case she took offence. They had known each other such a short time.

He went to the kitchen area to put the kettle on, then realised he had no kettle, cups, coffee, tea or milk. He picked up his phone to stop Angie. How could he have her here without even offering tea? Before he had typed a letter, the doorbell rang. Petro opened it, smiling a welcome. Angie grinned back and thrust a bottle of prosecco into his hand. He led her into the living room. She looked around approvingly and said, 'Is it a bedsit?'

'No, but that's the only furniture I have. Let me give you a tour.'

Angie admired everything and when they got back to the living room, she sat on the bed.

'I'm afraid I don't have any cups, glasses or anything. I don't even have a kettle to offer you a cup of tea. I moved in last night and this is all I've got.'

'You've had no breakfast or even a drink?' He shook his head. 'In that case, let's go out, grab a cappuccino, and make a list of essentials. Before we go, put that bottle in the fridge, we might want to share it later and it's better chilled.' Petro happily allowed Angie to organise him. He had felt lost and miserable. Now he felt himself tingling with excitement.

They left the flat, soon arrived at their favourite café and the making of the list began. The amount was daunting and Petro wondered if his bank account could cope.

'We don't have to get all of this today,' he said. 'I just need enough to get by. Big things like a table and chairs, settee and so on can wait. I might even be able to stay after work and make some of it.'

'Good thinking. Let's circle essentials. You've got to be able to make yourself breakfast and an evening meal. We could probably get most of this locally. Let's begin by walking to North Shields and exploring. You can often get bargains there.'

They did this and only returned to the flat when they could carry no more. Now Petro could put the kettle on and make a cup of instant coffee or tea. Angie washed all the crockery and glasses, checked how clean the cupboards were and put them away. By five o'clock, they were finished.

'Let's open that bottle now and drink a toast to your new home,' said Angie.

Petro willingly did as she suggested. An hour later, both tipsy having finished the bottle, Angie leant back on the pillows, holding out her arms to Petro. He needed no more encouragement and soon they were naked, discovering each other's bodies.

After that, Petro fell asleep and when he awoke, Angie had gone. He got off the bed, pulled on his pyjamas and called. She really had gone. He was worried but then his phone pinged with a message.

'Sorry, I had to go. I've got school tomorrow and there were things I had to do. Thank you for a lovely day. I enjoyed ALL of it. Can we meet next weekend? xxx.'

Petro smiled and messaged back. He made himself a sandwich and went to bed early. He had his first day at work tomorrow.

Petro was a happy man. His first week had gone well. Mr Moore had praised him, and he had been allowed to stay late and make a kitchen chair for himself. He left work on Friday, carrying the chair. Mr Moore had been very kind and refused to let him pay for the materials he'd used.

'So how many chairs do you need?' he'd asked.

'Well, two would be great. I only have a bed to sit on at the moment.'

'Have you got a table?'

'No. I'm thinking of buying one this weekend.'

'Wait, Petro, come and look at this.' Mr Moore led him into the woodstore. At the end of the room was a door which he'd assumed went outside, but it was another room. 'I call this my junk yard. I know there's a table that was discarded because it wasn't perfect, but you could probably make use of it.'

He stopped and began to take part-made chairs and a coffee table off the top of a medium sized table. He stepped back so Petro could have a look at it. Petro ran his hand over the surface looking for an obvious defect. The top was perfect but one of the legs had a slight crack in it.

'Why didn't you just make a new leg?'

'It was made to fit a customer's exact measurements and he cancelled the order. They'd decided to move to a larger house and this table would have been too small.'

'I hope you charged him for all the work and materials.'

'I was going to and then he gave me a much bigger order, a table to seat ten people and chairs to match. I decided to waive the cost of this one. So, it's yours if you want it.'

'That's fantastic, but I can't get it home. I don't have a car.'

'You carry the table out while I go and sort out a bit of paperwork and then I'll give you a lift.'

Petro stood, alone in the junk yard, and his eyes filled with tears. If a new leg was made, the table would cost about £1,000 and Mr Moore was giving it to him. He sniffed, brushed the tears away as they began to run down his cheeks, and lifted the table. It was solid and very heavy, but he managed to carry it out into the workshop. Then he went back and tidied the junk yard, putting the chairs and the coffee table where his table had stood.

While he waited for Mr Moore to come out of the office, Petro carefully measured the cracked leg and decided he would make a new leg next week, after work.

Angie arrived on Saturday morning. Petro held out his arms and she snuggled into them. They kissed and then she said, 'I've missed you. Have you had a good week?'

'Yes, come and see.' He gestured expansively to the beautiful table and single chair. She moved close and ran her hand over the table. 'This is beautiful.' She then turned and did the same to the chair. She sat on it and said, 'It's really comfortable. Did you make all this in one week?'

'No, just the chair. Mr Moore gave me the table. It had a flaw and was discarded but I can make a new leg for it and then it'll be perfect.'

Angie grinned up at him. 'Well, this is obviously my chair. Where are you going to sit?'

'If I work hard, I might be able to bring another one home next Friday. Anyway, I'll make us a cup of tea and you can tell me about your first week back at school.'

Later that day they went into Newcastle to look for a sofa and matching chairs. Petro liked the idea of reclining at the pull of a handle and settled on a leather settee, with two armchairs in a sandy colour. It had to be ordered and a deposit paid. It would be about six weeks before they could deliver it. *That's good. I'll have been paid again and will be able to afford it,* he thought.

'This buying of furniture is exciting,' said Angie, pushing her arm under his and hugging it to her. 'What are we going to buy next? A television?'

'No. That's not high on my list. I managed without one for seven years so it can wait. In fact, everything else will have to wait until I've earned some more money.'

They spent the rest of Saturday together, Angie stayed overnight but went home after breakfast so she could prepare her lessons for next week. They agreed that Petro should come to her house the following weekend. Petro asked why they couldn't meet in an evening during the week. Angie said she wished she could, but she used her evenings to organise the following day's lessons.

'It seems to be a very demanding job. No wonder you need lots of holidays,' said Petro.

'It is but I love it. I don't think I'd get the same satisfaction out of any other job.'

They kissed before she left, and the flat seemed empty. Petro thought of similar quiet moments he'd had in the other dimension and wished he could visit his friends and go to the diner. He wanted to tell them about Angie and his new job. He sighed, then did the next best thing. He wrote a letter to Arthur.

Chapter 32

2022/23

'I need to tell you quickly, before Dad comes in, because I told my parents a lie. I said I was abducted. The truth is, I did fall through the picture into a deep river. I swam to the side and, as it was still dark, I sat on the beach, by a cliff and waited 'till morning. I then got picked up by a boat and when I got to the jetty, there were all these people crowding around and welcoming me. It seemed I was expected.

Later I found out they had a lovely cottage hospital with an operating theatre and badly needed a doctor. My questions went unanswered so I decided to just go with the flow until I could find out more. They called the place the other dimension and there were no mobile phones, computers, televisions or anything. It felt a bit like an Amish community, but there was no religious side to it. Everyone worked for their bed and board. Alice and I still live and work there. The community is lovely, and I've made lots of friends.

When I found out there was a way to leave the community and go back to the real world, the first thing I did was go to see Mum and Dad. Then I discovered Mum had cancer and Dad was at his wits' end trying to cope. I'm sorry I didn't get in touch, Mike, and I'm really pleased to see you and Fiona tonight.'

'Wow, that was quite a speech,' said Mike. 'All this time I thought you were dead and, I must admit, I felt a bit neglected when your Mum invited us. I thought you just hadn't wanted to get in touch. It's a very strange story – takes some believing.'

'It's true,' said Rich. 'The picture was some kind of portal. I've spent quite a lot of time there, building a hydroelectric plant.'

Dad came and sat down with them.

'How's Mum?' I asked.

'She's fine, just tired. When I got up there, she wanted a glass of water. By the time I got back upstairs with it, she was asleep. I looked in on Sandy while I was upstairs,' he said, looking at Alice. 'She's fast asleep too. Now, have you left me any pudding?'

Alice served Dad and the conversation turned to the time and whether we should get the Prosecco ready.

It seemed we had about ten minutes to go so I got up to muster champagne flutes while Mike turned to Rich.

'If the hydroelectric plant is finished, what are you doing now?'

'Nothing. I'm out of work but I've got an interview next week.' Before anyone could ask, he said, 'It's to build a wind farm. There's a lot of support for renewable energy but the attitude changes when something like that is suggested in a rural area. Then it's, 'We're not having it close to our village,' or 'Not on my farm.'

'If you're going for an interview, does that mean one near here has been agreed?' asked Dad.

'Yes, but not on land. It's to add to those already off the coast. I'm excited by the challenge and hope I'll get the job.'

There was an explosive pop as I pushed the cork out of the bottle. Everyone cheered and I poured wine into the glasses while Dad put the television on. The scene was London's embankment as the crowd was counting down to midnight. At the first stroke of Big Ben, we all shouted, 'Happy New Year!' We clinked our glasses together in a kind of complicated dance of arms, sipped our wine and then there were hugs all round. When we sat down again, we watched the fireworks on the television making suitable oohs and aahs.

Dad turned the television off when the fireworks finished, and Rich and Olivia stood up to go home. Mike and Fiona stood up too and in just a few minutes there were only three of us and it was blissfully quiet. I'd opened two bottles of Prosecco, so I refilled our glasses and we moved to sit in the living room.

Dad was the first to break the silence. 'I'd call that a successful night. What do you think?'

'It was lovely,' said Alice. 'I just wish Mum had been able to see the new year in with us.'

'It would have pleased her more to have heard what you just said. She would be delighted if you'd call her Mum,' said Dad.

Alice grinned, 'So can I call you Dad?'

'Please do.'

'In that case, Dad, would you mind if we all went to bed and cleared up in the morning? Sandy will be up, as usual, at seven and I'd like some sleep before then.' There was a nod of heads and we went to bed, tired and content.

The following morning Alice and I were up first so, while Alice made cups of tea for everyone, I cleared the remains of last night's dinner. By the time Mum and Dad arrived downstairs everything was clean and tidy, and we were having breakfast.

'Morning,' said Dad. 'You've been busy, thank you.'

We chorused, 'Morning' and then I added, 'It was a lovely dinner last night, Mum, thanks for organising it.'

Mum smiled and joined us at the table. 'Dad told me the rest of the evening went well. I'm so pleased. I know you're going home today, but I hope you won't leave it too long before we see you again. I want to know about your wedding plans. Are you getting married here or where you live?'

There was a silence as Alice and I looked at each other. I couldn't get married without Mum and Dad being there. Finally, I said, 'We haven't discussed it. There's nothing to stop us having two celebrations.'

'Don't worry, Mum,' said Alice. 'We can't get married without both of you being there, and it won't be until the summer.'

About an hour later we were packed, hugging goodbye and repeating our thanks. I noticed Mum's eyes filling with tears as we waved and set off towards the warehouse.

'Your mum and dad are lovely people,' said Alice. 'I feel all cosseted when I'm with them. They seem to love Sandy and feel she's their grandchild even though she's not your daughter. They have so much love to give.' I nodded as we walked along the road. I was pushing Sandy with a rucksack on my back and bag on the rack underneath the pushchair. Alice was carrying a bag too.

'I was thinking,' I ventured. 'After we're married, if you would consider having another child, mine? You know I love Sandy and if you can't bear the thought of going through pregnancy again, I'll accept that.'

'I've thought about it too.' I held my breath. 'It wasn't so dreadful last time, and I'll have a doctor for a husband, so, yes.'

I stopped for a moment, hugged and kissed her. 'I wanted you to say yes but I knew I shouldn't persuade you. You're so special, Alice. You do realise we'll need to practice a lot.' I had a wolfish grin and she hit me on the arm, laughing.

I rang Eve as we neared the warehouse. She said she would be there in ten minutes, so we slowed our walk.

When we arrived Eve looked serious, no smile of welcome or even a happy new year wish.

'Has something happened, Eve?' I asked.

She nodded, then said, 'I think I'm responsible for an outbreak of chicken pox. Abe must have caught it just before school broke up. We went to our cabin for Christmas and now it seems there are several other cases. I'm so sorry.'

'It's not your fault, Eve. These things happen. It's an uncomfortable disease but can be eased with antihistamines. Make sure he's drinking plenty and ask him not to scratch the scabs. It'll leave a scar.'

'Thank you, doctor. I'll let you in now.' Eve seemed very tense and there was little conversation in the lift. When we got to the bottom, she let us out and went back up herself.

'She seemed very worried, Phil. Should I be fearful for Sandy and keep her away from other children?'

'I'm tempted to say yes but chicken pox is far worse in adults. If she should get it now, it will protect her from getting it again.'

'I'll see what the nursery's doing. If they're open for business, I'll take Sandy.'

We got home and as we unpacked, I felt pleased to be home. We'd talked about leaving in a couple of years, but I didn't want to think about that.

The following morning was business as usual. I found the waiting room busy with itchy, fractious children and by lunchtime I was feeling quite tetchy myself. I was tired and the parents were all blaming Abe and Eve. I kept reiterating, 'Abe couldn't help getting this disease. It's very infectious and Eve had no idea he had it because the spots don't appear until you've been infected for a week or more.'

I was just writing my notes when there was a lot of shouting.

'Doc, Doc, we need help!'

I rushed into the waiting room to see four men carrying another, moaning and covered in blood.

Chapter 33

2019

Arthur received the fifth letter from Petro, but he hesitated to open it.

'What's up? Open it. I want to know how he is,' said Diane.

'It's just, well, every time I read one of his letters, he's so happy.'

'What's wrong with that? Don't you want him to be happy?' she saw him shrug, and said, 'Give it to me. I'll open it.'

Arthur thrust it towards her, his movements irritable. Diane opened it, commenting on the number of pages. It took her a few minutes to read and at one point she gasped and smiled. Finally, she looked up at him.

'They're getting married. Angie's pregnant.'

Arthur took the letter from her, then said, 'Married, a baby on the way and we can't be part of his life. We'll never see his child. He's never going to see Ben growing up.

What's the point of keeping a friendship going by letter? He'll expect a reply giving all the little happenings here, but he's left and never coming back. I miss him so much even after nearly a year.'

Diane's face creased with concern. She moved closer to him and kissed him. 'I miss him too, but he's made his choice and it's worked for him.'

'Could it work for us? I've been thinking about this for a long time. What kind of education can Ben get here? He'll learn to read and write and understand basic maths but what if he's clever and could be a scientist or a techno-whizz kid? He'll need to go to university for that.'

'That's too much now, Arthur. I'll think about it, and we *will* discuss it but now I must take him to nursery, and I need to get to the diner.'

They all went out and Arthur trudged up towards the farms to help with the harvest. There wasn't just wheat, oats and barley but all the ripe produce in the orchards and greenhouses.

The weather was warm. He removed his jumper and stopped a couple of times to wipe sweat from his forehead. He heard the bark of a fox and turned to peer through the trees, but he could not see it.

When he arrived, Jason B. thrust a glass of ale into his hands. 'This is just the stuff to quench a man's thirst, Arthur. It's good.'

Arthur took it gratefully and had glugged nearly all of it before he realised it was not the usual brew. It contained alcohol and he felt the effect immediately.

'Wow, this is the real thing. It's superb. Can I have another?'

Jason B. shook his head. 'There's only a small barrel so we're saving it until lunchtime. If you're feeling fit, we're ready to get to work.'

Arthur stacked bales until his back was too painful to do any more but, all the time he was working, he was thinking of that promised lunchtime drink. Nagging at the back of his mind was the feeling it was dangerous for him to get a taste for alcohol again, but he dismissed it because there was not enough available for him to get hooked.

At lunchtime, they sat on bales and ate what they'd brought with them. There was enough of the special brew for everyone, and the alcohol was clearly felt as they told rude jokes and giggled.

'When is there going to be another brewing of this elixir?' asked Arthur.

'I think there's one on the go already, but we don't have the equipment to make much at a time. Generally, if we need something, we ask Adam but he's not likely to agree, is he?' Solemn faces and nods responded to Jason B.'s words.

Raymond stood, ready to go back to work. 'I think it's a crying shame there's no alcohol allowed. It's enough to make a man want to go back to where there's pubs and supermarkets full of the stuff. I like working here, the cabin's great, my wife likes it and we've made friends, but I *don't* like the lack of choice – to smoke or not smoke, drink alcohol or not. Anyway, enough grumbling, it's time we got on.'

Everyone went back to work and Arthur thought about Raymond's words and their way of life. Adam had saved him when alcohol had brought him to his knees. He owed Adam a lot but still, he felt unsettled. He put a lot of energy into the rest of the afternoon, doing the work of nearly two men to try and eradicate his negative thoughts.

That evening, when the children were asleep, Diane brought in a glass of lemonade for each of them. She sat opposite him and said, 'This morning you were talking about the future and whether we should stay here or go back. I've been thinking about it, and I believe we should give Ben the best start in life we can. At the moment, this *is* the best. We eat healthily, breathe unpolluted air, and live in a safe environment. There's no crime here, no social media, no unhealthy competition. At school or nursery there's no uniform, no fashion statements to make a child feel they're not conforming. It's a good life.' She paused and sipped her lemonade. 'How do you feel?'

Arthur wriggled with discomfort. 'Today I drank some alcoholic ale. Someone up at the farms has been making it. It was delicious but I felt in such a muddle. I wanted to drink more. Yes, it was hot work, but it scared me how much I thought about it. There was some feeling of resentment amongst the men that alcohol was forbidden. Young Raymond said what everyone else was thinking.' He had been looking down as he confessed this but now, he looked at Diane and saw she was frowning. He had thought of keeping quiet about the ale, but he told Diane everything and knew he had to share this.

'That's quite shocking news. Should we tell Adam?'

'I don't think it's harmful because they can only make a small amount, and I don't want to be the tell-tale.'

'I can understand that. Let's ignore it for now. Have you also been thinking about leaving?'

'I have and my conclusion is the same as yours. We stay until Ben is at the secondary school age, say ten or eleven. Our school will have increased in size by then and, hopefully, will be following the National Curriculum.'

'You said, "hopefully," but surely you can influence this? You're the mayor and close to Adam. You've been here the longest, and he listens to you. He also has Abe, who's older than our children. Let's see what Adam decides for his own child's education.' She moved to give him a hug and was pulled onto his knee. She smiled and kissed him. 'We're so lucky to have had a second chance. Let's enjoy every moment of being here.'

'If I wasn't so exhausted, I'd make love to you.' He turned his head away and yawned. 'I think we'd better go to bed, and straight to sleep.'

Chapter 34

2023

Nurse Jane told the men to carry the patient to a bed in the hospital, but after a very quick look, I asked them to take him into the theatre.

'What's his name?'

'Raymond.'

'What's happened to him?'

'It were a fuckin' enormous wild boar. It knocked him flyin' then gored him with 'is tusks. Took all of us to get the beast off 'im and then Mark killed it. Cut its throat.'

'No-one else hurt?' Heads were shaking. 'Right. Leave us now to see what we can do for him.'

Nurse Jane cut the man's clothes off. He had bruises, already black, on his thighs but his torso was lacerated with deep wounds. There would almost certainly be internal damage. I decided to anaesthetise him, so he was unconscious while I worked.

'Raymond?' There was an answering groan. 'I'm going to put you to sleep while I sort out your wounds. Okay?'

'Shall I run for Gary?' asked Jane.

I stifled the desire to shout, 'Why can't you just phone him?' and said crisply, 'Yes, I'll give him some morphine and start cleaning and stitching the lesser cuts.'

It was half an hour before Gary and Jane arrived in the operating theatre scrubbed and gowned. Mark's chest was crisscrossed with neatly stitched wounds but there was one, covered in gauze, that was so deep it may have punctured a lung. I wasted no time on recriminations but just said, 'He's getting weaker, Gary. Give him just enough and watch him closely. I'm not sure he's going to make it.' We worked quietly and efficiently until the last suture was in place then I sighed.

'I can't do any more. It's in the hands of the gods, now.'

Raymond was taken to the ward and Jane monitored him for the rest of her shift. My afternoon surgery had been cancelled and I went home exhausted. There was no need to tell Alice what had happened – everyone knew.

'You poor dear, you're exhausted. How's Raymond?'

I shrugged, almost too tired to talk. I sat on the sofa, while Alice made a cup of tea and a sandwich but fell asleep before she returned.

While I was asleep, she went quietly out to collect Sandy from the nursery. Then she went on to the library. Sandy looked at the toddler's books while she put the returns on the shelves and dusted them. When her jobs were done, she sat with Sandy on her knee and read her a story.

She told me later there was a part of her that didn't want to leave the peace of the library and face an irate fiancée. It was likely I would talk about leaving again. It happened every time there was a medical emergency where a telephone or ambulance could have saved a life. She fervently hoped Raymond would survive his ordeal.

Sandy began to whine, 'I'm hungry, Mum.' She repeated it until Alice could stand it no longer and stood up. 'Come on then, let's go home and have tea. Daddy will be there.' The whining stopped with the action of going home and Alice hurried as snow began to waft tiny flakes around her.

The body of the wild boar had been carried, trussed onto two long poles, to a barn where it was hung from a hook and then gutted. The farmers promised themselves a feast when Raymond recovered. One of them muttered, 'If he dies, then it'll be the best wake a fella can 'ave. I miss meat so bad, I could almost eat that beast raw.' There was a murmur of agreement.

When Alice arrived home, I was awake and had eaten the sandwich she'd made and drunk the cold tea. Alice asked me if I knew how Raymond was. I shook my head and managed a wan smile. 'They'll come and fetch me if he deteriorates. A wound that bad could easily become infected but I've given him antibiotics so...'

'I'll put the kettle on and make Sandy her tea. We can wait until she's in bed for our dinner.'

'What are we eating? I'll start on the veg. I don't want to sit here and brood. I need to do something.'

'Okay, peel potatoes, carrots and butternut squash. We'll have curry, with naan bread.'

We worked companionably in the kitchen as Sandy ate her pieces of raw carrot and cooked broccoli, finishing with an apple and carrot cake.

Later, when we had eaten our meal and Sandy was asleep, Alice snuggled up to me and whispered, 'Thank you.'

'What for?'

'For not ranting about the lack of telephones and ambulances.'

'We agreed to stay here for a few more years and, although I was angry, I knew I had to accept life here as it is. Changing the subject, I've been thinking about that wild boar and wondering if they intend to eat it. I suspect they will. I would. We've had a lovely meal tonight but just thinking of roast pork makes me salivate.'

'They shouldn't because it's against the rules.'

'I know, but the rules are made by Adam. Can he enforce them? I don't think so. We've no police because there's no crime. What happens if there is?'

'I assume Adam banishes them.'

'He can't banish all the farmers; the place would collapse.'

'We all rely on each other and that's its strength, surely. Anyway, we can't alter anything ourselves, so...' she yawned, 'I'm going to bed.'

Chapter 35

April 2020

Arthur shrugged on his thick jacket. It was nearly Easter, but the wind was blowing hard from the north. Diane was working in the diner, and he had nothing to do. Since Petro left he felt at a loss and needed friends. He was now looking forward to joining the farmers up on the plain, high above the village. He only went up there on invitation for they were a clique but, as he willingly helped at busy times, they were allowing him in.

He strode briskly, the wind ruffling his thinning hair. He shivered and put up the hood of his anorak. Somehow the wearing of the hood accentuated the feeling, no, the knowledge, that he was about to do something illegal. There was to be a barbecue and they were not cooking corn on the cob. It was probably venison. His mouth watered just thinking about it.

Adam had decreed that their commune should be vegetarian, but he rarely visited the farms. As long as the produce continued to arrive, he trusted they were abiding by the rules. The venison would be accompanied by bread, not baked by Diane. The farmer's wives generally baked their own because it was too far to go to the shop just for a loaf of bread.

Arthur felt warm by the time he arrived. Jason B. met him, and they walked for another fifteen minutes to the furthest farm, run by Mark. Mark's farm was acres of greenhouses, and everyone was gathered in one of those when they arrived. It was filled with tomato plants at various stages. Some had tiny green tomatoes and tiny yellow flowers, others were no taller than a few centimetres. Staggering the planting enabled them to have a longer growing season. Some would be ready in late May, others ready in October.

At that moment, the people were not interested in what was growing. They were near the barbecue, most of them with a glass of real ale in their hands. The smell of cooking meat assaulted the senses, and it was all Arthur could do not to go straight to it and grab a slice of sizzling steak between two slices of bread. He quelled that thought and shook hands with everyone. Some slapped him on the back and Mark offered him a glass of ale. He smiled, thanked him, and tried not to glug it in one go. He knew ale was made in small batches and he had to make it last.

There was a shout, 'Grub up,' and people went to the table with their own plates, helped themselves to bread, and stood patiently as Mary expertly wielded tongs and served them with the meat. There was homemade chutney or tomato sauce and Arthur added both to his. When he bit into the sandwich, he rolled his eyes and grunted with pleasure. The steak was so tender, the sweet pickle complimenting it. It was heaven in a bite.

As they ate, there was very little talking. He looked at the people around him. Mark stood tall and lean, a mop of black afro hair making him look even taller. His wife, Jeanie, petite and nimble contrasted with him as they stood together. Jason B. was stocky with a florid round face, made redder by the hot food and ale. Arthur, with his build, felt at home with these people but there was no-one special. They were still acquaintances rather than friends.

There were no seats, and as people finished, they thanked Mark, Jeanie and Mary then went back to work. Arthur had no work to do so he lingered and helped Mary clear up.

'That was delicious. Don't tell Diane, she'd be furious, but your bread was tastier than hers.'

'That's quite a compliment, Arthur. Your Diane makes good wholesome bread. Mine's plain, white bread. It's not so good for you, no bran or fibre.'

'Maybe not but it tasted wonderful. What do you do with the barbecue? It's too hot to move and it's very, erm, obvious here.'

'We just leave it. We use it two or three times a week, whenever we have meat, so there's no point in moving it.'

'Aren't you afraid of being caught? What would happen if Adam visited?'

She looked at him, a broad smile on her face. 'He never visits. He's too busy doing whatever he does in the other world. If he did, we'd offer him a sandwich. I bet he'd eat it too. What are you worried about? There's nothing he could do. The village cannot manage without our produce, and we work hard every day. As far as I know there's no law enforcement, so he couldn't do anything.'

'He could banish you. Send you back.'

'As I said, if he did, the produce would cease. The vegetarians would starve. The place would collapse. Don't worry, Arthur. We don't.'

He nodded. There was nothing more to be done, so he thanked Mary again and set off walking back home. It was easy, being mostly downhill, and he thought about Mary's confidence. It had never occurred to him that there were so many people, especially the farmers, that everyone else relied on.

This thought made him think of their doctor. He worked in a hut the same size and shape as everyone else's. There had been talk of building a proper hospital. Adam had an architect working on the plans. He wanted it to have all the latest equipment and be finished to the highest, hygienic standard. Adam had told Arthur they'd begin the build next week. Tomorrow, the site was going to be cleared and he was looking forward to working again. They had four able builders, including Arthur, but none of them had the flair and expertise of Petro.

He decided to write to Petro when he got home and tell him what was happening. Petro would appreciate what a difference a hospital would make but he wasn't sure he should tell him about the farmers eating meat and brewing alcoholic ale. Petro was a straight up sort of guy. He stuck by the rules and would probably be shocked to hear Arthur was joining in, especially with the drink. He knew Arthur had almost been an alcoholic.

When he was nearly home, he met Doctor Greg. He stopped and they chatted. Arthur began, as British people do, talking about the chill wind but then he asked if he was looking forward to having a proper hospital to work in.

'Yes, but I hear it's going to have an operating theatre and I'm not a surgeon. I must ask Adam if he intends to get us a surgeon, although there really isn't enough work for two doctors, full-time.'

'I doubt if he'd agree to having a surgeon on call for when we need him. It seems if you leave here, you're not allowed back because Adam wants our village to be secret. A surgeon on call would be difficult.' They both nodded and then Doctor Greg moved away, his shoulders droping and head down.

That man never smiles, thought Arthur. Had he chosen the right career? It seemed too much for him. Thoughts of Doctor Greg were forgotten as he entered his house. It stank of vomit. There was a trail leading from the front door to the bathroom and he could hear retching. He stepped carefully and quickly rinsed a flannel to bathe Diane's forehead, murmuring, 'You poor thing. I wonder what's set this off.'

'Sorry Arthur,' she gasped. 'I'll clear up the mess. Tried to reach the bathroom but...sorry.'

'Stop saying you're sorry. You can't help being sick. I'll fetch a glass of water if you think it's stopped.' She nodded and he half-filled a glass in the kitchen. She took it, sipped, and waited, kneeling in front of the toilet. She handed the glass back to Arthur and then tried to stand. He helped her up and persuaded her to go into the bedroom for a rest.

'Will you bring me a bowl in case it comes back?' He did that, then set about cleaning the mess. When he'd finished, he looked in the bedroom and saw she was sound asleep. *I wonder what she's eaten to cause that? If she's eaten something other people might be sick too. Then again it might be a virus.* He dismissed that last thought because colds and flu were rare. They were a small population and the only interaction with the outside world was Adam and Eve. They were a healthy pair. Arthur had never known either of them to be ill. But they could have brought something in that didn't affect them but set off Diane and possibly others. *Perhaps people who had been in the community five or more years were less likely to have antibodies. Was this true? Doctor Greg would know. Petro hadn't suddenly caught a cold or flu when he went back. I must write to him but first I need to see if anyone else can take Diane's place cooking the evening meal and cover for tomorrow.*

When Arthur got to the diner, there was a note on the door.

'Sorry we're closed due to sickness. Will re-open tomorrow for breakfast.'

It was signed by Clare. *Had she got the bug too?*

Arthur walked to Clare's cabin and knocked before opening the door. Clare came towards him, her face the colour of a lily. 'Don't come any closer, Arthur. If you've seen Diane, you'll know I'm the same.'

'So, who's going to open the diner tomorrow?'

'I'm just hoping one of us will feel well enough. Are you any good at cooking breakfast and baking bread?'

'Sorry. Mary, Jason B.'s wife, bakes her own bread, but I don't know if she can do it on a big scale.' If he wanted to ask her, it would take him at least two hours, and he was loathe to leave Diane much longer. 'I'll ask her tomorrow if neither of you have recovered. I hope you feel better soon, bye.'

When he got home, Diane was still asleep, so he went out again to collect Ben from nursery.

While he was collecting Ben, there were mothers collecting their children and they all knew someone else who had the sickness bug.

'Seems we've almost got an epidemic. The advice is to eat nothing for forty-eight hours. Doctor Greg's dishing out rehydration stuff. You should get some for Diane, Arthur. We can't manage without the diner forever.'

Arthur didn't know the mother's name, but her advice was good. He nodded, then pushed Ben in his buggy to the doctor's house. He collected sachets for Diane and Clare, then went home.

Chapter 36

Easter 2023

I was taking Sandy for a walk while Alice was baking for the Easter celebration the next day. We were both wrapped up warm against the chill wind. It was slow going because Sandy was helping me push the pushchair but that didn't matter. My mission was to keep her out of the way so Alice could do some baking. Sandy loved helping Mum bake but, because they were going to share the food at a faith supper, Alice wanted to concentrate and didn't want anything landing on the floor.

This is a strange place. I've been here nine months and there've been no church-type gatherings and now everyone's talking about Easter. There's going to be egg rolling down the hill and a street party for everyone. Diane and Clare are not doing the food. Everyone must bring something to the table. They call it a faith supper. I suppose you just have faith that there will be a variety and enough for everyone. I can't see it has anything to do with religious faith. I don't think there'll be any chocolate eggs and I'll miss that but there could be hot cross buns. My mouth watered at the thought.

'Hey, Phil, wait for me.' Rich came running up the hill. His face was pink with the cold wind and the effort of running. 'I saw you up ahead but I'm so unfit, I've no breath.'

'It's great to see you, Rich. I didn't know you were coming.'

'No, if you had I'm sure you, or rather Alice, would've baked a cake.' He was grinning but his grin changed to a query at Phil's grimace.

'Don't talk about cakes. That's why we're walking, to give Alice a chance to do exactly that, but not in your honour.'

'No, I heard about the Easter celebration from Adam. He asked me to come and check the hydro plant and the wind turbines and do any maintenance needed. I have a full-time job so the only time I could do it was over the Easter break. It's good to see you.'

'You too. The last time we met was at my Mum's at New Year. What've you been doing since then?'

'I've got a girlfriend.'

I could see he was itching to talk about her, so I smiled and said, 'Go on then. Tell all. Do I know her?'

'Yep, it's your sister.'

'You're kidding! I never thought you two would get together. How did that happen?'

'I was getting fat, not enough exercise and too much unhealthy eating, so I went to a gym. I'd been going for about three weeks, been on a diet too, so I was feeling good about myself, when I met Olivia at the gym entrance. It turned out she went to karate on the same night. We went for a drink and laughed a lot. We just kind of clicked. Amazing after knowing each other for so long.'

'You'll have to stop being a slob. She's such a tidy person.' I saw him nod, and then smile as if remembering something.

'I invited her to come to mine for a drink. It took me an hour to clear up the kitchen and dust and vacuum the sitting room. Then I remembered the bathroom, did it in a panic and when she rang the doorbell, I still had rubber gloves on!'

I laughed. 'I hope they weren't pink.' I looked at his expression and added, 'Oh my God, they were!' Our laughs were so loud Sandy looked up at me, her face unsure whether to laugh or cry. I picked her up and hugged her to me. 'Sorry, Sandy. Uncle Rich said something funny. We didn't mean to scare you.' I turned to Rich. 'I assume you're staying at my cabin, as usual, but I've not been there for a while, so you'll need to stock up on some milk and so on.' I saw him nod then added, 'Are you going to work now?'

'Yes, I was just going to make a start. I'd better get on with it. Bye, bye Sandy.' Sandy waved saying goodbye quietly, a little unsure of Uncle Rich. *Woah, he might be a real uncle if he married Olivia.* I realised I didn't mind the idea. Mum would be ecstatic. She's not been able to understand Olivia's disinterest in finding a husband. In her day, if you were over the age of twenty-five and not married, you were considered an old maid.

'Right, Sandy. Let's pop you in the pushchair so I can walk a bit faster. I'm feeling cold. We'll go up to the first farm then home.'

On the way I saw Arthur putting up bunting around the front of the diner. I wasn't going to stop and chat, but he called out to me. 'Hey, Doctor Phil. Any idea what the weather's going to do tomorrow?'

I shook my head. 'You'll have to ask your farming friends. They usually have a good idea. Were you intending to have the faith supper out here?'

'Yes, if we can.'

'Have you got help setting it up?' His face twisted into uncertainty. 'What time are you starting? I'll come and help.'

'Ten-thirty should be soon enough. Everyone's due to bring food at twelve. Thanks, I'll see you then.'

I waved and set off up the steep hill leading to the first farm. It belonged to Jason B., and he was mending a fence post. 'Hey, Doctor Phil. It's a been a while. Do you fancy a cuppa? We usually have one about now.'

I nodded and followed him along his lane to their cabin. It had an extra door and porch on one side. 'You've two doors. Did you add that yourself?'

'Yes, we've all done it up here. Visitors go through the front door. The other one leads into a boot room with a connecting door inside. Come on in.' He held the door, and I went in, carrying Sandy, as he kicked off his boots, leaving them outside.

'Mary, we've got visitors.'

Sandy struggled to get down when she saw toys on the floor and a little boy, Sam, sitting in the midst of them. Mary stood up as we came in and smiled broadly.

'It's lovely to see you. I worry that Sam doesn't have any little friends and today, he has Sandy. I'll put the kettle on. I've been baking for tomorrow but I'm sure there'll be plenty, so would you like a chocolate muffin?'

'Sounds great, thank you.'

We settled down with our drinks and cake. Sam and Sandy shared one and soon there were crumbs all over the floor and icing around their mouths and on their hands. I offered to fetch a cloth from the kitchen, but Mary wouldn't hear of it.

'You sit there and relax. I'll clean their hands and face and the crumbs on the floor can wait.'

'It's chill out there. Would you like a drop of spirit to warm you up?' Jason stood up to fetch it and I didn't know what to say. This was an alcohol-free society, and I hadn't expected to be offered any. I didn't hesitate for long. 'Yes, thank you.'

He returned a few minutes later with a tiny, bone china cup. The liquor inside was golden – whisky. I took a tentative sip, expecting it to be raw and rasping on the throat but it was smooth and delicious. 'That's amazing. Did you make it?'

Jason smiled and nodded. 'It's taken a few years to perfect. My first efforts tasted like medicine. You're drinking my best so far.'

'Does Adam know?' I saw Jason shrug and shake his head.

'He won't hear about it from me but it's tempting to come and visit more often. By the way, changing the subject, the party is outside tomorrow. Any idea what the weather might do?'

'It should be fine. My barometer's steady, though there might still be that chill wind.'

I stood up. 'We'd better go, Alice will be making lunch, although I don't feel that hungry after your hospitality. Thank you very much. Come on, Sandy, Mum's waiting for us.' Sandy began to cry; she was enjoying playing with Sam and his toys. I picked her up, hugged her and thanked Mary and Jason again, then went outside. I put Sandy into the pushchair and walked quickly down the hill towards home.

Chapter 37

2021

Petro and Angie had bought a house together in Tynemouth. It was furnished in the cottage style, mostly made by him during his lunch hour. There was a lot of motivation when your girlfriend was pregnant.

It was evening. He had come home from work and was enjoying a cup of tea. On the floor was their daughter, Clare, laying on a blanket surrounded by colourful toys. He sighed and smiled at Angie. 'We're so blessed, to have all this.' He waved his hand expansively. 'But more than that we're so lucky to have each other.'

Angie came and sat next to him and kissed his cheek. 'I know you're right, but I'm worried about the pandemic. Thousands of people are still dying and they're talking about another lockdown in April. When will it end? We've had our vaccinations so why don't I feel safe?'

'We've coped before with lockdowns, and we can do it again. As long as we stick to the rules, keeping two metres away from other people when we're out and wearing a face mask, we'll be fine. Let's watch the news tonight and see what the situation is.'

During the previous year, Mr Moore had delivered wood to Petro so he could work from his garage during lockdowns. When the items were finished, Petro phoned him, the furniture was collected, and more wood delivered. It worked well and financially things were the same.

When the news programme was finished, Petro turned it off, a frown creasing his face. Clare chose that moment to begin to cry. Could babies pick up anxious vibes? He thought they probably could. Angie picked her up and began to breastfeed her. While she was doing that, she thought about when they were first told about this nasty virus, Covid-19. She remembered Boris Johnson demonstrating how to wash your hands. Then there was hand gel available at the entrance to shops, even paper and special liquid to clean your supermarket trolley handle. The worse thing was the creation of special Covid isolation hospitals in buildings like warehouses and the regular news announcements of the number of deaths.

She felt herself tensing and tried to relax, to think of Clare at her breast. She began to talk soothingly to her.

'You're such a beautiful girl, Clare. I love you very much. We'll stick to all the rules so that bad Covid-19 never comes into this house.'

Clare let go, satiated and tired. Angie put her over her shoulder and was rewarded instantly with a burp. She stood up and went upstairs to Clare's little bedroom where everything was to hand to change nappies and then a cot with a 'cosy toes' sleeping bag in case she kicked off the blankets.

Petro found them there half an hour later in time to kiss his sweet-smelling daughter goodnight.

While they were having their evening meal, they avoided talking about the pandemic. They focused on holidays they would like to have. Petro wanted to go abroad, somewhere warm and sunny so Clare could paddle in the sea and play in the sand.

'It might even be possible to do those things this Summer. Let's just think positive,' said Angie.

Angie ordered all her groceries online during the lockdown. It was the highlight of the week when the order was delivered. Her last order had been received on Maundy Thursday and now she was cooking a proper Easter Sunday meal: roast lamb, mint sauce, roast potatoes, roast parsnips and broccoli. Petro had taken Clare out in her pram to allow Angie to cook without interruption. They arrived home just as she was testing the lamb to see if it was done.

'Hello, you two. Perfect timing. It's almost ready to carve.' She looked up at Petro and her smile dwindled. 'What's up? You're white and you're shivering. Is it that cold outside?'
'I don't know. I don't feel well.'
Angie moved towards him and felt his forehead. 'You've got a temperature. Go to bed and I'll bring your dinner up. I'll find some paracetamol too.'
'Thank you.' She heard his slow footsteps on the stairs and spoke to Clare who was still wrapped in layers in the pram. 'Daddy's poorly. You'll be poorly too if I don't take some of these layers off.'

Two hours later Angie had breastfed Clare and put her down for a nap, ate her own solitary lunch and taken Petro a dinner on a tray, only to find him sound asleep. Before she sat down for a rest, she found a Covid-19 testing kit and read the instructions. There was no real hurry. They were not going to get any visitors or see anyone. She put her feet up and shut her eyes.

The following morning, she gave Petro the Covid test. It was positive. She warmed up yesterday's meal for him. He ate some of it but complained it had no taste. Angie felt annoyed, knowing it had been delicious when she ate it but remembered the symptoms of the virus and let it go.

Over the next few days, Petro, the fit, workaholic man she loved, shrunk as he wheezed and complained he couldn't breathe. Angie was frightened, phoned for help and he was taken to hospital. She was told visiting was not allowed. When she rang to see how he was, they said he was in intensive care on a ventilator.

The situation became desperate. The nurse said he was struggling. Then, he was deteriorating. Shortly after that conversation, the hospital rang her. Petro had died.

Chapter 38

2021

'Oh my God!'

'What's the matter? What's he say?'

'You'd better sit down, Arthur. The worst news ever. The letter's not from Petro; it's from Angie. Petro caught a virus called Covid-19. He was taken into hospital, intensive care but they couldn't save him.' She whispered, 'Petro's dead.'

Arthur had not sat down while Diane was talking, but now he sat down heavily and put his head in his hands. His shoulders shook and his breath came in gasps. Diane put her arms around him but knew there was nothing she could do to ease his pain. Tears began to run down her cheeks as she remembered Petro, his face alight playing the fiddle for them all to dance. It was hard to believe he was gone. She thought of his wife, Angie. They'd never met her, but she'd made Petro happy. They had a little girl, Clare. How were they going to manage without him? What was this scary bug?

'He's being cremated on Saturday and only thirty people are allowed to attend because the virus is so catching. Please, Arthur, don't go to it. Petro knew how you felt about him, and he wouldn't want you to risk your life, or all our lives.' She knew he was listening when she saw him nod, unable to speak. 'I'll put the kettle on. It won't make anything better, but a hot drink is soothing.'

Diane had just made a pot of tea when there was a cursory knock and Adam walked in. 'I've had a letter from Angie too. Have you read yours?'

'Yes, we know about Petro. It's shocking. Would you like a cup of tea? I've just made a pot.'

'Yes, thank you. I can't believe it. You've not been able to hear the news but it's a dire situation. Eve and I have been vaccinated but Eve's refusing to move from here and go back to our house in Tynemouth, for fear of catching it.' He looked towards Arthur. 'I'm sorry, Arthur. I know you were great friends. Petro was a skilled craftsman but was also a delightful, gentle man.'

Arthur looked up, his face blotchy red. 'I've been missing him so much I'd even thought Diane and I should move back so we could see him again. There's no point in doing that now. I didn't know there was a virus going round.'

'It's worse than that. They call it a pandemic because it's everywhere in the world, except here. We're all safe here.'

Diane handed him a cup of tea and said, 'You've been going back and now you're here. How do you know you haven't brought the virus with you?'

'I'm only going to my office. I can work from my computer and telephone. I don't meet any other people and I come home here every night. The virus is passed between people. If I don't talk to a person, face to face, I should be safe. I must keep working because we still need a lot of things we can't make ourselves. My aim is for us to be ultimately self-sufficient but even then, we will want modern medicines.'

'Thanks for explaining about the pandemic,' said Diane. 'I was thinking I should give you a wide berth.' She saw Adam smile, but Arthur didn't respond. He seemed almost unreachable in his grief.

Adam finished his tea, stood up and placed a hand on Arthur's shoulder. 'I'm sorry Petro's gone. I had hoped he'd return to us one day. Now there's no chance.' He sighed. 'I must go.' He stopped and turned to add, 'Would you like me to ask Clare to open the diner this afternoon?'

'No, thank you, Adam. I think having to work will be therapeutic. I might even get Arthur to peel some potatoes.'

Adam smiled and said goodbye but there was still no response from Arthur. He stayed, hunched, head down. He only looked up when he heard Diane say, 'Will you collect Ben from playgroup? I'm going to the diner, and you can bring him there

for lunch or make him lunch here. Either way, I need to go.'
She saw him nod, collected her coat, shrugged it on and left.

At the diner Diane went through the motions, her brain elsewhere. By the time people arrived for lunch, the fish pie, a great favourite, a vegetarian stew, and all the makings of an omelette were ready, plus a small selection of puddings. The favourite was Diane's Damson Pie.

As she made up plates of food, she was thinking of Angie. How was she going to cope with a baby and no husband? There would be no income unless she went to work, and her baby would have to be in a nursery. Perhaps Angie had her mum nearby. Then she might babysit. Diane wondered how she would have managed without Arthur. He was her rock, but since Petro left, he had become less buoyant and much quieter. It was going to be worse now. What could she do to prevent him sinking into a depression? She knew this had happened before. She also knew alcohol was available at the farms. It was a dangerous situation and it worried her.

'Penny for 'em, Diane?' She woke from her reverie.

'Hello, Doctor Greg. What can I get you?'

'I'll just have a cup of tea and a piece of pie, thanks.' He waited while she organised that and when she returned with a smile, he said, 'I heard about Petro. I'm so sorry. We all liked him and miss his cheerful face. Arthur must be gutted.'

'Thanks, he was very upset this morning. I've been thinking about his wife, Angie, and wondering how she'll cope.'

He nodded. 'It'll be a very difficult time for her. Well, I mustn't let this tea get cold. Thanks, Diane.'

When Doctor Greg stood up to leave, Diane went to clear his table and asked him if he intended to vaccinate everyone.

'I didn't know anything about it until this morning, but I've asked Adam to get a supply and some testing kits.'

'That makes me feel safer already. I also wanted to ask if you like your new hospital.'

'Yes, it's beautifully equipped. So much easier than having patients coming to my home. Now, when I leave after surgery, I can put work behind me properly. People can, of course, still come to my door but most try not to.'

When the lunchtime rush was over, Diane closed the diner while she tidied up. She decided she would write to Angie. In her letter, she would say how upset they all were about Petro, and she'd invite Angie to come and visit them once the funeral was over. This might be putting them all at risk of getting Covid and perhaps, Adam wouldn't allow it. She would ask him first and only add that to her letter if he agreed. Having made that decision, Diane walked home preparing herself to meet a tired Ben who would resist his afternoon nap.

Arthur and Ben were not at home and there was no note. It was not worrying. They were certainly at someone's home or had gone for a walk. She hoped it was the latter because Ben would get his nap in the pushchair. This would give her time to write a letter to Angie. She could write two, one inviting her to come and stay, and one where she just sent her condolences. Then she could give Adam the appropriate one to deliver.

The letter took a long time to write, and she found it hard not to cry as she imagined the distraught Angie opening it. The second letter was easier, mostly a copy of the first but the invitation added. When it was done, she stood stiffly and took both letters to Adam's house. He might not be there, but Eve would. Diane liked Eve. Some of the other women were wary of her because she was Adam's wife – number one lady. Diane had known her a long time and considered her a close friend.

When Diane returned from Eve's, having drunk tea and cried together over Petro, she was surprised there was still no sign of Arthur or Ben. She needed to go back to the diner to prepare for the evening meals and she felt anxious now. Still, she thought, he'll know where I am. Perhaps he'll bring Ben in to have his tea there.

He didn't. It was a difficult late afternoon and evening. Everyone knew about Petro and there was little talk of anything else. When, at last, she closed the door and went home, she assumed Ben would be ready for bed or at least in his pyjamas but the house was still empty.

Diane sat down, rested her head in her hands and let tears for Petro and anxiety for Arthur and Ben flow.

It was nearly dawn when Diane was woken by a tapping on her door. The door then opened. She felt a frisson of fear as she slipped off the bed, still fully clothed and went towards the entrance. The first thing she saw was a sleeping Ben in his pushchair. Then she saw a dark figure.

'Hello? Who is it? Where's Arthur?'

'I'm Jason B. from Thistle House Farm. I'm sorry it's so late but Arthur was drowning his sorrows. We had a wake for Petro. Then Arthur just fell asleep, on the floor and I realised he'd be in no fit state to look after Ben in the morning, so I decided to bring him home.'

'Thank you. I've been so worried. I was waiting up for them but then I fell asleep. Would you like a drink of water or a cup of tea? It's a long walk back.'

'A cup of tea would be grand, thanks.'

He followed her into the kitchen and she indicated he should sit at the table. He did so, put his elbows on the table and covered his face with his hands.

'I've never seen anyone drink like Arthur did. It was like he was driven. He said very little, just sat there, morose and drank.

When he passed out on the floor, I was worried and checked his breathing, but he was just asleep. I'm so sorry. If we hadn't brewed beer and distilled whiskey, this would never have happened. I feel responsible.' He took a sip of the hot tea, then another. 'This is good.'

Diane cut a loaf of bread, spread the slices with jam and sat opposite him. She watched him eating with relish and took a piece of bread too. The tea and bread revived them both. She took a deep breath and said, 'You weren't to know that Arthur was an alcoholic when Adam recruited him. I think Adam saved his life but now he has access to drink here, I worry he'll never be able to resist it.'

Jason B. shook his head. 'I had no idea. We've always welcomed Arthur up at the farms because he works so hard just when we need it, especially harvesting. He's a good man. I don't want to ban him from coming, but if he comes, it'll be hard to refuse him a drink. Everyone else drinks sensibly.' He stood up, drained his cup, and said, 'I must go home. I'll send Arthur back when he's feeling capable of walking. Thanks for the early breakfast.' He let himself out of the door, shutting it quietly behind him. Diane lifted the sleeping baby from the pushchair and laid him carefully in his cot. Then she undressed and went to bed.

Chapter 39

2021

Alice was unable to sleep. The baby was kicking, she was too hot, and Dan was snoring and wheezing. She got out of bed and opened the window wider. There was a little breeze squeezing into the room. It was not much but enough to make her feel she wanted to just stand there and breathe it in.

'What are you doing? It's the middle of the night.' Dan's voice had a hard edge to it.

'Sorry, I couldn't sleep, too hot.'

'Get back into bed and try again.' Alice obeyed. She almost always obeyed Dan.

Before they were married, they went dancing every Saturday night. He was athletic and danced with lithe, sexy movements. He was also handsome, tall with thick black hair and brown eyes that shone with enjoyment. Sometimes she could hardly believe that a man like him could fancy her. All her friends were envious. He was considered a great catch.

After they married, Alice had expected their dancing to continue but Dan seemed to have lost interest.

'I only went dancing to get a girl, and I got you. Now you're mine I don't need to go dancing anymore.'

'But I thought you liked it. I miss going out. It seems all we do now is sit and watch football every night.'

'Come on, Ali, it's the Euro 2020 final. Be fair.' Alice was about to protest again and then changed her mind. She believed in her church vow, 'til death us do part,' and really wanted the marriage to work.

Everything changed when Dan lost his job. He was sacked because he made a mistake that resulted in a house fire. He had been the only electrician on the site and the fire brigade said it was an electrical short that had started the blaze. It spiralled Dan into a depression that he tried to relieve with alcohol and then drugs, which only made everything worse.

Adam, at that time, was looking for an electrician. The story was in the newspaper, so he contacted Dan. Dan was intrigued and met him. Adam explained the situation, and, without consulting Alice, Dan agreed.

'I'm going, Alice, whether you like it or not. You can come or you can stay here but then you've got the rent to cope with, on just your salary.'

'I'm paying the bills now, Dan, and have been doing ever since you lost your job.' She was standing up to him for almost the first time, her hands on her hips. He had a sneer on his face as he shrugged and turned away. Alice stood, her fists clenched on her hips and thought, *I find it hard to believe he feels anything for me at all.*

They put their furniture in storage, gave their landlord three months' notice and moved into a cabin just before the Christmas of 2020. Dan and Alice both loved their new home and quickly made friends. Alice worked in the pharmacy. There was no television, and they were both enjoying their new life, so Dan was keen to have sex as often as possible. They had talked about having a family and when Alice announced she was pregnant, they were both delighted.

She was now five months pregnant and beginning to feel fat and uncomfortable. She got back into bed and turned over, trying to shut out the sound of Dan's laboured breathing. In the morning, she thought, I must ask him to see Doctor Greg. He must have a chest infection.

He was irritable when he woke up and said he had a wiring job to do at the furthest farm and hadn't time to go and see the Doctor. Alice went to work and told Doctor Greg she was worried about Dan.

'I know he's much in demand. I'll see him after hours if he'd like to come to my cabin, when he gets back from work.'

He did not come back from work. One of the farmers knocked on her door at 7 pm and said Dan was exhausted so was staying the night. Alice thanked him for telling her, ate a solitary meal and hoped he was not ill as well as tired.

Dan arrived home the following evening. His face was ashen and his breathing laboured.

'You sound terrible. I'm fetching Doctor Greg, and don't argue.' He said nothing, just kicked off his shoes and fell onto the bed. Alice ran to the hospital. He was not there, so she ran to his cabin.

'Doctor, please come and see Dan. He can hardly breathe.' Greg grabbed his bag and they walked quickly to her cabin.

He helped Dan sit up and listened to his chest. 'You've got pneumonia. We must get you to the hospital so you can have intravenous antibiotics.' Dan nodded and tried to get up. Greg and Alice supported him and then, as they crossed the road Dan lost consciousness and they could no longer hold him. They lowered him to the ground and Greg ran to get a wheelchair. The dead weight meant they struggled to lift him into it. 'Alice, go to Nurse Jane's cabin and ask her to come while I get Dan inside.'

By the time Alice and Jane arrived, Greg had managed to drag Dan onto a bed. The drip was quickly set up and everyone breathed with relief.

'Can I stay with him in case he wakes and wants a drink of water or something?' asked Alice. 'I won't sleep if I go home.'

Both Jane and Greg nodded. Then Jane added, 'There's tea, milk and you can make toast too, if you want it. I'll go home, but I'll come back and check on him in a couple of hours.'

Alice looked at her husband and tears fell. *Please, God, make him better.* She went into the kitchen to make a cup of tea but went back to see Dan while the kettle was boiling. She didn't want to miss him opening his eyes. The kettle clicked off, so she made the tea. She moved a chair beside him then sank into it, sipping the hot liquid. *I'm so tired*, she thought. *I'd like to curl up next to him and go to sleep.*

Nurse Jane came in quietly and took Dan's temperature. Alice had fallen asleep, so she failed to see Jane's frown. She did not see her set up a monitor that showed Dan's heart rate. She missed the weakening bleep. Jane left, just as quietly and went to Doctor Greg's cabin. She had to wake him but then he moved quickly and soon they were both working on Dan. Alice woke up.

'What's happening?'

'I'm sorry, Alice, but I think we're losing him. His heart's giving up. I've done all I can.'

Alice stood up. 'No! Please. There must be something else.'

Greg took her in his arms. 'He's not responding to any of my treatment. He's in God's hands now.' He continued to hold her as she cried. Eventually she pulled away from him and sat beside Dan on his bed, holding his hand.

'Jane and I will be in the waiting room if you need us,' said Greg. They left her alone and Jane made some tea.

'It's tragic to die so young. If only he'd come sooner, we might have saved him,' said Greg. They sat in silence after that, and both heard the monitor's urgent, continuous beep as Dan's heart stopped.

Chapter 40

2023

'I'm going back home today, can't wait to see Olivia,' said Rich. 'I've cleaned and tidied your cabin. I know, don't look like that. I do know how to clean, just don't like doing it. Anyway, it's a bank holiday at home. In fact, it's a month of bank holidays.'

'What do you mean? There's been two holidays in May for years,' I said.

'Yes, but there's an extra one next week for the King's Coronation.' Rich saw Phil frown. 'You did know the Queen died last September? Prince Charles is now King Charles the third and his coronation is next weekend, and we have another bank holiday?' He saw my rueful smile.

'You needn't look as if the world is passing you by. You're better off here. There are strikes and protests everywhere because the cost of living has rocketed. Even doctors and nurses have been on strike for better pay and conditions.'

'Really? I'm not sure I could join in a strike. I suppose there's pressure from colleagues and certainly hospital doctors work extremely long hours.' Rich waited as I paused, then sighed before going on. 'You've made me feel ignorant, not knowing what's going on. I also feel I'm procrastinating here, marking time, making no progress in my career.'

'Don't think like that, Phil. The people here need you. They like and respect you and then there's Alice and Sandy. It's a good place for little ones to grow up, away from media pressures. Your mum and dad are doing fine, and Olivia gets me to do any little jobs they need.'

'Now you're making me feel guilty that you're doing the things I should do.'

'No, I don't mind. I said that so you could feel better about being here, not to make you feel worse! Anyway, I need to go. Give my love to Alice and I'll see you next time I'm here.'

Rich called at Adam's cabin to be escorted back to the lift. He was invited in to report on the work he'd done and when the next service would be necessary. Rich refused a cup of tea or to sit down, explaining that he wanted to get back to see his girlfriend. Adam nodded and said, 'Let's walk and talk then, if you're in a hurry.'

In the lift, Rich asked Adam if he thought the people should be told of important things happening in the real world.

'That's worried me for a long time. I suppose you're thinking now of the coronation and maybe the war in Ukraine. I think the people here should be able to lead a good healthy life without carrying those extra burdens put on us by the media. In the time before fast communications, news arrived slowly, and people were generally less harassed. At least that's what I believe.'

They arrived at the door of the warehouse and Adam thanked Rich for his help. Rich went to his car and drove to see Olivia. They were not living together. She liked her house, and he liked his, so they met every weekend to spend time together. He sent her a text, asking her to put the coffee on, finishing it with a love heart.

As he entered her door, Olivia went to meet him and after a big hug and several kisses that threatened to get out of hand, she pulled away saying, 'Coffee's ready, as instructed.'

'I didn't instruct. It's just that in the other dimension, there seems to be mostly tea. I've missed coffee and I've missed you. It's not fair to have had to go away on a weekend, especially when it was unpaid work.'

'Yes, but you got your bed and board and you saw Phil. How is he?'

'He's well but said he's worried that his career's static.' He saw Olivia frown and knew she thought it was too.

'Did he mention getting married? He was full of engagement delight at new year but there don't see to be any plans unless he's got married there. He hasn't, has he? Mum would be so disappointed. She keeps asking when he's going to visit again.'

'He didn't mention marriage so I've no idea. I've been working more than socialising. Anyway, what are we doing with the rest of this lovely, sunny May holiday?'

'Let's walk down to the Fish Quay in North Shields, and see what restaurants are open. If there aren't any, we'll be able to buy fish and chips.'

They walked, talked and laughed – happy just to be together. There were flags flying everywhere, preparations for the Coronation of King Charles the following weekend. There were posters advertising events and a general air of anticipation.

'It would be lovely if Phil and Alice could come next weekend. Mum would be thrilled and then, if she babysat, perhaps the four of us could go to Newcastle to see the concert on the big screen. If I write him a letter, could you get it to him?'

'Yes, no problem. You'd better write it when we get back because Phil might need to find a locum if he comes for the whole weekend.'

It was lunchtime. I was in the diner with Alice when Adam came in waving a letter. 'I hope it's not bad news, Phil.'

'Me too, thanks, Adam.' I put my knife and fork down and tore open the envelope. Alice was watching me, a worried frown on her face. I saw her brow clear as I smiled.

'It's not bad news. Apparently, it's the King's Coronation next weekend and Olivia wants us to come and stay at Mum's. What do you think?'

'I'd like that. We had a lovely time at Christmas. Can you find someone to stand in?'

'It's only really two nights away so I think people will cope. I'll also have my phone so Adam could get in touch if there was a real emergency. He's still here, I'll go and have a word now.' After a brief chat I went back to Alice with a broad smile on my face. She looked pleased but then her expression changed to a slight frown.

'What's up?' I asked.

'Your Mum will quiz us about our wedding plans, and we haven't organised anything. Perhaps we should set a date that we can work towards. I feel we must have it where your family can come.'

'What about September – not too hot or too cold. If I could get Steph to stand in for a week, we might even be able to have a honeymoon.' I was warming to the subject but then I remembered we had no income.

'What's up? One minute you're all animated and then you look like you've sucked a lemon!'

'I just remembered that weddings and honeymoons cost a lot of money and I don't earn anything.'

'It doesn't have to cost that much. I've been married before so no need for a white dress. We can have the ceremony in a registry office. It's cheaper than a church. We can keep the guests to just family, and Rich. He's practically family anyway. It seems to me the only real expense would be a wedding breakfast. We need some sort of celebration.'

I nodded, liking the sound of her economy wedding. 'Perhaps hiring a hall and getting caterers would be cheaper than having it in a hotel?'

'But I'd like some music so we could dance. Let's discuss this with everyone this weekend. I feel so excited I want to pack up and leave right now!'

I laughed and hugged her. 'When you get home, look at the calendar and choose a date. I'll be happy with any Saturday in September.'

Chapter 41

2021

It was harvesting time and Arthur tentatively mentioned this to Diane. He had not visited the farms since his descent into depression after Petro's death and his alcoholic lapse. He was ashamed of himself, contrite and had done his best to make Diane realise he would not do it again.

'Do they still make non-alcoholic beer?' she asked.

'I don't know. I'll ask, and if not, I'll drink water. Please, Diane, I need to show you I can manage without a drink.' He could see her wrestling with the desire to say no.

'They need your help and I trust you, but if you decide to stay over, send word with someone so I'm not worried, please.'

'I won't stay over.' He stood up and kissed her on the cheek. 'Thank you,' he said and collected his rucksack. He packed it with a sun hat, a thin jumper and a bottle of water. The farmers would give him whatever tools he'd need. He finally kissed Ben, who was playing on the floor.

Ben put his arms up to be lifted but Arthur crouched down and said, 'I can't pick you up and play now because I've got to go to work. I'll see you later. Bye.' Diane picked Ben up, settled him on her hip, and followed Arthur to the door. He turned, gave them both a hug then set off along the lane.

He walked quickly but knew when he reached the hill, he would slow down. It was a steep climb and when he'd left the village behind, it felt like he was entering a different country. In a way, it was, because the farmers were more self-sufficient than any other group. They supplied the village and used the shop rarely.

Jason B. met him with a whoop of delight. 'I wasn't sure you'd be allowed out to play with us – the wicked farmers.'

Arthur grinned. 'I've had a few conditions: no alcohol and I mustn't stay over.'

'It's great to see you, and there's a lot of work. You'll earn your lunchtime barbecue. The wheat's being cut, and we need a strong man to stack the bales. You know where to go. See you later.'

A month earlier Angie had arrived, escorted by Adam, who gave her Petro's old cabin. He had put a new bed in it and a cot. Angie cried when she saw it, recognising her husband's furniture.

'Adam. It all looks wonderful, but Diane said everyone works to earn their keep. She said you needed a primary school teacher. I don't see how I can work in a school when my baby's so young. I'm still breastfeeding.'

Adam smiled. 'Don't worry about that yet. Get settled and make some friends. There's no rush. We currently have a teacher so you can act as an adviser to begin with. There might be other skills you can bring, so give that some thought. When you're hungry, go to the diner. You'll find Diane there and the food's free.'

'Where's the diner?'

'It's just up the lane. You can't miss it. Unpack, then go for a walk. Our village is very compact.'

Angie walked around the cabin, touching the smooth perfection of Petro's furniture managing not to cry any more.

'Your daddy was so clever with his hands, Clare. I was lucky to have him even if it was such a short time. Adam's been so kind, and you've even got a cot and all the bedding. I must try to count my blessings.' She looked in the fridge and found oat milk, eggs and dairy free spread. In a cupboard there was tea, instant coffee, some bread and a jar of jam.

When everything was unpacked, she tied baby Clare around her body and walked along the lane. The diner was obvious, and she went in feeling like a new girl starting school. The woman behind the counter called out to her with a dazzling smile.

'Angie! I'm Diane.' She lifted the counter flap and rushed to give Angie a careful hug, not wanting to crush Clare who was asleep.

'I'm so glad you decided to join us. Come and sit down. Would you like coffee, tea, a meal? The menu's up on the chalk board.'

Angie felt almost overwhelmed by Diane's welcome and found herself smiling as she said, 'Petro told me all about you and Arthur and of course I read Arthur's letters. Thank you for inviting me to stay. You've made me feel at home already. I'll start with a cup of tea and then the savoury pie sounds good.'

'That's a good choice. As it's lunch time I'll be very busy but if I come to your cabin about three, we can have a better chat and I can show you around.'

'I'd like that, thank you.'

A month later

Diane called on Angie and was welcomed in with the offer of tea and cake. They had become friends very quickly and met whenever Diane was free. They chatted, as young mothers do, about their children and Angie could now talk about Petro without crying. Sometimes Eve joined them and told her stories of the early days when the cabins were being built and the close friendship between Arthur and Petro. Today, it was just the two of them and Diane mentioned her anxiety that Arthur would start drinking again with the farmers.

'I have to trust him, Angie, but I can't help worrying.'

Angie nodded and then stood up. 'To take your mind off Arthur, let me show you what I've been working on.' She went over to the kitchen area and came back with some crude sheets of paper.

'These are my first efforts and I'm sure I can improve to make them smoother.'

'Wow, you can make paper. Adam will be delighted if you can do it on a larger scale. How did you do it?'

I was thinking about using waste products and saw, in the shop, a pile of cardboard boxes. Years ago, I went on a craft course, and we made paper, so I knew what to do, but I had to make a frame and find some mesh. My mesh wasn't fine enough. I'm not sure where to get something better.'

'You must tell Adam. He'll get you the stuff you need. All the letters I wrote to you were done on paper Adam bought. It would save him a lot of money if paper could be homemade. Perhaps you could also make toilet paper? We get through oodles of that.'

'I believe paper can also be made from fibrous plants so I'm going to experiment with that, too. The prospect of making a real contribution here is exciting. I could also utilise the workshop attached to this cabin to upscale my efforts. The good thing is, it can all be done at home, so I can still look after Clare.'

'It's brilliant, Angie. The annoying thing is you also make excellent cake,' she said, scooping up the last crumbs. 'That's my skill and I can see I've got competition. Anytime you want to make a batch, you can always bring it to the diner to share.' She saw Angie looking uncertain and laughed. 'It's really good cake. I mean what I say. The diner is not my sole prerogative. We always welcome cake makers to bring their spares.'

'That's a relief. I thought for a moment I'd annoyed you.'

Diane got up and gave her a hug. 'I'm so glad you came. I've got to go now and do some prep for lunch.' She picked up Ben and he whinged, struggling to get down again.

Angie said, 'Why don't you leave him here for now? Clare's asleep, he's happily playing with her toys. I can bring him to the diner for lunch.'

'Thank you. I'll see you all later.'

It was lunchtime at the farms and there was a choice of slices of venison in bread or rabbit pie. Arthur was torn but solved that by having both. The others laughed as he said, 'I'm a big man and have a big appetite.' Then he was quiet as he took a big bite of the pie and nodded his appreciation. Jason B. offered him a non-alcoholic beer that quenched his thirst but did not make him crave more.

Four hours later, exhausted but happy, Arthur arrived home. Diane had finished in the diner and was bathing Ben. Arthur joined them in the bathroom and asked if he could top up the bath when Ben had finished so he could wash away the grime of the day.

An hour after that, there were two clean males in the house and the little one was sound asleep. Diane and Arthur enjoyed sharing their day as they ate a simple salad meal.

That night they both slept soundly, the spectre of alcoholism settled, for now.

Chapter 42

2023

I was pleased to see Rich and Olivia on the Saturday of the Coronation of King Charles. We all crowded into Mum's living room and watched the ceremony on her modest sized television. There was a fervent wave of patriotism on the screen and in the room. Dad was the first one to wilt with the length of the event and quietly went out to make tea for everyone, bringing it in with the muffins Mum had made, iced in red, white and blue.

Sandy was mesmerised at first. She'd seen very little television, but then she fell asleep on the floor, surrounded by cushions and toys.

After lunch, Olivia said she needed a walk and asked who wanted to join her. Mum and Dad shook their heads but suggested we left Sandy who was playing happily. This gave us the freedom to stride out and get some exercise after being stationary for so long. Down at the Fish Quay, we sat outside with a drink and Olivia said, 'I don't want you to think I'm interfering in your life Phil...'

I laughed and finished her sentence. 'But you're going to do it anyway.'

'Yes.' She smiled but I could see she was desperate to tell me something, so I nodded, and she went on. 'I've been looking online for jobs for you. There's a brilliant one in Durham. They're looking for a GP with a surgical qualification. That's you.'

'Well, I didn't expect that. I don't know what to say or think. When's the closing date for applications?' I watched as she pulled a piece of paper from her bag.

'The details are on here and you have until the fifth of June.'

'Thank you. We've been talking about coming back but had thought we'd wait until Sandy was older. On the other hand, it's difficult coming home and knowing I have no money to spend. This is tempting. What do you think?' I asked, turning to Alice.

Her face screwed with uncertainty then she said, 'I think you should apply.' Rich and Olivia both cheered and I found myself grinning, realising that I wanted to get a job and return to the real world.

'Just one problem. Mum and Dad don't have a computer. Can I come round and use yours tomorrow?'

'Yes. We're going to a barbecue about eleven so you can have the place to yourself.'

'That's great, and thanks again for doing the research, even if nothing comes of this.'

Mum and Dad were excited to think we might come back from the commune and almost shooed me out of the door the next morning.

Alice kissed me, and wished me luck, adding, 'It's going to take you a long time. You'll have to write a CV and I've no idea how you're going to explain what you've been doing for the last nine months, and what about references?'

'Don't worry, I didn't sleep well last night thinking about it, and I've got a plan.' I looked at my watch and she nodded as I said, 'Best get going.'

I walked briskly the two miles to Olivia's house. When I arrived, the door was open, and they were ready to go out. There was a delicious smell of coffee as I entered.

'You can, obviously, help yourself to coffee, there's lots in the pot but there's also food in the fridge so you can make yourself some lunch. Good luck.' Olivia gave me a hug, and, to my surprise, Rich joined in.

He let go, slightly embarrassed, and said, 'I've missed you just as much as Olivia and your mum and dad. I hope it's successful.'

When they'd gone, I poured myself a coffee and went into Olivia's study. The computer was on, so I sat down to find the site and then download the application form. I was very slow, writing and revising every sentence. By lunchtime, I had finished my CV and had begun the form. I made a sandwich and hardly remembered eating it, worrying about references. Early ones from university were easy. In normal circumstances I would ask for a reference from the hospital where I had been a junior surgeon. But, when I'd fallen through the picture, I'd failed to let the hospital know where I was or formerly resigned until several months later, when Mum was ill. I'm ashamed to say I'd used Mum's illness as an excuse. I decided to swallow my pride and ring my former head of department, Jeff. I had his number in my phone because we'd become friends, often going out for a drink together. It could be difficult; he would have felt hurt that I hadn't told him about Mum. I phoned him, apologising for interrupting his weekend.

'To be honest, Phil, I'm tired of all this coronation pageantry. Do you fancy a drink at our old watering hole?'

'Great, in half an hour?'

It was a much easier meeting, over a pint, than I had anticipated. I told him about the commune and how I had been working as a GP and surgeon when necessary. I explained about the lack of phone signal and internet. I asked about his family and told him about Alice and Sandy. Finally, I told him about the job near Durham and asked him for a reference.

'Not a problem. I can send you one by e-mail or wait until I'm contacted.'

'I'd prefer you to wait until you're contacted because after this weekend, I'll be back in the commune.'

'Fair enough. Anyway, I'd better let you get back to your application form.' He stood up and held out his hand. I shook it and he said, 'Good luck, Phil. Let me know how you get on.'

'Thanks, Jeff.'

We parted and I went back to Olivia's house feeling much happier than when I'd left it. I printed a copy of all the documents, so I had a record and then sent them by e-mail. Then I stretched in my chair, stood up and looked at my watch. It was six o'clock. Mum and Alice would be serving dinner. I left a thank-you note for Olivia and set off at a brisk walk.

When I arrived, my dinner was being kept warm and they had almost finished. Before I ate, I sat with them and told them about my day. Everyone seemed so happy. Mum was positive

I'd get the job, one of those 'nobody is as good as my son' moments. It made me realise how much I missed being able to see them easily. I wanted this job very much. Then Alice thought of a problem.

'How are you going to know if you've got an interview? We go back on Monday morning and then you've no internet.' There was a horrified silence that I was quick to fill.

'I used Olivia's computer and e-mail address so any communication that way will come to her. She'll let me know through Rich. He can get me a message. I also gave my home address as here so if a letter comes for me, you can give it to Rich. So, it's not a problem.'

The wedding had not been forgotten in all the excitement of my job application. While I was at Olivia's house, Mum, Dad, and Alice had discussed it and settled on the 16th of September. Dad had promised to find out about the hire of village halls and caterers but said we would have to contact the registry office ourselves.

'We'll do it when we come back here next time. We can't do it on a bank holiday weekend.' I tried to sound excited and enthusiastic, and I think I achieved it because everyone was smiling, but I felt so tired after the concentration earlier in the day.

The rest of the weekend went quickly and soon, it was Monday morning. We left early and I was only a few minutes late for morning surgery. There were a lot of patients. I worked hard but felt resentful. Everyone in the real world was having a bank holiday and I was having to work.

Chapter 43

2022

Angie had perfected making smooth writing paper out of cardboard and was now, in her spare time, working on making paper from plants. There was such a demand for her paper that she asked Alice to help when she could. Sometimes, this help simply consisted of taking baby Clare for a walk to get her to sleep while leaving Sandy on the floor, surrounded by cushions, banging saucepans with a wooden spoon.

On this beautiful day, Angie felt a surge of happiness followed by a wave of guilt. *Life's such a rollercoaster. Losing Petro had been so traumatic, but Clare was a huge consolation. Then there was this place, paradise compared to my previous, manic existence. The people were friendly, the pace of life was slow and had a calming effect. Why did Petro leave it? It was my fault. He'd been on holiday and meeting me had pulled him away.*

Angie made herself a cup of tea then went back to work. She concentrated, and the time went so quickly she was amazed when Alice returned, declaring it was feed time for Clare and lunchtime for Sandy. They all went to the diner. Alice had assured her that breastfeeding there was accepted with no comments. It was busy and Doctor Greg stood up, offering his table to them.

'I've finished, so come here. How are you all?'

'We're fine but you don't look so well yourself. You've left most of your lunch,' said Alice.

'No, it seems whenever I eat, I feel full after just a few mouthfuls.' He laughed, 'Perhaps I need to see a doctor.' Then he left them.

'I think he does need to see a doctor. He shouldn't dismiss a problem like that. He should know better,' said Alice.

'So, what does happen here if you have something that needs specialist treatment like surgery or chemo?' Angie had a frown on her face, but Alice couldn't reassure her.

'I don't know. Perhaps, Doctor Greg ought to talk to Adam. Most of the people here are young and a problem like that hasn't occurred. The lifestyle here is healthy with no pollution, a vegetarian diet and less stress. I'm sure a lot of illnesses are made worse by tension and anxiety.'

Angie nodded, then suggested they ordered their food. Arthur then arrived with Ben, now a sturdy boy of four years. His dad had just collected him from nursery school and brought him to have lunch. Arthur moved a table up to theirs so they could all chat together. He sat Ben next to Sandy, who offered him a piece of her bread. He took it and devoured it hungrily, then looked for some more.

'That's enough, Ben. Don't eat any more of Sandy's bread because your dinner's coming now.' He turned to Angie, 'How's the paper business coming on? Have you found a suitable plant?'

'Not really. I know they must be dried first, so my workshop is full of plants and twigs drying in great bunches. I've also had some success with onion skins, so I've got Diane putting them aside for me.'

Arthur and Ben's dinners arrived and as they ate, Alice told Arthur of her concern for Doctor Greg.

'That's interesting,' he said, waving his fork, shedding pieces of mashed potato. 'I saw him yesterday and thought he'd lost weight. Do you think I should talk to him or tell Adam?'

'I think it would be better to speak to him. It seems like telling tales to the teacher if you talk to Adam.'

Just a few days later, Arthur cut his hand on a saw and the wound needed stitches. Doctor Greg soon had him stitched and neatly bandaged but then listened when Arthur spoke to him. He sighed and sat back in his chair.

'I'll tell you, in confidence, Arthur. I've not only lost weight but I've lost heart. I don't want to be here anymore.

Everything's an effort and I probably should see an oncologist because I'm fairly sure I've got stomach cancer. It's difficult because I'm the only doctor. Could you help me, by telling Adam? I just hate the idea of letting him, and all the people here, down.'

Arthur stood up. 'I'll do that, Greg. I can't shake hands,' he said looking ruefully at the bandage, 'But I can wish you luck.'

The clinic was closed on Monday 13th June. A notice on the door said:

Doctor Greg has left due to a serious illness. The clinic will be open tomorrow for minor problems that can be dealt with by Nurse Jane and Midwife Madeline.

I am searching for a replacement doctor.

Adam

When people met in the street, in the shop or the diner, there was no other topic of conversation. It was not that Doctor Greg had been particularly liked. He was generally business-like and almost brusque when working and had made no friends. He would not be missed by anyone in particular but missed by everyone because he was their doctor. There was a general feeling of unease. What would happen if someone had a serious accident or got pneumonia? Was Nurse Jane able to prescribe antibiotics?

Nurse Jane was not an independent prescriber. She wished now she had done the course. She spoke to Adam about it.

'If the occasion arises, Jane, you must prescribe antibiotics if you think it necessary.'

'But it's illegal because I'm not qualified.'

'Yes, but better to save someone's life than be hidebound by rules that don't have to apply here. There's no police or legal system. If you deem it necessary, please prescribe.'

'Thank you, Adam.'

Weeks went by and Adam was deeply worried. He felt the weight of responsibility heavy on his shoulders. They had to have a doctor. He had contacted many who were retired, but they had all refused. He was walking on the quayside and saw Leo, the pavement artist hard at work on a new creation.
'Morning, Leo.'
Leo looked up and smiled with pleasure. He stood, stretched and held out a chalk-covered hand. As Adam took it, Leo said, 'So how's it going? I suspect there's a problem as you're here. How can I help?'
'We need a doctor. I've tried asking lots of retired GPs but they're all enjoying life and don't want or need to work. I've had my eye on some young hospital doctors. They have a tough life. Long hours and huge responsibility. I just don't know who or how to approach them.'
'Leave it to me. Now I know what you need I'll try to work it that a doctor falls through the picture.'
'What's it going to be when it's finished?'
'A chasm with a broken plank of wood half across it. The gap must be jumped.'
'Sounds good, Leo. How will I know if you've nabbed a doctor, bearing in mind I must pick him up in my boat?'
'I'll text you, but you have to be at the warehouse or anywhere that's got a signal.'
Adam nodded. 'I'll be there all over the weekend and if that doesn't work – all next week. Thanks, Leo.'
'No problem. I really want your commune to work.'

Adam went back and told Eve what he'd arranged.
'It might be good if we organised a welcome with lots of people at the slipway all cheering. Maybe a banner or something,' Eve said. 'If you let me know when you come down to get the boat, I'll see what I can do.'
'That's a brilliant idea. It shouldn't be hard to arrange; we're all desperate for our clinic to be back to normal.'

Chapter 44

2023

I was excited and scared when Adam arrived with a letter for me. I was in the clinic but hadn't yet started my morning surgery. It didn't look very official, and the handwriting was Olivia's, but there could only be one subject – my application.

'Thanks, Adam. It's from my sister. I'll open it later. I need to make a start.'

'No problem. I hope it's not bad news. See you later, Phil.'

I went into my consulting room and saw by the pile of folders on my desk that Grace was the first patient. I knew she just wanted to tell me all her aches and pains; she was a hypochondriac but pleasant with it. She could wait. I opened the letter.

Hi, Phil, got an e-mail inviting you to an interview on July 4th. I've printed it and enclosed. I bet that's got you all of a flutter! Would this be a good time to warn that chap in charge, oh, how could I forget his name, Adam? I'll leave that for you to think about.

Fingers crossed for you,
Love,
Olivia xx

I read the formal letter. It said they had contacted my referees and were satisfied with their response. I made a note to take Jeff out for a drink, but not until I'd got the job. Would I get the job? I stopped musing, put the letter to one side, and called Grace to come in.

Grace was forty-five, married, with no children. I suspected she was bored and thought about nothing else but her imaginary ailments. I smiled, gestured her to sit and prepared myself, putting on my sympathetic, but interested, face. As soon as she spoke, I was in no doubt she did have a very sore throat. Her voice was husky, little better than a whisper. A quick look confirmed it was very red and sore. I listened to her chest for any wheeze or crackling but there was none. I prescribed gargling with salt water and paracetamol for the pain.

'Can't I have antibiotics?' she asked.

'No, I have to save those for infections. You have a sore throat, probably just a cold and it doesn't warrant antibiotics. But, if you follow my instructions, it should be better in a week or so. If not, or you have any other symptoms, come back.' I stood up and she reluctantly did the same. I opened the door and as she exited, I called the next patient in.

The morning seemed interminably long. I wanted to see Alice and show her the letter. I wanted to ask her if I should be honest with Adam, or just invent a reason to see my family.

My lunch hour finally arrived, and I walked home quickly. Alice wasn't there and a note said I'd find her in the diner with Angie. Damn! I couldn't talk to her when she was with other people. I thought about making myself a sandwich but knew the note, although it hadn't said as much, meant meet me there. I grimaced and went to the diner. Adam was there too. He was sitting with Arthur. What was I going to tell Adam and when?

I gave my order in at the counter and sat with Alice, Angie and the children.

'What's up? You look worried,' said Alice.

'No, I'm fine, there's no problem.'

The children took our attention, and I got through lunch, somehow, with my mind in turmoil. Then Adam came to our table.

'I just wanted to say that if that letter was bad news about your mum, don't hesitate to ask me for leave. Perhaps you could get Doctor Steph to stand in? All the women loved her.'

'Thank you, but my mum's fine, but I might need to see if Steph's available early July.'

'No problem, just let me know.' Adam left with a cheerful wave encompassing everyone.

'I knew you had something on your mind,' said Alice, looking a bit put out. 'You've got an interview, haven't you? Why didn't you say so earlier?'

'I was unsure because Angie was with you.'

'You needn't worry about me,' said Angie. 'Alice already told me you'd applied for a job. Congratulations on getting an interview. I don't want either of you to leave but I wish you luck in July.'

I had stood up when Adam came to the table. I sat down now. 'I'm sorry, Angie. I didn't know you knew, or I would have told you both. Anyway, it's on July the 4th.'

'American Independence Day, but that's not relevant, is it?' giggled Angie.

'Some people might be celebrating so perhaps it's a good omen,' said Alice. Their conversation was interrupted by Clare who suddenly started to cry, stuffing her little fingers in her mouth, her cheeks bright red. Angie looked frightened and tried to comfort her baby.

Alice said calmly, 'She's teething. She needs something to chew on.' She picked up a set of bright plastic rings that Clare was supposed to play with and gave them to her. She awkwardly got the toy to her mouth, and they all watched as she managed to get one of the rings partly in it. She dribbled but calmed a little.

'It's always less painful once the tooth has come through,' said Alice.

'I was really worried then. Thought she'd got some illness. I'm grateful to have you to turn to, Alice. It's hard being a new mum.'

'Who needs a doctor when Alice is around?' I said standing up, grinning. 'I've got to go back to work. See you later.'

That evening, with Sandy in bed, Alice and I had time to talk.

'Should I tell Adam the truth, even though I might not get the job, or wait until I've got it, assuming I do?'

'I think you should tell him the truth and also get in touch with Steph, as Adam suggested. I know you only have to be away a day for the interview, but if Steph hasn't got a job at the moment, she might be interested in taking over here, permanently.'

'I think Steph will probably have a job by now, but there's no harm in asking. I'll talk to Steph first, then talk to Adam.' I felt calmer, having made a decision, but there was still the awkwardness of having to ask Adam if I can go back to the other life in order to make a phone call.

It seemed to me impossible to live here without having any contact with the life going on in the known world. I knew Adam's ultimate desire was to have us totally self-sufficient, but it was a pipe dream. People needed modern drugs, vaccinations and general medical items that can't be made here. They didn't want to manage without tea, toilet rolls, pencils, pens or books. That night I struggled to go to sleep, worried about our future and the future of this idyllic rural life we led and the people in it.

The following morning, before surgery, I knocked on Adam's door. I had a plan but found myself telling him about the interview and my need to ring Steph. I saw him frown and it was obvious the news upset him, but he came with me to the lift, opened it and we went up together. I used his office phone while he went into the warehouse.

Steph picked up on the first ring and I was surprised. I explained the position and then there was a long silence.

'Steph, are you still there?'

'Yes, but you've upset me with your news. You see I've applied for that job in Durham too. We're competing for it.'

'I'm sorry. I obviously had no idea. Perhaps we should talk again when we know the results of the interviews. I can't wish you luck because I want it as much as you do.'

'Bye, Phil.' She clicked off, leaving me in turmoil.

Chapter 45

2023

Angie and Alice met at the nursery school.

'Today's the day then. How was Phil this morning?'

'I don't really know because he was up and out before I woke up. He had to collect his car from his Mum's house, then drive to the Durham clinic for 10:30. I'm not even sure he'll come back here tonight. These interviews can be protracted affairs, sometimes. Needless to say, if he doesn't, I won't sleep a wink.'

'You poor thing. Come on, I'd treat you to a frothy coffee – my cure for all ills – but we can't do that here. What about a cup of tea at my place and some serious paper making to pass the time before we pick the children up?'

Alice nodded, adding, 'I miss frothy coffee too, but I'll settle for tea.'

The paper they made that morning was fine writing or drawing paper. It was much better quality than Angie's earlier efforts. Alice was given the job of guillotining the sheets into neat rectangles. She then collected the pieces that were cut off and put them into a tank holding water. Eventually they would be recycled to make more paper.

They made a good team and by lunchtime, there were sheets of paper drying on every surface and a tall, neat pile of finished ones.

They walked back together to the nursery and Angie said, 'This afternoon, if I can get Clare to have a nap, I'm going to use an even finer mesh and try my hand at toilet paper. It seems a lot of effort when it's going to go down the toilet but then it would save Adam buying it in such quantities. In the olden days, people used newspaper torn into strips and hung them on a nail in the privy. That's a thought; perhaps I should try to make newspaper. You could write the articles.'

'About what?' Alice laughed. 'Nothing newsworthy ever happens here and word of mouth is all that's needed.'

'If Adam told you about important events happening in the real world, then there would be something to write.'

'I'm not sure Adam wants us to know. The wars, shootings, epidemics would just make us all anxious. I think he feels we're all better off in blissful ignorance.'

'Adam's not God and we're not children. Who is he to control what we should or shouldn't be told?'

'Adam found this place. It was, and still is, his dream of a sanctuary where people can live and work happily, without stress.'

'Yes, but it's too tightly controlled. Only vegan food, no alcohol, his or Eve's choice of clothes in the shop. I can appreciate the life of calm he's created, and I really found it therapeutic after Petro's death, but it's also boring.' Alice frowned, not sure if she agreed with Angie, who, seeing her expression added, 'I'm sorry if I've shocked or upset you.'

'No, not shocked, just surprised. I've never been bored here. I'll happily go back if Phil gets the job, but I'll miss the serenity. I'm not looking forward to panic making broadcasts on television, the radio and social media. So do you want to go back to teaching and trying to juggle work with childminders?'

Now it was Angie's turn to grimace and then shake her head. 'Not yet.'

They collected their children and went back to their respective cabins. Alice made a simple meal of sandwiches and then went for a walk. She took the pushchair, but Sandy wanted to push it. This made walking very slow but that didn't matter. If Sandy walked far enough, she would be tired and willing to get into the pushchair and have a nap. They walked up the hill towards the farms. It took them nearly an hour as they stopped to look at wildflowers, which Alice named, and the butterflies, bees and birds. It was surprising how many small species of birds they saw, not just the raucous seagulls. It was warm and at one of their stops, Alice breathed deeply, knowing how much she would miss this natural haven.

Eventually, when Sandy had given up and was asleep, they reached Jason B.'s farm and, as the front door was wide open, Alice called out to Mary. She came to the door, face all smiles, recognising the voice.

'Have you brought Sandy to play with Sam?' she looked down at the pushchair. 'Oh, she's asleep. Bring her into the hall and we can have an almost quiet cuppa. Unfortunately, Sam is wide awake and full of himself. I can't get him to have a nap in the afternoon. The only blessing is he's usually asleep by 6:30.'

While this monologue was going on they went into the kitchen where Sam was trying to bang pegs into tight holes. Alice thought Mary must be lonely and vowed to go and see her more often. Then, with a frisson of anxiety, she remembered she might not be here much longer.

Mary caught her facial expression. 'Is something wrong? You can tell me.' When she noticed Alice's hesitation, she added, 'If it's a secret, I promise it won't go any further.'

'It's not really a secret. Adam and Angie know. Phil's gone for an interview and if he gets the job, we'll be moving to Durham.'

'Wow, I didn't expect you to say that. I thought you were both happy here. What'll happen to us? We can't be without a doctor. Phil was brilliant when my Jason's leg was such a mess. I kind of hope he doesn't get the job.'

'He really wants it and we're getting married in September. It could all work out perfectly for us. Adam will just have to recruit another doctor.'

'Sorry, I was being totally selfish. For your sakes, I hope he's successful.'

'Mum, Mum, I want to get out.' Sandy was obviously awake now.

Alice got up and unclipped the harness holding her into the pushchair. She ran and sat down with Sam to play. He stopped banging, much to the relief of both mothers. Sandy picked up a car and put it on the ramp of a wooden garage and watched it roll down. Sam got another car and did the same thing.

They were playing happily so Mary got up to get drinks of oat milk for the children and some biscuits. When they were eating and drinking, she collected two wine glasses and half-filled them with a pale pink liquid.

'You've got to give me your opinion of this. It's rhubarb and I made it myself. Jason's been perfecting spirits, but I prefer wine and I'm quite pleased with this.'

Alice took a delicate sip and nodded. 'It's lovely.' She drank some more. 'Very easy drinking. I can feel the effects of alcohol already!'

'Yes, I think it's quite potent but I've no way of measuring the alcohol content. I'm glad you like it.'

It was about an hour later, having drunk two glasses of wine, that Alice decided she should take Sandy home.

'I could feed you both. There's plenty of stew.'

'Thanks, but I want to be at home when Phil gets back. You've already been so hospitable. Why don't you pop in when you're next in town?'

Mary agreed and they all went to the front door together.

When Alice got home, she eagerly opened the door, but Phil wasn't there. She sighed, turned around and went to the diner. At least there would be people to chat to there and it would take her mind off the anxiety of not knowing if he had got the job.

Chapter 46

July 2023

Adam had taken Phil up the lift and seen him off from the warehouse door. He wished him luck with his interview, while privately hoping he did not get the job. As he turned to go back inside, he heard a voice calling his name. It was Leo.

'Good morning, Adam. Have you time for a little chat?'

Adam looked at the artist and felt anxious. 'I've time to talk but I'm surprised to see you here, Leo. Is there a problem?'

'I think there's going to be a big one for you and your project.'

'In that case come into my office.' Leo followed and sat on the chair opposite the desk. Adam sat behind the desk, and looked at Leo, expectantly.

'So, what's the problem?'

'I've visited your farms. They're well run, and the people work hard producing high quality produce. I'm sure you know that.' Adam nodded but made no comment.

'Did you know they go hunting and eat meat most days?'

'No, I'd no idea. It's years since I visited. I was just satisfied they were producing what we needed in the village.'

'Now I don't know how much eating meat causes any problem. To tell the truth, I'm not sure why you made the village vegetarian. That's not the main issue. The real issue is the beer, wine and spirits they're making and enjoying. How would you feel if they offered to stock your shop with some of these products?'

Adam frowned. 'Arthur worries me. He helps at the farms regularly. I suppose that means he's eating meat and drinking. I can't bear the thought of him becoming an alcoholic. He's got a wife and a child now.'

'That may well help him to drink sensibly so perhaps you should trust him. What I saw when I visited was two communities. The farmers and the villagers. The only reason the farmers need to come down to the village is the hospital and I understand Doctor Phil is thinking of leaving you.'

Adam looked up, sharply. 'How did you find that out? He's gone for an interview today. Are you even more of a magician than I thought? Perhaps you can tell me if he gets the job. I'll certainly need your help to find a replacement.' His voice had a hint of anger and he now stood. Leo stood too, making a placating movement with his hands.

'I've no idea if he'll get the job. I found out by chatting to one of the farmer's wives. Look, I know I've dropped a bombshell on you, but I did have a thought. The farming community is self-sufficient which is what you wanted all along, but the village is totally dependent on what they and you supply.'

'Yes, you've said that already. Does this matter?'

'Perhaps not and as you say, it's not my project, but I've been watching it develop with great interest.' He paused and then said, 'I think I should go. Have you still got my card? In case you need help recruiting a new doctor?'

When he saw Adam nod, Leo walked to the office door. He had a jaunty grin as he turned and said, 'Do I need to be escorted off the premises?'

'I'll see you out,' said Adam tersely.

When he got back to his office he felt restless and could not settle to work. *What was Leo trying to say? I'm not sure I like him, but I might need him.*

He knew part of his concern centred around Phil. He had to come to the warehouse to return to his cabin so Adam would find out then if he had got the job. The idea of losing Phil made him feel even more irritable than the artist's visit. He answered the phone abruptly, tapped the keys of his computer vigorously and by mid-afternoon, he'd built up a head of steam that needed venting. He went down in the lift determined to see the farmers himself.

He walked quickly nodding to people who waved a greeting but did not stop to talk to anyone. The walk had a calming effect and he slowed, enjoying the sea breeze and noticing the screaming gulls wheeling overhead, and then saw Alice just leaving Mary's cabin. He thought he ought to stop and say something, but her face was creased with anxiety. She managed to give him a brief smile but pressed on past him, the pushchair wheels whirring as she headed down the steep hill.

Adam knocked at Mary's door which was quickly opened by a smiling Mary. Her smile wavered when she saw who it was.

'Adam, this is a pleasant surprise. Come in.' She stood back and he entered, the delectable smell of meat stew making his mouth water. 'Please sit down. Can I get you a cup of tea, or would you like something stronger?'

'What do you mean, stronger?'

'Well, I've just given Alice a taste of my own rhubarb wine, but we also have ale and a rather good whisky.'

Adam felt wrong footed with Mary deliberately offering alcoholic drinks to him. He frowned then said, 'I'd like to taste your whisky, thank you.' She went to fetch his drink and Sam brought Adam a toy car. 'Thank you. It's a racing car. Do you want me to play?'

Sam nodded and Adam knelt and pushed the car across to Sam. 'What's your name?'

'Sam. It goes fast.' His little hand grasped the car and slid it back to Adam. He was a healthy, sturdy boy and Adam compared him to Abe, who had been paler and thinner at Sam's age. Perhaps eating meat sometimes was not such a bad thing. His mind felt burdened with uncertainties.

'Here, try this,' said Mary offering him a glass with a small amount of golden liquid in it. He sipped, rolled the liquor around his mouth, then swallowed. A smile told Mary everything she needed to know.

'We're just about to eat. Jason will be in very soon. Would you like to join us?'

'It smells wonderful, thank you. I'd like that very much.'

There was a clunk as Jason B. threw his shoes off and then walked in.

'Daddy!' A delighted Sam rushed to his father who picked him up with ease and swung him into the air.

'Hello Adam. It's been a while. What do you think to my whisky?'

'It's smooth. Delicious.'

'I've invited Adam to stay for dinner and he's agreed. It's ready, so shall we sit at the table?' Jason put Sam into his highchair and Adam sat where Mary indicated. The stew was as delicious as it had smelled and was served with fresh bread in chunks. Mary had poured glasses of her wine and by the time the meal was over, Adam's face was flushed with hot food and alcohol.

'That was a wonderful meal, thank you, Mary. You know I came up here to see you because I'd been told you ate meat and had produced your own alcoholic drinks. I was full of righteous indignation. On the walk up I mellowed and now I can't understand why I felt like that.'

'Perhaps it's because you began this community and stated rules that you expected everyone to abide by – being vegetarian and no smoking or booze. Well, I can tell you no farmers smoke, but we all hunt now and again and share the meat between us. We see nothing wrong with eating what nature provides in abundance. We eat a lot of rabbit, deer and occasionally we find wild boar. We work hard, enjoy our food and liquor. We don't make enough whiskey to get drunk on. Our life is good, and we're happy, as you can see.'

'I can,' said Adam, nodding. 'And you make me wonder about those rules I made. I'm not sure how I can change them now.'

'If everyone in the village is happy with it as it is, perhaps you don't need to,' suggested Mary. 'I also think we'd find it difficult to keep a regular supply of meat to the shop or diner, but we could do it occasionally if we're blessed with more than we can consume. What do you think?'

'I think that's a good idea. A meat feast now and again. I'll look forward to it.' He stood up, thanked them profusely for their hospitality, and walked thoughtfully down the hill. He called into the diner on the way to the warehouse and asked Diane what she thought of an occasional meat feast.

'That's a great idea, Adam. I hate waste and if there's a surplus of meat, I'd be happy to cook it.'
'Good, well, I'd better get back to work. Bye.'

Adam sat at his desk and considered how much happier he felt now than when he left several hours earlier. His resentment against the artist had gone and he felt he had achieved something, although he was not sure what it was. Perhaps it was the alcohol that made him feel mellow and relaxed. It felt wonderful.

His meditation was rudely interrupted by the telephone. It was Phil saying he was staying the night at his parents' house and would be at the warehouse late the next morning. He also asked Adam to tell Alice there was no news. He was going to get a call in the morning once the panel had made their decision. Adam agreed and put the phone down. Then he tidied his desk and closed down his computer for the night. He was looking forward to seeing Eve and Abe and telling them about his unusual day.

Chapter 47

I got the job. I was so excited I gave no thought of what it would mean to leave the other dimension. Alice had more of an idea. She had lived there much longer than me. Her friendships were deeper, and the wrench would be harder.

We decided to move on a Sunday and Alice suggested we cleaned our cabins from top to bottom. It was not my idea of how to spend our last day, but I left her singing as she cleaned out the kitchen cupboards, placing everything back as it was before.

I went to my cabin. Rich was not there so I didn't have to work around him. I didn't sing as I worked while feeling slightly resentful but there was no choice. Alice had spoken. The only thing to do was to work hard and get the job done.

While wiping down the worksurface, I worried about Alice, leaving friends and this peaceful existence. I just hoped my love for her and Sandy and our marriage in just over a month would be enough to soften the loss.

When I had finished cleaning, I went back to Alice's cabin, carrying a rucksack of clothes. I was going to leave them there while we walked to the diner for our last Sunday lunch. It was going to be a meat feast day and I was looking forward to it. I'd no idea why Adam relented on the strict veggie diet but I'm glad he did. Sandy enjoyed venison sausages a few weeks ago and her stomach coped with the new food perfectly. Mum will be pleased she doesn't have to make special meals for Sandy anymore.

I walked towards her cabin excited to be starting a new life, looking forward to having a telephone in my pocket and ambulances to send people to hospital. I hated running up the hill to the farms in an emergency. The frustration, anger and breathlessness made it so much harder to cope when I arrived. I knew it would be different. I was unlikely to get to know my patients personally because there would be so many of them, but I hoped I could give each one my best diagnosis and treatment.

I pushed open the door calling, 'Hello, I'm ready for lunch, are you?'

Alice kissed my cheek, smiling. 'Definitely. Let's go to the diner now, I have a feeling there may be some sort of farewell planned.'

'I hadn't thought of that. There might be cake, Sandy. You'd like that.'

'Cake, cake, I like cake,' chanted Sandy turning towards the door.

We walked to the diner and there, as Alice had predicted, was a long banner, 'Thank you, Doctor Phil. Good luck to you, Alice and Sandy.'

'That's lovely,' said Alice. 'I bet Angie made that.'

As we went through the door, there was a cheer that brought tears to Alice's eyes and my own were pricking. The room was full of well-wishers who stood and came over to us shaking my hand and kissing Alice. Glasses of something that looked like wine were offered to us and then it all went quiet as Adam raised a hand.

'There's hardly anyone here who hasn't been to see Doctor Phil for some ailment or other. He has served us well and we wish him good luck in his future job. Raise your glasses for Doctor Phil!' Everyone raised their glasses and drank but Adam held up his hand to show he hadn't finished. 'But we're also saying goodbye to Alice who, years ago, worked in our pharmacy and since having Sandy has quietly helped at the library and also made paper with Angie. We will miss them both and wish them health and happiness in their forthcoming marriage. Once more raise your glasses to Phil and Alice!'

'Phil and Alice,' was the communal response as more wine was drunk. People began to sit down as Adam led us to the seats of honour behind which was an enormous cake, iced with three little figures on top – the bigger ones holding a hand of the child between them.

'Look Sandy, that's models of us on the cake,' said Alice.

Sandy looked solemn and said, 'Can I eat *that* Sandy?' We both laughed and nodded.

Then I added, 'After you've had your dinner, you can have a piece of cake and that tiny Sandy. Are we going to try the meat feast today?' Alice and Sandy nodded, and I went to the counter to order.

Diane was serving and came up with a broad smile. 'What can I get you all?'

'Two normal size and one small meat feast please and a huge thank you for that amazing looking cake. Sandy can hardly wait to eat herself.'

Diane laughed then said, 'I don't think you realise just how much we're going to miss you all. I just hope Adam's got someone in mind to replace you.'

'Don't worry, I'm sure he has.' There were other people waiting to give their food orders, so I moved away and sat down.

'It makes me feel sad to be leaving all our friends and having to start again,' said Alice.

'I feel the same, but I know it's the right thing to do. Being here has taught me to expand my horizons. I never thought of being a GP but having done it here, I realise it was what I should have done all along. I just wish we were moving into our own place instead of staying with Mum and Dad but buying a house takes time and money.'

'Can I join you?' It was Arthur, with Sam wriggling in his arms shouting, 'Get down. Play with Sandy.'

Sandy then asked to get down, so I released her from her highchair and the two children ran to the corner of the room where there were some toys. Arthur joined us, smiling at our children.

'Sam's going to miss Sandy. I wish you weren't going. I understood when Petro left but I missed him so badly.'

'Phil never knew Petro, but I did, and I know you two were very close. I'm going to miss Angie, too.'

The conversation was saved from becoming maudlin by the arrival of our dinners. Arthur and I collected the children and once they were stowed in their highchairs the talk was of the food which was delicious. We had just finished when there was an announcement from Adam that they were going to cut the cake and would Alice and I please come and do the honours. At the sound of the word 'cake', Arthur released them from their seats so Sandy and Sam could join us, their noses practically touching the cake.

'You cut it, Phil, while I hold these two back from that sharp knife.'

I did and there was a shout for a speech. I shook my head but then there was a noisy repetition of, 'Speech, speech, speech,' until I nodded and put up my hand. It went very quiet as I looked around the faces, recognising all of them. I swallowed, took a deep breath to steady myself and began.

'I arrived here just over a year ago, bewildered but touched by the warm reception you gave me. Since then, I've done my best to help anyone who was ill.'

I was interrupted by a hearty shout, 'And a damn good job you've done,' followed by affirmative noises.

When they'd finished, I went on. 'The wonderful thing about being here has been the pace of life and the great people, but then the icing on the cake was meeting Alice and Sandy.' There was a cheer then. 'So, I just want to say how much I'll miss you all but also to thank you for giving me the experience of being a GP. Finally, I want to thank you for this memorable send off and this beautiful cake, Diane. So, let's all get our teeth into it.' With the final cheer, I sat down and blew out my cheeks.

'Well done, Phil,' came a voice from behind me. It was Diane balancing a plate piled high with slices of cake and little plates. Alice took enough for all of us, and we all ate with relish.

It was depressing arriving back at Alice's cabin seeing the rucksacks and bags waiting. Adam had rounded up a small party of helpers to carry all our things to the lift, so these were quickly hefted, and we were on our way.

Chapter 48

Adam phoned Doctor Steph, biting his lip as he did so. Phil had told him she had also applied for the job in Durham but obviously had not got it. Would she consider helping him again, with no pay? Should he offer to pay her? No, that went against everything he believed.

She answered. He explained what he wanted.

She laughed, 'What took you so long? I've been expecting you to call when Phil was offered the job.'

'Phil and Alice left this afternoon. That's why I didn't rush. He was still our doctor until he moved away. So, what's your answer?' He crossed his fingers.

'I'd love to come, as long as I don't have to share a cabin with Rich.'

Adam laughed, with relief. 'I have two empty cabins so you can choose.'

'I think I'd like to have Alice's cabin. I can start in a couple of days, say Monday? I need to tidy my life here before I come as I don't know how long I'll be with you. It is temporary, right? You're not expecting me to be permanent?'

'I'd like you to be. Would you consider it?'

'Thanks, Adam, but no, not permanent.'

'I understand. I'll see you on Monday, here at the warehouse. Bye.'

The problem of a doctor or surgeon was not solved then. He'd have to keep looking. Suddenly Adam felt tired, weary of the problems his dream life was causing. People were a responsibility and he had not realised how much that weighed on top of his family and his job. He rubbed his eyes and stood up, going round his desk towards the entrance to the lift. As he went down, he wondered how long he could continue the work involved, ordering goods for the shop, things they could not make for themselves, keeping the electricity going by calling

Rich, finding a new doctor. That was the big one. Perhaps Leo would come up with something.

Adam shut the door of the lift, then the outer door and walked, head hanging, towards his cabin.

Angie saw him and called out from her doorway. 'Adam. Come and see what I've made.'

He lifted his head, managed a smile, and went into her house and then into the workshop. He could never do this without seeing Petro in his mind's eye, but he would never say that to his widow.

Angie handed him a bundle of fine paper held together with a piece of string at one corner. He took it from her, bemused until she said, 'Toilet paper. I got the idea from the historic use of newspaper hung on a nail in a privy. What do you think?'

He grinned before saying, 'You're a marvel but I'll have to try it out. Can I use your loo?'

Her eyes opened wide, not sure if he was joking and then he laughed.

'If you could get a production line going, then this could save me a lot of money.'

'I'll need regular help. Alice used to work with me when Sandy was at nursery but to fulfil the amount required for all the people here, it would have to be a factory. There are quite a few women with children at nursery or school and they might be persuaded to join me.'

'Arthur would help too, I'm sure. He's needed in the farms when they're pushed but there are days when he complains of being bored. Would you need a bigger workshop?'

She nodded, then waved her arm encompassing the room. 'This much again. It would help if this extension was enlarged rather than another separate building. There is space behind.'

'I'll get that organised. I'd better go now but I must tell you, I was quite depressed when I was passing your door, but now I feel buoyed and excited. Thank you.'

Adam's pace was quick, and his heart felt light as he walked the short distance to his own cabin where Eve was making sandwiches.

'Hello love.' She looked at him carefully and smiled. 'I thought you'd be sad, depressed even, with Phil and Alice leaving but you look surprisingly cheerful. Have you solved the doctor problem?'

Adam then told her about Steph and then Angie's invention. Eve laughed, then said, 'It'll save you a small fortune. She's amazing. I'd like to work with her on that. I know I work in the warehouse while Abe's at school but on the weekends, I could make toilet paper. Abe might like to help too.'

'It won't happen overnight. We need to extend her workshop. I'll talk to Arthur tomorrow and see if he can muster a team to do that.'

Later that evening, Abe in bed asleep, they sat with a cup of tea and Eve snuggled up to him.

'I've something to tell you.' She paused waiting for him to respond.

'Mmm?'

It was not an interested reaction, so she sat up. 'You need to know this. Listen. I'm three months pregnant.'

'What? Really? That's wonderful. Abe will have a new brother or sister. Six months, that'll be January. Nowhere near my birthday, thank goodness, and you can have it at the hospital instead of the diner toilet.' He kissed her, then did it again, his hands wandering over her tummy. 'It's hard to believe a baby is growing in there.'

'I'm a bit worried Abe might be jealous. He's had all our attention for six years and now he'll have to share it.'

'That's true but some of the time he'll be at school, so he won't see all the fuss then. We'll just have to give him lots of extra attention when he gets home. I've assumed you'll be happy to have the baby here but if you want to have it up top, that's fine by me. I just want you to be safe.'

'I suppose that rather depends on whether Steph stays on. If she doesn't, then that's an unknown, The NHS is struggling with insufficient staff and low pay. The junior doctors are on strike next weekend. That doesn't make me feel safe. If we have a doctor, then I'd prefer it to be here.' She grinned. 'We could always call on Jason B. in an emergency.'

'That's not funny,' he said then laughed. 'Shall we have an early night? I'm feeling like a celebration.'

'Definitely,' she said undoing her blouse as she walked into the bedroom.

Chapter 49

There was just one week to go before the wedding and Alice was sitting with Mum going through the finer details of the big day and what, if anything, they still had to do. I had just got home after a morning surgery and had been hoping to find lunch ready. Instead, I'd been asked to take Sandy to the park so the women could concentrate.

I pushed Sandy on the swing, and we sang *See Saw, Margery Daw*, then we moved onto the climbing frame. I watched her, worrying she might fall but knowing she needed to try all these things. Eventually she said she was hungry. I agreed wholeheartedly, and we walked quickly home. Now delightful smells wafted, and I said, 'Grandma's made soup.'

We ate lunch and Alice told me the things we still needed to do before next Saturday. This afternoon, we had to collect the cake and pay for it. Then go to the florist and choose the flowers for Alice's small bouquet. She thought it would be nice to have the arrangement in a basket. After the ceremony it would be taken to the private room in the pub we had hired for the venue, to be a table decoration.

We chatted in the car, going to collect the cake, about where we were going for our honeymoon. Mum and Dad had agreed to have Sandy for the week so we could, as Mum put it, 'Be free to enjoy yourselves.'

Our plan was to go South to North Yorkshire. I had found a bed and breakfast place in a small town called Boroughbridge and the plan was to explore the North York Moors and the towns of York and Harrogate. Alice also wanted to see Fountains Abbey. We both got excited as we talked.

'I hadn't realised how narrow my life had been when we were in the commune,' said Alice. 'Now I feel we've the whole world to discover.' Her hands spread apart as she demonstrated her words.

I laughed. 'Just at the moment, our finances won't run that far. Let's start with North Yorkshire. But I agree we had a comfortable life, but a very limited field of experiences there.'

It was quiet for a moment. Both of us thinking of what we'd left. Then I said, 'I still miss Arthur and Diane, Adam and Eve, Jason B. and Mary, not forgetting Angie.

'I miss them too. I also miss having a house of our own. I do love Mum and Dad, but we need to shorten your journey to work and find somewhere to rent in Durham.'

'We do but let's work on that after the honeymoon. Coping with my new job and getting married is enough for the moment. There's also the issue of money. I've had one month's wages and most of that has gone, or is spoken for, already.'

The conversation ceased until our jobs were done and we were back in the car heading home, the cake box sitting on Alice's knee.

'You know I might be able to get a job. I'm a trained pharmacist but I could also work in a shop or something if Mum and Dad would look after Sandy. Just part-time, I mean.'

'That's a good idea but if we found a house to rent near or in Durham, you'd have to give it up.' She nodded her reply just as we reached home. I got out of the car, then took the precious cake off her knee, so she could get out.

When we went indoors, the cake was greatly admired, and Mum wanted to know what flowers Alice had chosen. Dad looked at me and gestured me to come closer. When I did, he said, 'I'm up to here with the talk of weddings,' he'd gestured to the top of his head. 'Do you fancy a pint?'

I nodded and when we told the women where we were going, they barely registered.

'That's better,' said Dad as we swung down the road. 'Just being outside is a relief. We could just go for a walk.'

'Let's go for a walk to the Fish Quay. There's plenty of places there to have a pint and we could probably sit outside. The best of both worlds.' The sun shone, seagulls wheeled and screeched, and I found myself feeling so happy I could burst. The emotion was strong enough to make my eyes water.

Dad said what I was feeling. 'You know your mum and I have never been happier than we are now. Mum loves Alice and Sandy and knowing you're going to stay nearby where we can phone you makes us feel safer too. I know we've had Olivia, and Rich is a great bloke, but we've missed you so much.'

'Thanks, Dad, but it works both ways and I missed you too. Anyway, enough of all this verbal backslapping – grab that seat and I'll get the beers.'

Two pints and a lot of chat about sport later, we decided it must be dinner time, mainly because everyone around us was tucking into delectable plates of food. We set off up the hill, slowly because Dad's arthritic knees were complaining. It was late when we did arrive home, and Mum looked at us and grinned. 'You've obviously had a liquid lunch. Do you want any food?'

We said, 'Yes please' simultaneously and then giggled.

'I think, maybe you've had a little too much beer. Come into the kitchen. I've plated up your dinners. They just need three minutes in the microwave.'

I woke up early enough to go to work and then remembered it was Saturday and I was not working because it was our wedding day. I now felt wide awake and slightly nervous. There'd been so much planning and talking about this day and I wanted it to go well, without a hitch. I sat up to find Alice doing the same.

'I didn't think I'd sleep at all, so excited about today, but I did. Just think this evening we'll be in Boroughbridge having our first night as Mr and Mrs Clarkson.'

I leant over and hugged her. 'I'm looking forward to it too. Do you want me to get you a cup of tea?'

'No, I've no time to lie in bed. I've got to be at the hairdressers at nine o'clock.' She leapt out of bed, rushed to the bathroom, then I heard her feet running down the stairs. Mum was already up. She was going to have her hair done too but after Alice. I then heard Sandy whining that she was hungry, so I got up. The little kitchen seemed overcrowded with everyone trying to get toast or cereal quickly. I felt I wanted to fire a gun like they do in cowboy films to get everyone quiet. Instead, I picked up Sandy, put her in the highchair and organised her breakfast. A cup of tea was made for me which I sipped gratefully amidst the chaos.

Alice and Mum went out, Sandy was playing with a toy having finished her food, so I now made some toast for me. Dad was hovering and I wasn't sure if he'd eaten so I offered him some.

'Nay, lad, I've had mine. You sit down and enjoy yours now it's quiet. I reckon we've two hours of peace before all the rest kicks off.'

The wedding ceremony at the registry office was booked for midday. After that, there was lunch with just our family, and Rich, at the pub. There was to be a rest gap and then we returned to the pub for a disco and buffet. This time, we were being joined by more distant family and friends.

I'd sent an invitation to Adam, Eve and Abe and asked if it was possible for our other friends to come too. He'd phoned and said Angie wanted to come plus Arthur and Diane, Jason B. and Mary, and finally, Steph. We were thrilled to think we'd be able to share our special day with them. It was going to be a real celebration with fifty people.

As we stood before the registrar, I glanced at Alice and saw she was nearly in tears. That set my own eyes pricking. I squeezed her hand and we both managed to get through it without crying.

The dinner at the pub was delicious, roast beef with enormous Yorkshire puddings and we needed a rest afterwards to digest such a feast. Sandy fell asleep watching television as did Mum and Dad. Only Alice, Olivia, Rich and I were left sitting in the kitchen, chatting.

'Your turn next,' said Alice, and Rich actually blushed.

'I must admit, watching you two today made me think seriously about it,' said Olivia. 'I know Mum would be delighted. She wanted us to have a joint wedding with you two, but I refused. Everyone should have their own wedding with all the memories that are made on that day. They shouldn't have to share it.'

'That was thoughtful of you,' I said, adding, 'Or was it selfish?'

Olivia and Rich laughed.

Three hours later we were back at the pub greeting all our friends. It felt odd having people from the other dimension in this one, but it was great to see them again.

Alice and I, with help from Sandy, did the first dance and then everyone seemed to want to dance too, and the space grew crowded and warm. I glanced across at Mum and saw her wiping her eyes for the umpteenth time today and smiled. It was lovely to see her so happy and knowing that it was because of us.

We had to leave the party early because we had over an hour's drive to Boroughbridge. Everyone waved us off as we drove away in a car adorned with clanking cans. We went about a quarter of a mile and then I stopped and removed the evidence.

Chapter 50

It was midnight when the party goers emerged from the lift. There was an unmistakable smell of burning wood and a glow that lit the dark sky. Smoke obliterated the moon and stars. Everyone began to run.

The conflagration seemed overwhelming, but Adam and the other adults rushed to help the chain of people bringing buckets of water up from the river.

Eve ushered Abe, who was crying loudly, down the hill to the jetty. Angie was ahead of them, holding a screaming baby.

'I'll stay with him if you want to help with the water,' she shouted. Eve tried to go but Abe clung on to her and she shrugged, ruefully.

'It's not fair to leave him. Step back a bit to let Mary and Diane join us.'

The noise of wailing children, shouting people and the crackling of flames was almost unbearable. One mercy was the wind, blowing off the sea, so they could breathe without inhaling the noxious fumes. That same wind was fanning the flames that were leaping from one building to another.

'Let's get into our boat. The rocking might help the children to calm down.' They did this and Eve spoke to Abe. 'We're safe here and I must put up the sides so the little ones can't see the flames. Can you let me do that?' Abe nodded and relinquished his grip.

The canvas sides hid the fire from sight but did little to mask the sound of crashing logs, splitting asunder and people shouting as homes and other buildings fell to the ground, throwing up a myriad of orange sparks into the smoke-filled sky. They huddled together in the boat for warmth and comfort. The younger children relaxed and slept.

'I don't think there'll be much left,' said Mary. 'I think, when it's over, everyone will have to come up to the farms. We have an empty greenhouse that we were going to fill with seedlings. It would be somewhere to shelter for a few days while we decide what to do.'

'I can't believe this is happening and I can't stop shaking,' said Angie. 'Just a few hours ago we were so happy, dancing at the wedding and now…this.'

'We're all in a state of shock,' said Eve.

Up the hillside, the passing of buckets of water was slowing. The distance to the fire was increasing as it ate through the village, and the people were exhausted. Arthur and Adam still had energy and were urging everyone to keep going but they could see the grey faces in the flickering light and knew the fire had beaten them.

'I think we should all go to the boats and get some rest,' said Adam, aware that he no longer had to shout to Arthur because the fire was up the other end of the street. 'Will you tell everyone? You've a louder voice.'

Arthur nodded and cupped his hands around his mouth to form a megaphone. 'Give it up, lads. Let's go down to the fishing boats and rest for what's left of the night.'

They made their weary way down. Adam, Arthur and Jason B. joined their families. The others went onto the decks of the two fishing vessels. They huddled amongst the nets and tried to sleep.

Everyone was up and out of the boats as soon as it was light enough to see. Tendrils of wispy, grey smoke curled up into the blue sky. The seagulls screeched as if nothing had happened, but there were no other birds and no insects buzzed as they toiled up the bank, in silence.

The sight that met their eyes was like news photographs after a bombing – total annihilation. Even the furthest cabin had gone. Trees, bushes, little gardens as well as the large diner and hospital were just ashes blowing about in the gentle breeze. The larger logs, covered in white ash still glowed.

They had lost everything. Adam stood, tears streaming down his face as he saw his dream destroyed. Eve and Abe hugged him, wanting to sooth but knowing nothing could.

Jason B. and Mary took charge, urging everyone to walk up the hill to the farms. 'We'll soon make breakfast for you all and then we can make plans.'

'Plans to do what?' asked Arthur, his voice harsh and bitter. 'Start again? Rebuild?' His voice croaked and it was obvious he was too overcome with emotion to say anything else. The women ignored the tension between the men, urging their children to walk on and promising them drinks.

When they reached Jason B.'s farm, the barbecue was alight and emitted a delectable smell of bacon. All the farmers and their wives were busy offering blankets and thrusting bacon sandwiches towards anyone that wanted them. There were pots of tea and milk for the children. The mood brightened as their tummies filled.

Adam went and thanked the farmers for their efforts. They were quick to explain they could smell burning in the night but there was nothing they could do when they saw every building ablaze.

'We just hoped there were no lives lost.'

'I think we've accounted for everyone,' said Adam. 'And I see Doctor Steph has already begun to work.'

Steph was checking minor burns and asking everyone about their breathing, making sure they hadn't inhaled too much smoke. Finally, having seen to her patients, she went up to the barbecue to claim her sandwich and mug of tea. Then she went to talk to Adam.

'My patients are better for some food but they're all in a state of shock. They have nowhere to sleep, no clean clothes, nothing. An emergency plan needs to be made, now.'

Chapter 51

Alice and I woke up to our first day as Mr and Mrs Clarkson and it felt good. The sun was shining through a gap in the curtains, and I felt a wave of love and happiness as I looked at Alice, her beautifully coiffured hair now a messy tangle. I rolled closer and kissed her cheek. She woke, smiled, and turned towards me. It was delightful to know that Sandy wouldn't come running in and we had this moment to ourselves. We made the most of it and arrived at breakfast just ten minutes before it finished.

The landlady knew this was our honeymoon and indulged us by producing a full English breakfast and lots of hot toast.

'I won't need to eat another thing all day,' said Alice.

'Me neither. What do you think to going to York? Not to go shopping but to walk around the walls. It's sunny and beautiful so we should be outside.'

'That sounds perfect.'

We enjoyed steeping ourselves in the history of the city, visiting the cathedral and walking by the river. It was lovely to be able to hold each other's hands, not Sandy's, and to hug whenever the mood took us. Inevitably, we chatted about our wedding day and seeing all our friends. I wondered how Steph was getting on and whether she would want to stay permanently. I hoped she would.

In the early evening, still in York, I phoned Mum and then Alice chatted to Sandy, telling her about our day and promising to bring her to York one day. Sandy then said she'd been to the swings with Granddad while Grandma was asleep. We were satisfied that Sandy was happy and my parents coping well so we enjoyed the rest of our day, returning to Boroughbridge when it was dark.

The following day, we walked from our digs along the canal and stopped to watch boats going through the lock. Then, back in the little town, we indulged Alice's sweet tooth and had coffee and cake for our lunch. In the afternoon, we walked to Aldborough and saw the Maypole and the stocks on the village green. When we walked up a steep hill, we discovered Aldborough had a museum of Roman artefacts and some mosaic pavements.

'I thought our area had lots of Roman remains, being so close to Hadrian's Wall, but it seems this part of North Yorkshire was also occupied by the Romans,' said Alice. 'Let's go more modern tomorrow and go to Fountains Abbey.' I laughed and hugged her. We were enjoying the freedom of having nothing to do except explore and have fun.

The next day the weather changed our plans and we went to Harrogate. It was raining heavily so we dashed from shop to shop and then went to the cinema to see, 'Indiana Jones and the Dial of Destiny'. We were both amazed at the clever way Harrison Ford was young and then later acted as he really was – an elderly man.

'I feel technology is moving so fast I can't keep up,' I said.

We ate our evening meal in Harrogate and chatted to another couple. When I mentioned the film, I was told actors in Hollywood had staged a demonstration against the use of CGI instead of real people. I quietly vowed to keep watching the news and reading reports, so I could feel up to date. Too much had happened while I had been away from the real world.

Fountains Abbey took us all day. We had morning coffee at the café then paid to become members of the National Trust. That allowed us in and gave us access to other National Trust properties. We both agreed we wanted Sandy to see all these wonderful, old, beautiful places and to appreciate her heritage. Alice wanted to know everything, so she stopped wherever there was a notice or a building holding artefacts and information. She came out of one grumbling.

'That Henry the Eighth did a hell of a lot of damage. These ruins must have once been wonderful, impressive buildings and the monks were looking after their communities.'

By the end of our week, we were saturated with history, had walked many miles and eaten far too much. We were also now thinking about going home and our future. We discussed where to look for houses to rent. If I'd not fallen through the picture, I might have saved enough to put down on a house. Then I would not have met Alice so there was no point in looking back.

We enjoyed our last breakfast in Boroughbridge and set off home.

There was a flurry of excitement on our arrival and then, when we were sat in soft chairs having a cup of coffee, Dad did a harrumph sound heralding he was about to say something important. He looked very serious, and I put my cup down on the coffee table and looked at him expectantly.

'While you were away, there was a serious fire in your commune.' Alice flinched and spilt some of her coffee.

'How serious?' she asked. 'Was anyone hurt?'

He shook his head, and I heard her sigh with relief. 'There were no fatalities and only minor burns. The biggest problem, apparently, was the entire village was destroyed. Every house gone and your hospital, the shop, everything. I'm so sorry.'

Tears fell down Alice's cheeks. We both thought of all the lovely moments we had enjoyed there with our friends.

'What are they going to do?' I asked.

'I don't know. I got this from Rich. We kept if from you because we didn't want to spoil your holiday.'

'Thank you. I don't know if there's anything we can do. There's no room for anyone to stay here.'

'Rich and Olivia both had their own houses, as you know. Rich offered his to Angie, her baby, Arthur, Diane and their child.'

'What a nightmare! It was just a week ago we were all having a great time at the wedding and now they're homeless. I think we must visit them, now.' Alice and I stood up, picked up Sandy and got back into the car.

Chapter 52

I knocked on the door and Diane answered it. She stepped forward and hugged me for ages and then did the same to Alice.

'Come in. Everyone will be so pleased to see you.' She was right. There were more hugs and some tears then we were told their awful story.

Arthur finished by saying, 'We spent a night in the new greenhouse while Adam phoned as many people as he could think of for help. Rich offered to move in with Olivia and lend us his home. On Monday, I'll look for work. I've two women and two children to support and we can't stay here for ever.'

'I'm going to look for a job too,' said Diane. 'Angie can be our live-in nanny for a while.'

'I'm also going to contact my last school. If I get a job, then Diane can be the nanny.'

'I hope one or all of you get a job soon. You can't manage here without money. Talking of that, how are you buying food?'

Arthur answered, 'Rich gave us a wad of notes and told us to buy what we needed, and Olivia gave the women some of her clothes. Unfortunately, Rich's clothes are too small for me, so I've had to buy a few things. I don't know how we'll ever pay him back.'

'Don't worry about that. Rich has a good job with high wages. Do you know what Adam's planning? Did he talk about rebuilding?'

'I've spoken to Eve,' said Diane. 'She said he's depressed and can't make any decisions. There are still people living there, up at the farms and a few of the homeless are staying with the farmers. They can manage for now.'

'What did Doctor Steph do?'

They all shook their heads. I wondered if she had stayed too. I wanted to go there but I didn't want to. Better to remember it as it was, not as a sad heap of charred wood. There was nothing I could do for any of them.

Eve opened the door to a man she had not met before. He introduced himself as Leo and asked to speak to Adam. She hesitated, not sure if she should let him in.

'I know Adam and I think he'll want to see me.'

She opened the door and allowed him in. Adam was sitting in an easy chair, doing nothing, his elbows on his knees, his head supported by his hands. Leo stood in front of him and gently called his name. Adam's face was grey with exhaustion and anxiety as he looked up. Leo crouched down. 'I know the fire has been a tremendous blow to you. I think we need to talk.' He turned to Eve. 'Would you be so kind as to make us a cup of tea?'

Eve nodded, went into the kitchen, and put the kettle on to boil. She busied herself getting out cups, putting a teabag in each while straining to hear what Leo was saying. She came in with the tray as he sat back on his heels and then stood. He moved towards a chair raising one eyebrow at her. She nodded and he sat.

'I need to tell you, Eve, that I once had an art studio where you now have your main warehouse. I found the trap door and the steps.'

'Oh. I'd no idea. I thought Adam was the first to discover it.'

'Once he did, I've helped a few times with finding suitable people. I wanted his utopia to work, and I still believe it can.'

Tears ran down Adam's face as he sobbed, 'I haven't the energy to start again, Leo.'

'I understand that and I'm not suggesting you do. I went yesterday and spoke to the people still there. They all want to stay and are willing to do so without the conveniences you offered – the shop, the library, the diner and the hospital.'

Adam wiped his eyes and looked at Leo. 'How will they manage that?'

'What they want is for you to entrust the key to the lift door to Jason B. He promises not to use it during the day and only to use it in an emergency. They promise not to call on you for anything but also, they want you to feel free to visit them whenever you want to. It seems to me a fair offer and takes the weight off your shoulders. You are free to live your life with your family without the burden you've been carrying all these years.'

His speech was rewarded by the glimmer of a smile, transforming Adam's earlier haggard appearance, and a whispered, 'Thank you, Leo.'

The End

Hazel Goss
AUTHOR

I was born in North London and my family moved to Harlow, in Essex, when I was 9. I met John, at a holiday camp, when I was 17 and after we married, we lived in a flat in Stevenage. I was a primary school teacher and John worked in electronics.

We moved to Boroughbridge in North Yorkshire, with our two small children, when John was invited to work in the north of England, by his company.

John had a gliding accident in 1989 and a few years later I retired. I was able to spend more time with John, but I missed the mental stimulation of my job. I found the solution when I attended a creative writing course.

Several years, and many courses later, it was suggested by writing friends that we should form a self-help group which we called The Next Chapter. The group flourished and we engaged speakers. One speaker, Jackie Buxton, an author and lecturer, offered to run a course for us called 'Write a Book in a Year'.

Out of this course came my first novel, *Forced to Flee*. It was inspired by a young refugee from Kosovo who joined my class for a few weeks. He described being in Pristina when bombs fell. I enjoyed doing the necessary research and placed my fictitious characters into the real events.

When the book was finished, I felt a sense of loss and used a short story I had written to expand into a time travel book. I called it *The Pathway Back*. I followed that with *The Pathway Forward*, using some of the same characters. When that one was finished, I wrote one more to complete the trilogy and called it *The Rocky Pathway*.

My husband and I have had many adventures in over fifty years of marriage, so my next book was a memoir called *When Life Throws You a Lemon, Adventures with a Wheelchair*.

My latest book is a called *My Poems*. It is an eclectic mix. Some are intensely personal while others are observations of nature and some, as in 'Santa's Stuffing', just fun.

You can find out more about these books and read some of my short stories and poems at my website:
hazelgossauthor.com

The book cover for Another Chance was designed by Victoria.
victoriaprintstudio@gmail.com

Printed in Great Britain
by Amazon